Praise for *Return to Oakpine*

"Engaging . . . The men and their tender, disgruntled families get almost enough to sustain them, but not quite enough to calm the inner cry. These characters will stay with you because that is how we are too."
—*The New York Times Book Review*

"As stirring and memorable and utterly rejuvenating a novel as you'll read . . . Carlson infuses these pages with such conviction, such perfectly orchestrated pathos . . . The book is as lean and structured as a sonnet, and it has a split-focus climax as sharp as an ax."
—*The Washington Post*

"Carlson's new novel, with its themes of male friendship and second chances, hoes much the same furrow as his lovely previous books *Five Skies* and *The Signal*. . . . Carlson's crafted an emotive yet pellucid prose style that conveys the profound spiritual satisfactions of homecoming."
—*The Wall Street Journal*

"In this new book of his, Ron Carlson has done a splendid job of making a reader feel at home in [Oakpine]. . . . Carlson can sometimes sound the music of the entire novel in a single sentence."
—Alan Cheuse, *All Things Considered*, NPR

"[An] eloquent and moving novel . . . Carlson's approach to fiction [is] to articulate with care and nuance the inner lives of characters who themselves may not be emotionally articulate: men, mostly middle-aged, living in the rural west and wrestling with the sense that opportunity has passed them by. . . . The tension that drives *Return to Oakpine* [is] between what we want to do and what we need to do, between our dreams and our responsibilities."
—*Los Angeles Times*

"With Carlson's typical grace and unadorned prose, his latest novel deals in the prodigal sons and promising footballers of Oakpine, a small town that seems to hold optimism only for its youth. . . . Carlson knits these multiple voices and perspectives together to capture the magnetic, sometimes damaging pulls of hometown and the memories of invincible youths that can never be restored. . . . Carlson excels in small-town Western Americana, in both embracing and interrogating nostalgia in quiet, controlled prose. . . . A humane portrait of the lives we lead and leave behind, peeling back nostalgia's gold veneer with grace, empathy, and a pragmatic sense of optimism." —*The Kansas City Star*

"In this novel by an American master, four middle-aged friends, once members of the same high school band, reunite in their Wyoming hometown thirty years later, reconciling the people they've become with the kids they used to be." —*O, The Oprah Magazine*

"Citizens in neighborhoods across America, despite occasional atrocities and outbursts of greed, learn to specialize in the labor of caring for one another. In eloquent detail, Ron Carlson shows us these processes working out. *Return to Oakpine* is simultaneously heartbreaking and reassuring, and infused with a continual, thoroughgoing beauty." —William Kittredge

"An exceedingly well-crafted book, straight and true as it deftly shifts between half a dozen characters, slowly revealing secrets, past and present." —*Orange County Register*

"Carlson is a fine, fine writer, and his alternately funny, sad, and heart-rending accounts of his characters' high school days will linger long after you close the book." —*The Star-Ledger* (Newark)

"Carlson tells a moving but quiet tale about a group of regular guys. . . . These men are immediately recognizable, making *Return to Oakpine* perhaps his most universally appealing novel." —*High Country News*

"A lean, weathered, and bighearted tale . . . Carlson shares his empathetic scope across three generations. . . . In Carlson's expert prose, the adults' midlife reckoning are revelations and the teenagers' discovery of adult agency are both touching and raw. . . . A moving novel about the importance of home, work, and friendships." —*Shelf Awareness*

"With spirit and grace, Carlson has caught the essence of what might have been, as well as the importance of friends and family. A touching and affecting work of literary fiction." —*Library Journal*

"Affectionately captures the rhythms of small-town life." —*Kirkus Reviews*

PENGUIN BOOKS

RETURN TO OAKPINE

Ron Carlson is the author of five story collections and five novels, most recently *The Signal*. His fiction has appeared in *Harper's*, *The New Yorker*, *Playboy, GQ, Best American Short Stories*, and *The O. Henry Prize Stories*. He is the director of the writing program at the University of California at Irvine and lives in Huntington Beach, California.

Return to Oakpine

RON CARLSON

Penguin Books

For Marianne Merola

Thanks to Michelle Latiolais and Josh Kendall

PENGUIN BOOKS
Published by the Penguin Group
Penguin Group (USA) LLC
375 Hudson Street
New York, New York 10014

USA | Canada | UK | Ireland | Australia | New Zealand | India | South Africa | China
penguin.com
A Penguin Random House Company

First published in the United States of America by Viking Penguin,
a member of Penguin Group (USA) Inc., 2013
Published in Penguin Books 2014

THE LIBRARY OF CONGRESS HAS CATALOGED THE HARDCOVER EDITION AS FOLLOWS:
Carlson, Ron.
Return to Oakpine : a novel / Ron Carlson.
page cm
ISBN 978-0-670-02507-7 (hc.)
ISBN 978-0-14-312559-4 (pbk.)
1. Homecoming—Fiction.   2. Male friendship—Fiction.   3. Families—Fiction.
4. Life change events—Fiction.   5. Wyoming—Fiction.   6. Domestic fiction.   I. Title.
PS3553.A733R48 2013
813'.54—dc23
2013001606

Printed in the United States of America
1   3   5   7   9   10   8   6   4   2

Set in Aldus LT Std
Book design by Alissa Amell

ONE

The Run

The way Craig Ralston found out that his old high school buddy Jimmy Brand was coming back to town was that Jimmy's mother had called him for help. There was a time when Louise would have tackled this whole project alone, but now it was too much and it had come up too soon. She called Craig at his hardware store downtown, and he came out one night after work. It was August. All the cottonwoods in his old neighborhood, pretty as a park so long ago, were now towering giants, clustering leafy cumulous that shaded the district and sounded like a river in the wind. They had split the sidewalks and dwarfed the old bungalows, half of which were still occupied by their original owners. The trees were the theme here, and Craig, who was happy for his move to the scrub oak mountain and the new mansion, felt them get to him as he went to her little porch. When he knocked, she didn't invite him in but came outside and took him around to the garage. It was a classic one-bay garage that her husband had erected with community help years ago, wooden frame, plank walls, wooden shingles, peaked roof, a one-paned window with a layer of dust on it thick as speckled paint, and a little side door. This place was the old band to Craig, the room where he and Jimmy Brand and Frank Gunderson and Mason

Kirby, who had lived three houses down, had practiced a hundred afternoons that fall. The little building hadn't been opened for ten or twelve years, maybe longer.

Craig Ralston had been a big kid, and he had played football with Louise's older son, Matt, who was long dead, and now Craig was a big man, square and strong, and though he was out of shape, there was something youthful about him. He still had all his curly hair and he spent his days hustling about the little hardware store, in which he knew where every hinge, every bolt, every flange lay, fetching things for people and kidding with them. There had been some talk years before, during the oil boom, about him starting his own construction business, but when his father nixed the plan, Craig came into the store. Building his house on the hill over the last year, though, had rocked Craig soundly; he loved such labor, and though he had stretched the work on his own house out as far as he could, he had finally poured the driveway last month and trenched the yard with a sprinkler system and sodded the lawns.

"What's the program, Mrs. Brand?"

"Can you open this door Craig? I've got a job for you."

Craig lifted and turned the old T-handle, but the bay door stuck. His hand came away rusty. They went to the side door, but that handle was locked solid, and she told him the key was long gone. Through the grimy glass Craig could see the dark space was full of stuff. Mrs. Brand was standing back from the edifice, her arms folded. The look of worry on her face promised to get worse.

Craig Ralston had eaten a lot of meals in her kitchen, hanging out with Jimmy. The fall of 1969, their senior year, she would feed the band after they'd practiced in Mr. Brand's garage. Edgar Brand told the kids he'd park his Chevy pickup, the one he drove to his job at Union

Pacific, on the driveway, "My beautiful vehicle will be out in the weather, boys, for the sake of the musical arts." The driveways up and down the street were two strips of poured concrete with a run of grass between them. In those days Craig could see Mr. Brand in the living room reading the paper and watching television while he and Jimmy and Mason and Frank ate hamburger steaks and sliced tomatoes and huge chunks of steaming squash covered with salt and pepper and melting butter. They had been Life on Earth, classic rock 'n' roll, and they had lasted one year, until graduation, when they flew apart like leaves in the wind. Craig Ralston went into the army and Vietnam with two dozen other kids from that class from Oakpine, and Mason went up to Minnesota for college, and Frank had spent a year at school at Laramie before returning and managing the Sears Outlet downtown and then buying the building. Jimmy Brand disappeared. Craig and Mason were home one Christmas, and Mason had gotten a card; Jimmy was in out in the world, having left Wyoming for good.

Until now.

Mrs. Brand backed away from the building as if realizing its size and the dirty window had defeated her. She was wearing a faded blue-plaid apron—Craig noted it as something he'd known from the past—and he saw that she was going to put her hands in it and give up.

"I'm glad you called," Craig told her. "You caught me daydreaming at the store."

"No, you weren't. Your father ran a good store, and so do you."

"It looks like we'll survive until they put in a Walmart, so that's something. I finished that house, you know, Marci's dream house on the hill—our dream house. I'm one of those characters who lives on the hill. You'll have to come by."

"Remember when that hill was the wilderness? I think the boys used to hunt right there—I can see the lights some nights," Mrs. Brand said. "This town is changing, but you're not one of the guys who live on the hill. They're all from California, aren't they?"

"Or Idaho. I'm glad Jimmy's coming back. He got out and did something. Those books. He's the only guy from Oakpine to write a book."

"Is Marci at the museum?"

"She is. She's doing what she wants now. Larry's a senior. You'll see him."

"My god," she said. "Those babies." She stood stiffly, having said all that she could manage, and she looked past Craig at the impossible garage, her eyes heavy now and laden with sadness and the weariness of all of time and time's sadness.

"Mrs. Brand," Craig started, "we all go way back. And Marci and I have that big house, and with Jimmy coming—"

"Don't, Craig," the woman said. She put her hand on his forearm. "We have to do it this way." She was looking at his face now.

"Just tell me what we need, Mrs. Brand. I'll get Larry, and we'll get this done for you."

A week later Larry Ralston came walking up the smooth driveway of the new house on the scrub oak hill, the house they'd just moved into last spring, taking those long rolling strides he took after a run, his hands on his hips, each breath three gallons of September, still a touch of summer in it, and he was smiling and shaking-his-head happy. He and his father had poured the cement for this concrete surface six weeks ago, and now he walked in a circle on the ramp "I ran around the town," he said. Larry Ralston was seventeen and had been talking to himself for two or three months. "That town is captured in its entirety." He turned in the new night and looked out over the dark world and the small pool of the sparkling network of lights of the town, and the knotted cluster of downtown Oakpine and the white halogen slash of the railroad, and beyond the dark pool to the colored lights in a distant grid, red and red, at the airport. It was the first time he'd run around the town, and he ran again now up the steps sweating and smelling the fall grass in the sod and the newness of the materials cut just this year, and it was funny not to tramp sawdust, as they'd done for weeks, into the kitchen.

There his mother stood now in her black bra, which was her nighttime ritual, doing the dishes in her underwear, her hair tied back in a ribbon, something she'd never done until this year, and it was almost seven. She said, "Where have you been?" thinking he'd been catting around, that age: seventeen, because it was what she was doing or about to do or considering doing or played at, and her thinking was that if her life had turned that way, then she saw it in everyone, even Larry, shining and breathing, and saying now, "I ran around this entire town." He wanted a glass of water but didn't want to get near her at the sink. "Mom, summer's over, grab a shirt."

She said the obvious thing: "It's my house."

And he, still having an ounce of humor about this woman and her black bra season, called out to the living room: "Dad, what is this with Mom?"

"Play through, Larry," his father called.

"It's a sports bra," she said. "It's a bathing suit, for Pete's sake."

"That's worse," he said. "They are all sports bras." And he called to Craig Ralston, his father, "Are you dressed, at least?"

"I'm dressed," she said. "Get used to it."

"You going to get a tattoo?" he said. "I'm sorry for asking, because your son is not a smartass but is dislocated by your behavior, but what's the answer: is a tattoo next?"

"What makes you think I don't have one?"

"Oh my god. Dad?"

"I'm saying: play through. Where have you been?"

His mother turned to him and said quietly, "This is my house. This is not indecent. Where have you been?" She turned, not waiting for an answer, throwing her hands out at him as if tossing a towel, and left the room. She'd been walking like an athlete for months now, long decisive steps. Larry felt an electric bite run across his gut, and he sat suddenly on the kitchen chair, his legs now rubber, paper, ash. He felt the day put its hard hands on his shoulders.

"I ran around the town," he said to the empty kitchen. The empty modern kitchen, the block kitchen island. It had been his mother, Marci, in the car tonight. He seized his knowing and boxed it and set it in his gut and stood up. He put his hand on his stomach. Maybe it was. But he had it boxed and set now, and his legs were back. Again now louder he called to where his father sat with the television: "Is the airport in Oakpine, Dad?"

"Of course it is. It's the Oakpine airport."

Larry found his burger under the bun in the cast iron frying pan on the stove and scooped it up with his left hand, dripping grease along his palm, which he licked away while opening the fridge with his right hand and grabbing the glass bottle of milk, half full, setting it down to pull the top off, and lifting it in a long cold drink.

"I mean in the town proper. City limits."

"It's in the county. The highway is the county line. Route thirty-one."

"Then I ran around the whole town." He was talking with his

mouth full, and he walked to the living room entry and dropped his shoulder against the wall there and continued eating. They were building an ice mansion on the History Channel.

"Look at this, Larry: wiring and everything."

"How's your project with Mrs. Brand?"

"Fabulous. I need you tomorrow after school."

"I've got football, but I can come on Saturday." He watched his father watch one of the men set the keystone ice block into the entry arch of their cold palace. His partner followed with a splash of water from a bucket, sealing the deal. His father, the hardware store owner, should have been the captain of builders. They'd had a crazy summer finishing this house, and Larry could not remember his father happier.

"Don't get any ideas from these actors," Larry said. "Such a gimmick. Ice walls. They're doing it to avoid that fiberfill insulation, for which I don't blame them. That stuff itches, but you stick with drywall or whatever. They'll put an ice house on TV, but it's crazy. It's a stunt, cool, but a stunt. It would be better TV to show us installing that garage door." Yesterday they'd fought the two steel L-trolleys for the door's rollers, adjusting each side for an hour.

"Where were you?"

"I ran around this town, Dad. I'm not saying it should be on the History Channel, though I'm sure I startled some ghosts and ran by the forgotten sites of four hundred short-lived romances, but I know it's a first, and I know it's a record. You could have done it in the day you and your buddies played that championship season, which I think was 1970 or so because the town was only Hackamore Flats and downtown, but it's different now." Larry finished the last bites of his hamburger and pulled his shirt over his head and wiped his face with it.

"These days such a venture is an hour and nineteen minutes running all the way, including a loop out around the silos and two crossings of the Union Pacific tracks at First Street, cornering at the old Trail's End Motel, may it rest in peace, and back again over the trestle at the river."

Craig Ralston regarded his son in the dark doorway. "Fall of 1969. We won every game, and Frank broke his leg. And you ran all of this because . . . ?"

Larry stood from leaning against the wall and held out his hands, which were suddenly this year huge. "Because I'm alive, Father." He turned and went up to his room on the thick stairway carpet, now hearing the *thump thump* of music coming from the huge bedroom wing, his mother suddenly playing music too loud everywhere, and he called once more: "I'm alive!"

He had started running at the high school, two laps after football practice with his buddy Wade, the cinders in the old track crunching as they jogged. Wade was quarterback and the coach's son, and Larry had known him since preschool. They'd jettisoned their helmets and pads into the end zone grass and were running in the gray team T-shirt and white gym shorts, and they felt light, and running was impossibly easy. When they came to the field gate on the second lap, Larry said, "Come on," and led Wade out across the parking lot and the street and up along the new roads leading to the new neighborhoods on Oakpine Mountain.

"You running home?" Wade said.

"No, let's circle out and come back through town."

"That's three miles."

"It's seven."

They'd run through the town all summer, meeting at dusk and

pacing each other through the twilight streets of the village for forty minutes, sometimes up and down the lanes of the two new developments, sometimes running out along the railroad trestle, nothing ahead of them but sage flats and antelope, and they'd run on each side of the railroad track for half an hour until Wade stopped and called at Larry's back. After Wade halted and clutched his hands to his knees, bent and breathing, Larry closed his eyes, and he could feel how strong he was, running in the wilderness. "I think I'll run to South Dakota," he said. "North Dakota. Canada."

He heard Wade call and turned to see that the dark had taken everything but the lights of town in a blister at the end of the silver rails, and he saw the dotted yard lights on Oakpine Mountain, one of them his house. It looked like it was on another planet. He'd run back then and found Wade exactly where he had stopped, and he approached Wade's pained face and ran by until he heard his friend running behind him. "You're overdoing it, Ralston. We're already in shape." Wade called this way for three or four minutes, falling farther behind. It was the way all their runs ended. Tonight Larry had followed the railroad back to the river and crossed at the trestle.

Wade slowed his pace precisely to short-step across on the ties, and he said, "See you later, Larry. I'm going to stop and see Wendy." It was what Wade said every night they went out. He'd run twenty minutes and then detour to his girlfriend's house. Wendy was in their class. Tonight Larry had crossed the river alone, smelling the rich clay before the reflection of the water appeared, and he dropped onto the new bike path, which drifted toward the park.

"I think I'll stop and see her too," Larry said, running in the middle of the unnamed road that marked the south edge of town. "For you are not worthy to touch her fair hand. Her little finger. Oh you could touch her little finger, say, if she were wearing protective gloves and you were giving her back a book that you'd borrowed, not that you'd borrow a book, unless it was just full of pictures . . ." And with a start Larry suddenly passed a couple walking their Irish wolfhound, a dog he and everyone else knew very well, Shamrock, known as Rocky, the largest dog in the county, four feet tall, but he didn't know the dog's owners except that they were the Drapers and they were older than his parents, and he had scared them by approaching at a run, a young man apparently yelling at someone. The large gray dog and the two people stood still while he drifted by, his long silent strides giving him just a chance to whisper a hoarse "Hello," in such a different tone than he'd been talking that it stilled them even more.

He took a dozen more long running steps and thought to turn and call back "Sorry," but they were lost in the dark now, and he was glowing with all his power, and he turned and loped through the weedy vacant lots between the little houses of old town and the highway department equipment sheds, and he said, "I'm sure your dog understood that I was making perfect sense."

There was a pleasure in the running now, and he took the ditch at the field's edge in a stride and continued the long miles beside the airport. He ran the packed ditch bank alongside the two-lane highway and drifted effortlessly by the lit edifice, a four-gate airport with a dozen flights a day, and here in the open world the wind bumped him once and twice, smelling of rain somewhere out in the prairie night. "Come on wind," he said. "Let's go."

He came to the end of the dark rocky lane, which years before had been a real road, when two bars and the Trail's End Motel lit that far edge of town, enough neon to beckon some and warn others. Now the two bars were unmarked ashy heaps and one garish chimney, and the

Trail's End stood mostly burned, squalid and gothic and ruined, its sixty-foot sign showing stars through the letters. There was a single car cocked in the glass-littered parking lot, utterly out of place. "Citizens," Larry said at the empty building shell, "sleep tight." And as he spoke, he was startled as a head appeared in the glass of the automobile, which wasn't a derelict at all but some kind of Audi, a face and then two hands, and then gone in the dark again. It was across the street, and he knew that he would know who was in that car with whom. The car was familiar, and he looked back again, but the headlights beamed, blinding him to further revelations, and the car, seemingly silently, turned a gentle turn through all the tiny fragments of broken glass and swept onto the abandoned street, two massive two-tone taillights receding into the night. "Or not!" he called to the vanished car.

There had never been a person running through this place, night or day, going back to forever. In the fifties the Trail's End had been a nifty motel waiting for the town to grow out to it, and it was even featured in a famous postcard on which it stood as a gateway for the village behind it, an emblem of the modern world, and then it slid for thirty years and had been empty almost twenty. Headlights now appeared, approaching, and Larry saw that this car could not see him, and so he leaped across the two-lane as it passed, another huge expensive import, a Mercedes of all things, and he cut through the old motel's broken landing, stepping high in the crumbling concrete, and now Larry found the corner and turned back toward his hometown, running ten minutes and then crossing the tracks and entering the congested little three-story downtown.

It was close and claustrophobic now to be among things, after having run out on the surface of the planet, and he seemed to be sailing unreasonably fast, up by the Antlers and around two blocks, even as he had done in the past, to greet his father's hardware store, where he worked part time, and then through the old city park under those thick leafy trees, which he loved, and where Wade always stopped running to turn for Wendy's house, and Larry always wondered if Wendy asked where he was and if Wade told her he was still running.

"Still running," he said now, and instead of steering through the village and up the hill home, he saw he was going to run around the whole town proper, which meant that he had to do a five-cent U-turn right in the street and loop out around Poplar Grove, the oldest neighborhood of redbrick bungalows and all the old tree giants, which were great to run under, but not tonight, tonight he was Magellan, and he ran out the cemetery way and up the unpaved sloping road, and he called as he passed the iron fence on the grassy plateau on the dark hill studded with gravestones and the old poplars, which were the most common trees in town, "Not yet, my dear friends." He called into the fenced graveyard. "Not yet." He thought he might see that car again up here, since the packed dirt parking for the cemetery was a place for that, but it was empty tonight.

The footing was tricky beyond the fence, and he slowed to find his way to the far slope, which was a sage hill untouched by the millennia. The snakes that lived here were direct descendants of those vibrated out of their dens a hundred and fifty years before by the first wagons swinging around this very hill toward the water, where the river bowed and then widened for a crossing at what was now Bank Street. "No snakes," he said, "no snakes," and he slalomed down in a sinuous course as if skiing, and when he felt the earth grow flat again, he took it as greeting, and he opened his stride and then opened it wider. He crossed from running into flight, a velocity at which he knew he would trip on a root in this blistered plain, and he didn't care. He could feel the night on his eyes, and he wondered what the sleeping coyotes might make of a man moving this way. His legs were on fire, and then beyond that they ached wonderfully as if he were growing with each breath, and he used the feeling to push, dropping into the ravine before Oakpine Mountain and skiing again, some of his downhill steps eight feet long, and he expected to be upside down at any moment.

Then suddenly he was on the bladed gravel of the snowplow turn-around and then on the pretty new asphalt of Oakpine Mountain Drive, the smoothest surface all night, his footfall a whisper, with only five or six blocks winding up into the new development of two-acre lots and the smell of scrub oak rich around him, along with the smell of rain, which the wind now delivered, having caught up with him again as he crossed the property line and turned and walked backward up the expansive well-made driveway, regarding the lights of all the lives below, and he said it. "I ran around the town."

Upstairs in his room in the new-carpet-smelling house, Larry felt a catch in his breath or an ache in his breastbone, and he looked out his window and saw the town again, glittering, and he saw the two yellow lights at the trestle where he had run forty minutes ago and all the dark houses he had circled, and he said, "What is it?" And then he knew that he wouldn't stay. He'd known he was going to go out of state to college, either to Wisconsin or Michigan, but now he knew he wasn't coming back. He sat on his bed in the space that they had painted Bay Blue from the big paint book, and he looked around at the bare walls, his few pictures still leaning here and there waiting to be hung, and he felt old now knowing the first long season in his life was over. He would play football and finish at Oakpine High in the spring and then go. So funny. He loved the town and was done with it. "There's your paradox, Mrs. Argyle," he said, invoking his English teacher's name, as in this year she had become audience and arbiter of his monologues, though she would never know it. "There's your ineffable conundrum, you gorgeous old lady, you mistress of the vocabulary cabinet."

His door opened and his mother in her robe said, "What?"

"Nothing, Mother, Nice robe. Lovely robe. You should wear it all the time," Larry said. He felt kindly for her now with his secret. "Come in for a moment and tell me to clean up my room and get to bed, and I'll say, 'Oh Ma,' and you say 'I'm going to talk to your father about this,' and I say 'Good night, Ma,' and 'I love you, Ma,' and you say, 'What a strange kid.'"

His mother looked at him, and then the smile. She shook her head as if it were too full to stay still.

"Goodnight," he said again. "You can go, so I can throw my clothes on the floor."

"Goodnight, Larry."

It took three weeks at the end of summer for them to complete the garage. Larry was a careful worker, fast but careful, but though he was handy and methodical, he wasn't keen on a life of projects the way his father was. He was worried by what he was beginning to hear when he was in the store and drove the weekend delivery truck; people were expecting him to come into the store, three generations of a hardware family, and what a good thing it all was for everybody. Craig never said anything to the folks who made the remarks, and he had seen from the beginning that the store wasn't a fit for Larry. The boy could go his own way and should. But the expectation was between them in the air as they worked; Craig could feel it unsaid.

But there was a lot of good labor in revamping the old garage:

lifting and some clean drywall work, and the boy was running for football, and he took it all as a kind of muscular play and fell to the work with rapacity. It was easy after all the projects they'd done on their house. First they'd had to get Mr. Brand's boat out of the garage, a new old boat. The boat from the story. It was thirty years old and hadn't been used for thirty, a red and white MerCruiser that was packed in amid boxes and house goods in such a way that when Craig and Larry finally pried the old garage door open, it looked like a wall of stuff and no boat at all. They moved every box, crate, and lamp into the backyard. There was a lot of gear and half an inch of velvet dust on everything. Then they found the boat trailer's tires flat and rotten at the folds. Craig didn't even tell Mrs. Brand about that because it would have seemed a cruel expense for her to have to replace them. He robbed the outside tires from the worn-out horse trailer behind his place, and he and Larry, pulling like mules, inched the pretty boat and its fine fur coat of dust into the daylight for the first time in thirty years. When they'd got the bow outside, Craig stood to wipe his brow, and he saw Mr. Edgar Brand standing at the back door watching them.

It was understood this was all done over Mr. Brand's objection. Mr. Brand did not want Jimmy back, wouldn't have him in the house. But when his wife stood before him and said that Jimmy would stay in the garage, that none of it would cost her husband a nickel, not one nickel, he relented. She was confused and heartbroken by this turn of events. Her grief in its layers had settled, she'd thought, and now it was blazing anew. She would take her son in. "He's our son," she said to her husband. He looked at her, a stony look that invoked all the past and the hard emptiness of the days around them, and he did not answer, not even with the dark rejoinder that he'd used so many years before, the year Jimmy Brand had finally left their house.

Larry, a strong boy and the promise of Oakpine High's fall football season, and his father drew the boat down the driveway and then pushed it back onto the lawn parallel on one side of the garage. All the boxes and gear on the Brands' back lawn had quickened the interest in a neighborhood that wasn't used to any change, and the appearance of this boat emerging from a building drew a little crowd under the high canopy of tree shade. A handful of kids, a couple of young mothers, and the Terry boys, who had been working in their yard, as well as Ed Hannah, who delivered for the Sears catalog store. They stood in a little crescent near the sidewalk and watched the two men struggle with the trailer. The original pale green canvas over the boat was rotted through in several places, and Craig cut it off, revealing the bright red and white craft, pretty as a toy. The life preservers and two wooden paddles were like new. He threw Larry his keys and told him to run down to the hardware for one of the extra large blue tarps, so they could wrap the boat against the weather.

Craig saw Mr. Brand on the porch in the overalls that he had worn forever, working at the railroad, around town, and at home. Underneath was a plaid flannel shirt, and Craig saw him there and thought, *Either he's got an endless supply of those shirts, or that one is thirty-five years old.* Craig raised a hand in greeting as he moved around the boat, making sure it was square on the trailer and checking the fittings. The gesture startled Mr. Brand, who moved down the steps for the first time in all of this.

"Okay, everybody," he said. "You can go on." He waved them back. "You've seen a boat before."

Carol Terry, who was almost his age, called out, "We've never seen that boat before. I didn't even know you had a boat, Edgar."

The little crowd dispersed slowly, some of them, while the kids hung around to watch Craig work, the way they'd been watching the changes all month. Mr. Brand came out across to the boat and put his hand on the bow.

"Sure is pretty," Craig said.

Mr. Brand looked at him.

There are a thousand things, a thousand stories, and their parts that never get said, Craig thought, looking at the old man. *It's just a boat and just a garage, but they've choked him all this time. I'm no better. Words don't weigh an ounce, and I can't haul them.* "We'll cover her right and tight," Craig said to the older man, who without a nod or a word went back into his house.

While Larry stapled insulation in the plank walls of the old garage, Craig refitted the little bathroom that Mr. Brand had installed so long ago. Sweating in the early September days, the two worked without speaking. At quarter to five every day, Larry set his tools in a milk crate, folded his tool belt on top, and drove off to football practice. His forearms were dusted with chalk from the sheetrock. Craig stayed on an hour and prepared for the next day, making a materials list. He stood at the little sink, the porcelain bowl crazed with the web of faint cracks from all the winters. He'd seal it, but he didn't have stand-alone hot and cold faucets of this type at the hardware store; he'd have to take them apart and fit them with new gaskets. He turned each, and the water bubbled and then ran clear, but they both leaked from under their silver letters: H and C.

These were funny days for Craig, which was his word, *funny*, because he felt something working in him, something that had been sparked by being back in the old neighborhood, the light through the mammoth cottonwoods and poplars on Berry Street, the smell of the Brands' garage, the turning year. He'd been ten or twelve years old when the structure was erected in a weekend, and he could still remember hearing the old gas-driven cement mixer churning, and watching the way the men shoveled and troweled the heavy wet concrete into the waiting floor forms. His initials were in some corner under a wall brace. The event had the feeling of picnic; there must have been coolers with beer. Craig remembered the bright wood of the framed walls lying on the ground and then being lifted by groups of neighbors, helping Mr. Brand. The yellow two-by-fours were swung up to vertical and nailed at the corners, and then the building stood where no building had been. When he thought of Jimmy Brand coming home, it seemed just strange, like a visit from a lost world. They'd been friends, close friends, a million years ago. The last time he'd seen Jimmy Brand was at the party at the reservoir two days after graduation.

Marci was surprised to hear of the prodigal's return. "He's a writer, I thought," she said. "What's he coming back to Oakpine for?" Marci had dated Jimmy in high school, had been his last girlfriend. "Stewart has shown me clippings at the museum from the book review. It'll be good to see him."

"He's sick," Craig told her. "His mother told me he's sick."

Marci came out of the bedroom carrying her short maroon coat and her shoes and her purse. She sat at the kitchen table by her half cup of coffee and pulled on her shiny pumps with a finger. She looked smart. When Larry started high school three years before, she'd gone back to work, having acquired a job she loved as administrative assistant at the museum. Stewart Posner had done everything he could to change it from frontier culture, as he called it, into a real museum.

What he liked to do, everyone knew, was shock the town at least once a year. He was the only guy in Oakpine besides all the Popes, who ran the mortuary, who wore a tie everywhere he went. Even the rodeo.

Marci looked good. She shopped through the catalogs and had a quiet taste. Her dark brown hair was parted to one side and fell to her shoulders. She looked just like she had in high school, to Craig. She'd been class historian and wore the Executive Board sweater and a kilt once a week and looked absolutely put together. They had married the year after graduation, and then Craig had gone to Vietnam while she stayed in Oakpine and interned and taught social studies and geography at the junior high. When he returned, he found Oakpine "all changed," that is, all his buddies were gone, and so he and Marci went to Clearwater, Florida, where a guy he'd met in the army ran a huge orange orchard, and Craig worked there "doing everything," which meant all the building and vehicle maintenance, while Marci tried to "do Florida" and grew homesick. When people go to Florida, the summer is hot and wet, but the fall is hard on them because their bodies wait to feel the change that never quite comes. Marci missed the changing leaves and walking in them, but she also missed the mornings with the furnace on and wearing sweaters even to the store, and the roadside stands of squash and pumpkins, and the rainy afternoons, and the twelve shades of gray a sky could go against Oakpine Mountain. Plus Marci didn't really care for the beach, and both times she went out in a boat more than a quarter mile, she became seasick. They gave Florida almost four years.

Craig wanted to get a job with the railroad or Chevron, where he could work, fix things, and not sell parts and tools to people, but there were slim pickings, and he went into the store with his dad and that was that. He put on some weight and became used to it all, especially

after he started to make a little money. Marci wanted a house in Oakpine Heights, and so the job made sense. By the time they'd moved in,
Craig was a hardware salesman. They waited to have a child even longer while she finished her degree, commuting to Laramie, which took
two extra years.

It had been a life. Hunting and football in the fall. The store.
Christmas with Marci's parents there in town, now that his were gone.
Spring cleanup and sales at the store. Fishing. The years. He hadn't felt
old, ever, except for twice. When they came back from Clearwater and
he started at the store, but he got over that. And now he felt it again
upon hearing Jimmy Brand's name, that he was coming back to
Oakpine.

"We've all changed too much," Marci said. "All the stuff we knew,
those times are long dead twice . . ."

"Thirty years," Craig said, not believing it. There was no way to
believe it. "It will be amazing to see him," he said, drinking his coffee.
His white nylon jacket had his name on a patch, and his white shirt
underneath also said CRAIG. He'd work in the store until noon today
and then go prep to paint the inside of the Brands' little garage guest
room.

"We'll have to have a dinner for this bona fide reunion." She stood
and saw the look on her husband's face. "Listen, don't brood over your
remodeling project for Mrs. Brand. It's going to be okay. I can't fathom
what the Brands are doing making him stay in that garage. I'm going
to run. I'll see you later."

Craig sat for just a minute looking out at the village of Oakpine
spread below him and, beyond that, the sienna steps of greater Wyoming layered to the west. Marci got in her blue Saab and drove through
the scrub oak along their gravel drive and disappeared. This was the

good life, and Craig was happy. He thought it again more slowly: *This is the good life, and I am happy.*

The garage project for Mrs. Brand was the best work he'd had since the back deck on his house. Before that it was sheds; he always tried to go with one of the guys when they built the little storage sheds that he sold as kits out of the store, but those only came up four or five times a year, most of them prebuilt and hauled away. He had the front double doors of the hardware store propped open every morning as the noonday warmed, and he helped customers and made keys, and in his head he planned the afternoon's work at the Brands' garage.

Larry worked in the store all day in the summers, and he made his disdain for such work very clear. This was his third year of cleaning the storeroom, repainting the rest room, dusting and washing some of the fixtures, weeding the alley behind the building, running errands, and making deliveries. Deliveries were his favorite, and he stretched them, swinging by to see his buddy Wade at his house to lift weights or drink a soda while the Ralston Hardware van sat out on the street. Craig knew all about it, and he knew that Larry thought working in a hardware store was beneath him, beneath everybody. Anybody with any dignity got out of Oakpine. Wade, who was the football coach's son, was going to play football at some college next fall, probably Laramie. Larry had no idea where he was going, but he was going, that was for sure.

At three, he joined his father at the Brands. Craig finished taping the drywall, and Larry came behind him with his sandpaper blocks. The garage door was lifted open in the late summer afternoon, and their sandpaper dust floated golden in the light. "What's she going to do about the door?" Larry said.

"We'll staple it with our heavy plastic sheeting," Craig told him.

"It won't be perfect, but the seal will keep the cold out. They're going to want to use this garage again."

"After your buddy dies?"

"That's what we'll do with the ceiling too," Craig said, pointing above them, where there were still a lot of boxes stored on planks on the bare rafters. "We'll do that tomorrow and then paint. Remind me to bring some solvent for this floor." Under all the sawdust there were oil stains in the old cement. The two stepped out into the sunlight, and Larry slapped at his pant legs, freeing clouds of chalk dust.

"When I come home years from now with all my problems," he said, "are you going to stuff me in the garage?"

"Are you coming home?"

"Should I wait for an invitation?"

Before Craig could answer, Wade pulled up in his black Nissan pickup, turning into the narrow driveway. It was a beautiful vehicle, and they could see Wendy, his girlfriend, in the passenger side.

"A new truck," Craig said.

"I don't need a truck, Dad," Larry said. "I'll see you later." He got in, and the three kids were gone to football practice. Craig remembered the summer workouts, running twice a day on the rough practice field behind the school. He'd never liked to run, but he'd never quit, and he remembered sitting on their truck tailgates after practice drinking well water from glass gallon jugs and smelling of cut grass. He could see it vividly, and the feeling he'd had climbed up his chest like some heavy thing in the great afternoon shadows: they could run for two hours; they could run until the sun quit and the dark came up. They would live forever.

He was losing the light, but he lifted the box of floor tiles and turned to see a gray Mercedes drive by on Berry Street slowly, and

Craig recognized the driver: Mason Kirby. Craig walked out to the front of the house and saw the big car drift slowly three houses down and stop in front of the old Kirby place. He waited, but the man did not get out of the car. Craig took the box and went back to work.

Craig got onto his hands and knees and laid adhesive tile squares on the floor of the tiny bathroom, cutting and fitting the pieces expertly. They were a speckled tan, and he looked into them a thousand miles. Alone like this, working carefully, Craig felt good. It was late in the day, and Mason would certainly stay a day or two. He had probably come up to sell the place. For some reason he remembered an afternoon standing with Jimmy in the Brands' backyard, plucking the last garden tomatoes and throwing them at Frank and Mason up at his place, laughing and dodging the incoming. *Memory*, he thought, *what is that good for? I'm fifty years old, and I'm on my knees in the Brands' garage, and I don't have anyplace better to be.* "Oh my hell," he said aloud, and heard the words. "You're lonely." *I'll put in a garden box with two-by-twelves*, he thought. *We've got the space. Marci won't want to, but I can grow some tomatoes, even if the deer eat them.* He took his time, and when he set in the last corner, it was almost dark, and the small piece of tile fit like a jewel, and he pressed it there with his hand and with the handle of his hammer until the seam disappeared.

TWO

Home

Mason Kirby had never been lost in his life, not even as a kid out of Oakpine in the real wilderness on backpacking trips or the like. Nor had he been lost in Europe, or in London, or in Alaska on a fishing trip, which was only business, or even drunk in college, or on one trip to South America, Caracas; and on that trip he became the go-to guy when it was time to find the small van that took the elite tour group around.

And now he pulled his plum Mercedes off the two-lane onto the gravel shoulder, and in the bland midday cloud cover and on the dry grass plain, he didn't know the number of the route or if he was still going north or northeast or east. He could see in all four directions the flat grassy earth. He was lost. He stood out of the car and noted that there were small weeds able to work through the cracks in the old road. He'd been driving for four hours, which meant he was either in Nebraska or about to come right back to Denver. He went back and opened the trunk just to see again the tangible evidence of his decision. His clothes were laid in a fan on one side, and he smiled to see he'd brought his suit. Maybe he'd have a job interview. His beautiful leather Dopp kit, the gift from Elizabeth six, seven years ago, his valise, swollen with the papers concerning the pending sale of his firm, and the black shoe box, which he now lifted and opened to see the $21,000 stacked there. A shoe box. It was such a raw maneuver, bringing that cash. He didn't need it, and in fact every time he'd had two or three thousand dollars cash in his wallet or in the console of his car, Elizabeth had said, What good thing can come of that? But he knew he'd gone to the bank and obtained all the hundreds in the zippered bag, not a tenth of what was in his account, so he'd have proof of his decision. Sell the firm, take a break, go. A shoe box; it was such a joke. He was so dramatic.

Again he scanned the horizon, not a hill, no smoke, not a clue. The sky was a seamless gray. He could turn on the GPS and know in a minute, but he hadn't turned it on after the first week with this car. The woman giving directions spoke French. That was okay, but he disliked the world jumping at him that way: *line line line, turn right, line line.* Plus, he had never been lost, and now he knew he was, and he felt it in the top of his stomach, the way a kid would. He felt the gravity of Denver pale and fade, and yet there was no pull from anything else. He'd never been between things; maybe that was it.

He stood and felt the realtor's letter in his sport coat pocket. Shirley Stiver, same class at the high school. His old house was in fact empty, the renters fled, and what to do? He could call her back from right here right now, assuming there was a satellite also lost above this place, and have it handled with four sentences, but no. He was lost, but he knew where he was going.

He thought of his BlackBerry but didn't check it, because he knew not to. He'd learned well as a lawyer to leave it until it beckoned. He looked at the thing twice a day on principle: first and last. He'd made sure it was off and thrown it into the trunk. Done.

Back on the road, still lost, he thought that like everything else in his life, this would last ten minutes. But an hour later the terrain had shifted to shallow hills run with sage, and dropping down a short incline, he came into the hamlet of Garrell, the two churches, the auto parts, the Grocery Basket, the old Rexall drug store, and the Bargain Barn, which had been in a former day a department or furniture store, and at the far end of town two bars, the Wasatch and the Divide, which didn't have a window in the front, even in the old painted red plank door. The two other license plates in the gravel parking were from Kansas. He hadn't had a drink in the afternoon for ten years, but now he was dislocated, feeling more like a blank page than he could ever remember.

"A man walks into a bar," he said, pulling the door open. "No," he said. "A lawyer walks into a bar." The bartender was sorting a rack of thick glasses, nesting them in rows behind bar, and he glanced over as Mason entered, looking for the person he was talking to.

"Just me," Mason said.

There was one other person in the place, an older man whose hair had been printed by the circle of a cap, but there was no cap on the bar. He was dressed in a blue oxford cloth shirt and khakis, and he watched Mason step up and sit two stools down at the bar.

"A dumb fat lawyer walks into a bar."

"What's that?" the bartender said. He was forty and thin-haired and pale. He was the owner. Mason could tell by the way he'd handled the glasses.

"Just a draft of Fat Tire," Mason said. "And a shot of whatever whiskey goes with it."

"They've all learned to go with it," the barman said.

"Any then." Mason turned to the other patron. "You want any Any?" he asked. "I'm buying."

"I don't know," the man said.

"Oh-oh," Mason said feeling suddenly like arguing. He'd been floating all day since he'd dropped off the keys to his loft with Allison at the office, and now he wanted to argue. "A truth teller."

"Yeah, pour me one, Gene," the man said.

"How long have you had the place?" Mason asked Gene.

"What's your guess?"

"I guess one year. The place is polished up, no dust on the shoulders of the bottles, even the old blue brandies, and optimism is in the air."

The man sitting at the bar turned, "And you're a realtor or a professor."

"I was a lawyer," Mason said.

"I won't ask," the man said. When Mason held his glance, the man said, "I manage the little satellite TV store in Farview."

"That's hardly bar-fight material," Mason said.

"Did you come in to fight?" Gene said. "Is that why you wore the sport coat?"

"I don't know. I don't know how I started the day. But since we're talking, I think I came in here to get hit."

The television representative shook his head. "You deserve to be hit?"

"Certainly," Mason said. "Should I provoke you?"

"Oh, I'm provoked,"

"Gene, your new bar is a powder keg."

"We haven't had a fight in here since I bought the place."

"People don't fight anymore," the man down the bar said. "They swear and they shoot each other later, but they won't fight. It's too genuine."

Mason tossed back his whiskey. He lifted his beer. "You want to hit me?" he said to the man.

"Let me just say it," the man said. "I wouldn't know how. I'd hurt myself, and I'm not provoked enough to want that."

Mason put a hundred-dollar bill on the bar and said, "Let's have another. Gene, can I buy you a drink?"

"Then you ask me to hit you? No thanks."

"No hitting," Mason said. "I can't remember the last time I made a fist. Is that good news or bad?"

Gene set the beer bottles out and poured the Jack Daniel's.

"Where you from?" Gene asked Mason.

"Denver. I'm out for a drive."

"Yes, you are."

Mason took in the room now that his eyes had adjusted, and he noted the four mismatched pool tables and the old red banquettes along the wall, and above each, high in the cinder-block wall, were windows made of six glass bricks. Those windows and the girder ceiling made Mason turn back to the barman.

"Is this the old Annex? Was it called the Annex?"

"It was called the Emporium and built by Wallace Debans when he came back from the war, and he sold furniture to all the ranchers out of this building, including washers and dryers, and as he used to say, the washer and dryer won the West. By that he meant that they had made this windy place habitable for women, and I think he also meant that he sold thousands of them and was able to retire. He's still alive and lives in Brook. Do you know where that is?"

"And then it was the café, the Annex, right?"

"You've been in here before."

"I was in this building thirty years ago on a night when we were coming back from a football game in Chadron, and our team ate at two long tables that were set along the wall there and there. I played junior varsity one year. I think this was a big chicken restaurant."

"The Annex was famous for chicken. Sundays were crazy. People would drive, sometimes from Denver, to have the deep-fried chicken."

"What town was it?" the man down the bar asked Mason.

"Oakpine. I grew up there."

"I've got an aunt in Oakpine," the man said. "Or used to."

"Where is it?" Mason said. "From here."

"Two hours and some. North on twenty-one until you cross the state line, and then you'll see the signs."

The owner, Gene, leaned on the back bar and folded his arms. "You going home?" he asked Mason.

Mason looked at the man. "I am now," he said. His voice had a shadow in it, and the barman looked at him seriously.

"What's the matter with you?" he said.

Immediately something rose in Mason to deflect this inquiry, and he had nothing ready in a second, the nothing he'd used like a windshield all his life, but the question touched the quick, and he knew his face had registered its canny accuracy, and he had another thought rise up: *Why hide it? Wherever you are, it's there too.*

"Five things or six," Mason said. "But the real thing is that I am simply over with the one life, I guess. I thought I wanted it, but what? Not really." He had to whisper the last.

All three men were still in the big room. And the silence ran along until the cooler motor shuddered on and the silence ran under that, and then Mason said quietly, "Do not say anything. I regret my remarks. It's okay."

The silence bore on almost another minute, and then the man down the bar said, "I'm sorry, man."

Mason used the blow to lift and drink his whiskey. "I'm not a drinker. And I'm not a fighter. I'm a lawyer who until ten minutes ago was lost in the West." And he knew that until ten minutes ago he was another man choking on his sublime unhappiness. The mathematics of everything had grown murky and was now impossible.

"You got any coffee?" Mason asked Gene.

"Let's make some fresh coffee right now," the barman said.

Three hours later, driving in the late summer twilight, Mason could sense a fence along the old highway, a fence he knew, and then the ruined tower of the abandoned wooden water tank along the railroad tracks off to the right, so old now it wasn't even photographed anymore, an artifact he knew from fishing trips with his father when he was five and six; it told him when they were almost out of town. Now the prairie still glowed, and he could see the empty shacks popping up on each side of the highway, places so desolate it would be hard to last a season in any, and the creatures who had lived there had been gone longer than Mason, and then the failed equipment yards, the broken fences and derelict vehicles and trailers, welcome home, and the lights now ahead of his hometown twinkling feebly as if unsure they would last the night.

Finally the road turned, and he rose over the railway on the one overpass and came into the west side of town, fitting into Mason's memory like a key he didn't want. Suddenly a figure flashed across his headlights, a tall boy running across the corner lot like a ghost, some lost soul running where no one rightly ran, but purposeful those strides, and now gone. Mason rubbed his eyes. Did he really see that? He closed his eyes, and the figure was printed there, a white runner. Well, and there in the rubble lot at the edge of his old hometown was the old burned husk of the Trail's End Motel, the nine units having been burned in 1985 or so by the first of the meth squatters, a charred skeleton lying under the crazy sign of the covered wagon and the feathered arrow. In the dark it came at him hard. He and Jimmy Brand had stayed there two nights thirty years ago, Jimmy hiding and about to flee. When Jimmy was finally on the bus, Mason went back and paid the bill to Mrs. Durfey, and he remembered it was some sixty-eight dollars. It was Mason who had taken Jimmy's handwritten letter in the motel envelope to Mrs. Brand. Beyond her and perhaps her husband, no one else knew where Jimmy was, and Mason didn't tell them. Now, in the Wyoming night, he drove past the old high school and took a room at the Best Western, in what had been an alfalfa field when he was a boy.

In the late twilight Craig Ralston pulled the little side door of the garage carefully closed and saw his reflection in the new glass. He wiped the window ledge again. The place would smell like paint for two days. After storing his tools in the steel box in the bed of his pickup, he went around and sat in the cab, one leg on the ground. He breathed on purpose and was glad for it. Up Berry Street as far as he could see, shadows webbed and traded on the patched roadway. It was like fatigue, but he wasn't tired. He climbed in and started the vehicle and drove back toward the store, but at Main Street he turned there for the tracks and dropped two blocks to park in front of the Antlers. He knew this town by memory, by heart, through every incarnation the storefronts had had for forty years. Frank Gunderson owned the Antlers, had for years, and five other three-story red block buildings down here. Craig was still wearing his Ralston's Hardware shirt, which was run with shorelines of dirt and sweat and full of chalk powder. It was the middle of September, and he had finished with the Brands' garage an hour before, rolling the bay floor with a coat of barn red, scraping and washing the paned window in the door, and then freeing up the doorknob. He'd had to disassemble and sand it before spraying the sleeve with lubricant. Tomorrow Larry and his friend Wade were going over to help Mrs. Brand move the bed and some other furniture into the room. When Craig had gotten the ancient doorknob to function, oiling it and then resetting the screws so that it registered fully closed, he stood there looking in, and he felt something, again funny, weird. He wasn't used to having the end of the day work in him in any way, and now he felt heavy, sad, and excited. He was proud of what they had done, but it was more. He hadn't been to the Antlers all summer, but here he was. It was just dark.

Wedged between the mountain bike store and Oakpine Java, the new coffee shop, the old black-tin front of the Antlers hadn't changed since he and Frank and Mason Kirby had painted it the last summer they were all together thirty years before. Inside, the place was half full because of *Monday Night Football*, and Craig slid onto a barstool. The old back bar was a hundred and twenty-four years old, an elegant monstrosity that the former owners had found in Bozeman and shipped down in four parts in two trucks sometime in the fifties. It was dark cherry and had fluted pillars and carved doors, and fourteen cherubs swam across the top, seven on a side, each big as a real baby, centering a figurehead nude, a placid woman with long hair and small breasts. She was seventeen feet from the floor, Craig knew, way above the two televisions at either end of the long, scarred cherrywood bar, so high nobody even looked for her up there in the dark. The beveled mirror was set in three huge sections, and the three bullet holes along the top of the center panel dated from prehistory, although they were featured as the punch line in a thousand stories, all about big jealousy and mistaken identity, and all sworn to be true and very recent.

Sonny was tending the bar, and Craig ordered a schooner of Cowboy lager, which was one of the two beers Frank's little brewery made out back. "You're still working here," he said to her.

Sonny set the tall beer in front of him and looked him in the face. "Meaning?"

"Sonny," he said. "Meaning nothing." She looked tired, a pretty woman with dark hair to her shoulders. She wore a man's blue dress shirt with a pen in the pocket. "I never said one thing in my life that had a meaning. I'm surprised to see you. I don't know."

"Well, hello to you too, Craig Ralston. You ought not to come in here in your Mr. Hardware shirt like that. The good folks will think we've got plumbing problems. Which we do." She glanced up at the television and started to move down the bar.

"Sonny, I didn't mean anything. I'm an oaf. Don't be offended by anything an oaf says. You know already that I like you just fine."

She softened and smiled. "I do know. And you are an oaf. And I'm still in town, and I still have a job, and this is my job, and I'm sort of happy and plan, frankly, to stay. Enjoy your beer. Frank's right around the corner at one of the tables if you want to know."

"You always had a way with women," the man next to him said. It was Al Price, who had spent more time in the Antlers than any man, even Frank, who owned the place. Once or twice a month in the winter Al would end up sleeping in one of the big booths in the back. He'd been in their class too, a tough guy who didn't play football and who lost a hand in his first month as a roughneck in the Chevron fields. He'd been nineteen. Now he was gray and grizzled, looking both wiry and soft at the same time, looking, Craig thought, as old as the rest of us.

"Hey, Al. Can I buy you a beer?"

"You ain't been in here for a while," Al said. He was cleaned up, comb tracks in his hair, his eyes bright.

"Life caught up to the good times," Craig said. "Larry's a senior, you know."

"Jesus Christ. I'd heard rumors that they kept that school open after we ruined it. A senior. What's he going to do to shame us all?

"He wants out of Oakpine," Craig said. "And he's not really picky after that."

"An idealist."

"And how's Marci? Don't even tell me. I know she's thriving. She's the one of us not to worry about. She's always been together."

"Right there, Al. She's at the museum. What you been up to?"

"Dribs and drabs," Al said. "I'm doing swing security at the transfer station. It's okay. Enough to buy beer, but not enough to get my teeth fixed." Al lifted his head and showed the two gaps on the sides of his mouth. "We're so old, our teeth have given up. You still got yours."

Craig looked at Al. It was a picture of two fifty-year-olds at a bar, Craig knew, but all he could see was this kid he had known who had been a smartass and careless and who'd hung on the periphery of things. All these years had passed, but it seemed simply impossible. "Yeah," Craig said. "I still got mine, but I never use them." Al snorted at this and began to laugh, a tight wheeze of a laugh, an alcoholic laugh overtly, and when his face settled, his eyes looked ancient. "I'm going to catch up with Frank," Craig said, standing. "Sonny," he called to the woman who now stood at the end under the television, "let's get Al a beer."

She pointed her finger at him and pulled the trigger. "You're an ace," she said.

"Thanks, man," Al said. "You're an ace."

Frank was in the first booth talking to his brewmaster, Ted Klein. There were papers spread on the table. "Well, Big Craig Ralston,"

Frank said to his old friend, "sit down." Craig greeted them both and tucked himself into one side of the table. "We just set our tanks in place today. Ted's in business. We're about to make some beer."

"Good deal," Craig said. "Congratulations. When do we sample the first batch?"

"We'll get the wrinkles out this week and start in," Ted said. "We're going to make an amber ale that should be ready about the time you get back with your first antelope."

"I like that," Craig said. "But I don't hunt anymore. I gave it up that time with Frank and Mason and Jimmy when we ran into the guy who'd been shot, remember?"

"You gave up everything, don't you mean, and years ago. We weren't exactly hunting, more like camping with guns."

"The point is to get out of town," Ted said. "If you hunt after that or not, it's okay."

"For god sakes, this old fart's not a hunter," Frank said to Ted. "We gave it up and went indoors, right, Craig? We're grass eaters now. I couldn't tell you where my rifle even is. Time cuts a guy real good." Frank called for Sonny, and she appeared around the corner and leaned her hip on his shoulder. "Bring us three more, dear," Frank told her. "Do you remember Craig?"

"I saw him already," she said. "He's glad to see me."

"I am," Craig said. "I thought—"

"He thought I'd run away so as not to ruin your former marriage," Sonny said, and disappeared.

"She gets right into it, doesn't she?" Frank said.

"How is Kathleen?" Craig said.

Ted pushed the papers into line and gathered them up, tapping the edge. He laid them back in a neat stack. Craig could see the diagrams of the vats on the top sheet.

Frank looked pained. "Everybody is fine. It's all old news. Sonny's a good woman, with her antenna out to here. She's sick of everybody assuming she's the deal, when it was just Kathleen and me crosswise. We've had some little moments, but everybody is an adult, and everybody is fine."

"Good, good," Craig said too fast. "As you know, I'm one of the few guys you know who wouldn't know what to do with an opinion."

Sonny herself appeared now with her tray and three glass pints of lager, setting them before the men. Without speaking or looking at any of them, she left.

"Sonny is staying," Frank said. "It turns out to be a free country, and she's staying in town." He lifted his glass. "Did you come out to take a census? I haven't seen you in months."

"I finished a project over at the Brands and had an hour."

"Are they selling the place?" Frank asked. "All the houses in that neighborhood are turning over."

"They finished the garage out back, insulation, the works. It's Jimmy. Jimmy's coming back. I guess he's sick."

"Jimmy Brand."

"There's a blast from the past," Ted said. "That's Matt Brand's little brother?"

"I thought Jimmy was dead," Frank said. "Where'd he live, New York?"

"Mrs. Brand said New York. Marci has some letters years old that were from New York. I think he's been out there all this time."

"Why the garage?" Ted asked. "What's the deal on that?"

Frank interrupted: "Jesus, we spent a lot of time over there, remember, Craig? We had a band, Ted, in high school and used to tear up the garage pretty good. Rock 'n' roll. Christ, talk about ancient history." Frank slid out of the booth. "Wait a minute."

He went behind the bar and returned with an aluminum step stool and set it up beside the jukebox and stepped up and reached the yellow bass guitar that was hanging there just below two mounted antelope heads. Wiping it with a bar towel, he brought the instrument over, grinning and plucking the strings. "Hell, maybe it will all come back to me." He handed it to Craig, who held it in his lap. The name RANGE-MEN was written along the shoulder in a loopy cursive in red enamel. "That name may have been premature," Frank said. "I'll have to take this over and show Jimmy. You still got your drums?"

"I think one survives," Craig said.

"Well, dig it out." Frank went on, "When we were little kids, Old Man Brand would stand on his front porch in those overalls and bellow for Matt and Jimmy. You could hear it downtown. Everybody knew it was six o'clock—you could set your damn watch by it. I think they ran the trains by it. Jesus, Jimmy Brand. He could play the guitar."

The beer had a heavy pleasant pull, and Craig sipped from his again. He'd last had this guitar in his hands thirty years ago as they unloaded somewhere, setting up for one of their few gigs. It had been fun. His old drum kit was in storage, a hole through one of the snares. Why had he kept it?

Frank saw Craig's face. "What? Is there trouble?"

"Mr. Brand won't let Jimmy back in the house, doesn't want to see him at all. This garage deal is her idea. I've been over there six weeks, haven't seen the old man except the day we pulled the boat out." Craig was thinking about the garage, what a good job it had been, how he was going to miss it. The store was wearing him out, all that smiling and the chatter. Any satisfaction he'd gotten out of finding someone the right hex nut was ghosted, gone. It was a good living, but it was eating his days.

"Jesus, that's right. I heard that boat was out of the garage," Frank said. "That's the boat that killed Matt, cut him up like a sausage. Our first real tragedy, I'd say. Holy shit, what a deal. So Jimmy Brand is coming back to old Oakpine. How sick is he? We'll have to get together. Somebody should call Mason, and we'll get the band back together."

"Mason's coming. He is selling his folks' place. Fix it and sell it."

Sonny appeared. "Another beer?"

"I got to get," Craig said. "Thanks."

Frank waved off, and she went back to the front. He raised the last of his beer. "This lager is pretty good, but it will be nice to have some of our own beer at last." He drank. They all drank.

"Is this good lager?" Craig asked Ted. "I mean, it seems real good to me."

"American lager is always a little green," Ted said. "They hurry it, age it with chemicals, and then drive it around in trucks."

"You can't truck good beer," Frank said. "Shipping kills it. It comes off like bus passengers, road shot and ready for nothing." The three drank up.

"I'll grab Mason and bring him down for some of this nectar. I'm giving it an A right now. You guys are perfectionists." Craig said. He set his glass on the wooden table.

"Thanks, Craig. We'll take it even though you don't know any better," Frank said. "Find your drums, big guy."

Craig smiled as he stood. He could feel the beer. He hadn't been in a bar after work for twenty years. *What am I*, he thought, *single?*

When Jimmy Brand returned home to Oakpine, Wyoming, from New York City, he was met at the little airport not by his mother or father but by Chuck Andreson, in the old Suburban he drove as a utility taxi.

Jimmy had four small trunks, everything he owned in the world. It had been thirty years, and he looked at the new terminal building and smiled. He was pretty cooked from the flights, and he sat in the wheelchair at the curb while Chuck pulled the big van around.

"You're Louise and Edgar's youngest boy," Chuck said.

"I'm the only," Jimmy said with no irony. "And no boy."

"I knew Matt," Chuck said. "At the high school. I was a year ahead."

"You go to Vietnam?" Jimmy asked the bearded man.

"No," Chuck said. "I got the diabetes." He closed the back of the vehicle and came around to where Jimmy sat. Jimmy was looking across the road, across the mowed field to the village of Oakpine, where it sat at the foot of the massive rolling forest of Oakpine Mountain. He knew it so well and had seen it in his mind a thousand times, and now his imagination fought with the vista before him and he had to keep blinking. The view encompassed forty miles. Above the village the ridges were still bright green but run with the red and brown of the canyons. The town kept slipping from Jimmy's vision as if it could be misplaced, and refocusing his eyes took as much energy as a deep breath. Could you mislay a town, let it get away?

"You pretty sick?" Chuck asked.

"I am," Jimmy said. "I'm sick. This is it for me. I'm home." His smile was weak. "Don't worry. Just help me with the chair. I can get in the car."

Exiting the airport, they passed a small herd of antelope grazing between the near runways. "You come from New York?"

"I lived in New York all these years."

"That's some from Oakpine."

"It can be. New York's a lot of places, really."

"Right, and Oakpine's just the one. You like it, New York?"

They entered town and inched along the street toward the high school. It would be okay not to talk; each answer felt like a chapter. Cars were double-parked and parked one wheel on the sidewalk and on the lawns here and there, angled into the narrow road as if abandoned in a hurry under the sullen skies. There was a raft of smoke still hovering over the large parking lot, which Jimmy could see was full of RVs and lawn chairs. Chuck wended to the far end of the field, and a place opened so they could see the game and all the people in colored coats in the stands. Two teams struggled in the gray afternoon, and the crowds seemed a waving blanket to Jimmy.

"I had a life there," Jimmy said. He pointed to the game. "Is it Friday? Who are we playing?" The *we* came from some forgotten place, and he smiled to hear it.

"Sheridan's down. My boy's out there. I'm going to swing back by after we get you home." Chuck craned his neck to see the scoreboard. "It's tied."

"Hey, let's just stop now. Park right over there and get out to the game. I'll sit here and take it in." Chuck looked over at him, so he added, "Seriously. There's no hurry about getting me out to Berry Street. I've been gone a long time."

Every two minutes the roar of the crowd at the football game nine blocks away lifted Marci Ralston's head from the drawings on her desk in the museum. They were all working on Saturday with a deadline for the new program. High school. This whole town is high school. She imagined her son running in the rain. The sound of the town all there in one place pulled at her, but she had this show to put together. Things were in motion at the Oakpine Museum. Three times a year the pace quickened in the run-up to a new show, and the days were twenty-hour days, six-day weeks. Marci Ralston loved these weeks. A month out the phone calls would double, and then it was shipping and insurance and the artists and their quirks or their agents' quirks or the estate's quirks, demands and tentative demands, and Stewart would give more and more to her to handle, and she wanted it. The fall show was called "Terrain," and there were two big sections, each involving eleven artists. After the initial decision to have the two motifs, one descriptive and one interpretive, Stewart balked on what to call them beyond that, and they needed the nomenclature today. The museum was the old train station in Oakpine, and the transition to museum had been surprisingly successful.

Stewart was Mr. Enthusiasm at the annual projection meetings, but as the shows approached, he became increasingly useless. Or maybe it was that he didn't become anything; he just kept his distance. One thing that was known as an empirical fact among the staff of six at the museum was that he had never, ever opened a crate. He loved to call a meeting to discuss the overview or the game plan or any wrinkles in the calendar, but he never took his jacket off. The headline on him was that his favorite mode was walking backward with his arms folded while he nodded like an expert. They all mimicked him, doing the walk and going *hmmm, hmmm, hmmm*. The opening was two weeks from Sunday.

They were well under way with "Terrain" now, but Stewart had still been going on about what he felt was important about this particular show at this particular point in time, when Marci interrupted: "We can go with 'Here We Are' for the descriptive and 'Here We Are?' for the evaluative." Everyone at the conference table had already picked apart their styrofoam coffee cups and placed the pieces on their ink-doodled notebooks like mosaics. They looked up hopefully, three young men who were glorified interns, and Wanda Dixon, who was Stewart's secretary. Marci was acknowledged as museum coordinator. Stewart leaned forward. "Say it again," he said. She knew it was his way of running a good idea through his posture, while everyone looked at his thoughtful face, and then making it his. When he had heard, he said, "I like it! We change the stakes with a single question mark." He stood up. "Marci, you are too bright for this town."

"You should be in Sheridan," Don Levitt said. He was from Sheridan.

Marci looked around the little conference room. She knew all about it. She'd been here for three years. It wasn't much, but it was what you got. You made enough money to order a few catalog suits, which you got to wear in Oakpine. You went to lunch at the same four places. You let Stewart grope you a little from time to time, just enough to feel you have a separate life, have made a decision. You have your own office with a door and a telephone, and you get to work with the interns and tell them what to do. And once or twice a year you suggest something that will be carved in the layered plastic signage that will tell people what they are looking at and which way to go. It was so close to being enough. She was in some kind of weird era. She recognized that if she stood still, she'd sink. It was hard not to hear the football crowd and sense that the game was the real business of this town.

Stewart came around the table and kissed her on the cheek, his hand briefly on the back of her skirt. When he left to go to his office and get on the phone, she looked at the interns and said, "You know the drill now. It's heavy lifting and fragile, fragile, fragile." She passed out a sheet with the numbered locations of each painting. "Let's just get everything we've got uncrated today, okay?"

It hurt Jimmy Brand to sit for so long. It always hurt, but now he'd been sitting for half an hour in the Suburban, and the pain had grown.

He tried to do the exercises he'd learned at the free clinic in New York, the imaging his group had done, isolating the feeling and then moving it piece by piece slowly back out of the body. He had a lot of places in his mind, and he'd written them from his deep vision, the desert reservoir with the blond clay banks in the sunlight and the sage knolls at each inlet, and the meadows and moose ponds up along the old road on Oakpine Mountain shadowed and surrounded by the dark wall of pines. But his default was Bleecker Street, around the corner from his apartment with Daniel, and then shop by shop up one side, the movie poster shop, the archaeological artifacts, the comic store, the cheap Italian shoes, the Bleak Arms, the green pub, and cornice by cornice to the grocer and his tiers of oranges and the nest of lemons, but he couldn't get a hold of it today, no image would take.

It had been raining now for a little while, and the water sheeted and merged as it ran down the windshield. It blurred the scene before him, the people across the football field in their coats, dots of red, brown, yellow, green, blue, three hundred people in the rain of Wyoming. They would blur and focus in the glass. He concentrated on them as they came and went. The rain was a soft pressure on the van. He lost it and then started awake and made a note to stay awake and lost that. It was a short step from the swimming windshield to his hallucinations to the high dreams. He could not feel himself breathing, and he made that note and then lost it.

Maybe he was already dead, these colored dots come to greet him, witness his induction, rows and rows of the dead blurring in this great gray room, a tray of apples. The dozen friends in New York, one by one, and suddenly the bottom dropped out. Eldon Rayalf had died in elementary school, shot one stormy fall out on the antelope hunt. He was shot in the head, the story was, and the second story was that his uncle, bored in the million-mile afternoon, had been playing with his rifle, up, down, shooting-bushes bored, and wheeling by the boy, he'd touched the trigger early, and instead of offering a noise that would have rung his ears for a week, he took off most of his forehead. Jimmy remembered the funeral in the Mormon chapel, the closed coffin, all the town it seemed, and then the ride to the cemetery. Was he the first? Jimmy's dad's hands were on his shoulder, and Jimmy could see Mr. Rayalf, the back of his head, his dark hair shiny from Brylcreem. Old man Rayalf would have been thirty-one or thirty-two years old at the time, and now he had something he would never get out from under, ever. It became the shadow, the pressure that would press his drinking, and he was a good, quiet, diminished man forevermore. But Eldon wasn't the first. There were two girls with the flu, and Boyd Mildone in junior high, drowned in the river, swimming or fishing. He must have been fishing alone before school, and his waders taken suddenly with the cold water like a scoop, he drowned. There was a place beyond the old Knop junkyard, the spillage of ruined cars, where the river bent and the cattails grew tall, and it had always been only one thing, the place where Boyd had drowned.

Now Jimmy focused suddenly on the furrowed windshield of Chuck Andreson's truck, and beyond he could see the rainy home-team stands, all black dots and yellow dots, raincoats and the red umbrellas here and there, and one green one, a golf umbrella. The plangent dizziness arrived like a breeze, and Jimmy wondered at it again, the merging of the world and idea; how could he ever parse what he was seeing from what he was thinking, especially now with the five kids killed in the car driving back from Cheyenne in the year 1967, all five, and he knew them, middle names and all. And now in a car humming with the impinging friction of the rain, he could hear their voices, Claudia DeSmet, who reminded Jimmy always for some reason of a goose, a girl with a great straight nose and a woman's body at fifteen, now dead thirty-three years.

Before him the clusters of dots, the people in the stands, shifted and reshifted, running in the rain on the glass, and he knew as an idea, as a thing, that he had been writing for them all. They were his audience. So strange. He'd written a thousand reviews for deadlines and for the magazines in New York, and all the stories and the novels, and he'd been writing for the kids they'd all been. He slowed his thinking down and started in sophomore year with homeroom, with Mrs. Scanlon, and he saw the classroom and went down the rows chair by chair looking for the dead. She had the alphabet, in large examples of cursive writing, in a lined banner around the top of the walls, and Jimmy felt the letters now, the weird feeling they'd given him where they were listed above the blackboard and the door and the windows that opened onto the great western desert running west to places that as a boy he could not imagine, though he had tried.

He was dozing lightly, the pain still a hard, untenable force along his spine, when Chuck came back. The big man was wet and smiling. "This one is history."

Jimmy looked at him, unsure for a moment who he was and what he was speaking of. History? "Craig Ralston's boy is the most amazing receiver we've had in some years—he can scramble. We've got Sheridan by two touchdowns with five minutes. You knew Craig Ralston, right? He runs the hardware?"

"I must have," Jimmy said. He felt as disconnected as he'd ever felt. He was going to be sick. Chuck backed the vehicle out of the field, each little bump flaring in Jimmy's bones.

On Berry Street the rain had stopped, and water dripped generously from the trees in the dark sky. Chuck pulled up and came around to Jimmy's door, but Jimmy could not get out. He smiled faintly at the driver and said, "I'm having a little moment here. We might need some help." As he said it, a woman came out of the front door of the house with a windbreaker over her pale blue housedress. She was carrying an umbrella, and at her first movement, he knew it was his mother. He had spoken to her once a year on her birthday, and there were times when she called him on his, but he had seen the woman, who was now coming toward him, only twice in thirty years. His head reeled. He had dreamed of this, this old place where he grew up, many times. And of course he had written about it. Seeing her there, he knew he had dreamed this too, his mother coming to him, taking his hand, her look of concern, her embrace. Her impossible cheek, cool and papery and sweet. The dreams were a blessing.

"Jimmy," she said. Her tears were on his neck. "Jimmy." Now her hands were on his shoulders and the side of his face, and it all rose in him, and he felt as if he were going to black out. He looked at his mother's face, and it registered like light throughout his body.

He whispered, "Mom," and his voice broke. "Mom, I'm sick."

"You're home," she said.

"I'm sick, Mom. I'm so sorry." He hadn't planned anything to say, and he said this, and then he began to cry. He hadn't planned on crying. He hadn't cried in almost a year. "Oh shit." She held him, drawing him out of the vehicle so he was standing in the gloomy afternoon. Chuck put the four bags on the porch, and now he stood out front of the Suburban. Mrs. Brand held Jimmy up, and they began to walk down the driveway. The rain dripping from the trees magnified itself in Jimmy's ears and became a crystal ringing. He could see through their yard to the Hendersons and the Dorseys and one more to the Kirbys.

"I'll get my purse, Chuck. Just a minute."

"Mrs. Brand. It is no problem, and there is no charge. Good to see you, Jimmy. Take care. I'm going to get back and see the end of the game. We're kicking Sheridan's butt, which has been long overdue." Chuck climbed in, backed carefully onto the wet street.

Louise Brand helped her son to the garage and showed him the refurbished room with some pride. He sat on the edge of the bed. There was only the faint smell of paint, almost pleasant. She turned on the lamp and showed him his bureau and the table where a television would go. She turned the light in the bathroom on and off, and she showed him the bathroom. He was burning with the day now, his body glowing with pain. It hurt to cry, so he sat still while his mother helped him with his shoes. Her hands at his feet sent him back to some ancient morning, and he thought he heard her say, "Now the other foot." The ghostly sound pushed Jimmy over, and he lay back and was asleep.

His dreams were like no other, not even the cinematic nightmares he'd toured when his partner Daniel had died. He was gathering everything he owned and putting it back in the basement of this, his childhood home. There were his baby toys and the two framed movie posters he and Daniel had had on their apartment wall in SoHo. It was an unending inventory, and no one was helping him. He saw some friends he didn't recognize at the house, and he saw his parents upstairs. They were young. But when he'd return with more stuff, these people weren't helping. Some of the things he'd brought back were gone again. It was hard work, and as he wandered through the dream, everything he saw was something of his, his responsibility. He marveled that he could carry such huge loads. His high school chemistry book, the bicycles, a tassel from the rearview mirror of his first car, an oatmeal box full of watches, a shell necklace, folded shirts, his guitar, his cowboy boots, a large glass stein from Germany, his journals, a wooden cigarette box, a ceramic clock from his kitchen in New York, and a fabulous kitsch rooster that Daniel had given him to remind him of his ranch-town home. Gathering the items was a kind of pleasure, but leaving them was worry. Every time he returned, more were missing. Maybe someone was taking them, but there was a chance they were just floating away.

The September rain moved steadily into Oakpine. It rained all week on and off, not all unpleasant, the stoic little town sensing the first real shift in the weather. The football team practiced in the old gym, running patterns in tennis shoes. These were always goofy sessions in the strange tight space under the yellow lights, the footballs careening off the walls, and the hours seemed rehearsals for some bombastic drama. Coach Nunley put in a new series of parallel passes that were aimed at his son Wade, who had showed he could move and catch the ball. Wade was to start downfield and, after five yards, cut parallel to the line of scrimmage as the other receivers streamed long.

At the museum, Marci had her hands full with the wet weather. In refurbishing the old station, they had never fixed an adequate loading dock. They used it only a dozen times a year, but on rainy days they had to move the crated paintings briskly into the building or cover them first. She had to be there every minute with a towel over each shoulder.

Downtown Frank Gunderson used the rain to find the two leaks in the Antlers roof he'd ignored all summer. They'd been too busy getting the little brewery on line. The one leak was easy in the front bar, dripping down the old light fixture, but the other that sent a rivulet of water wandering down the side wall was trickier. He stood on the roof of the old building in the rain in his old black cowboy hat holding a yellow crayon. He'd already swept the gravel off the one spot and circled the tear in the tarpaper. But along the side he swept but couldn't find it. He swept again, his shirt already soaked. He hadn't planned on being up here that long. Nothing. When he circled the three seams, he found the one that wasn't sealed and put an X in that circle. When he stood, he felt the old hot ache where he'd broken his leg, and he looked out over the village: a dozen rooftops, the park, the school, the houses and trees, and always across the rail yard, the larger western plain, as if waiting. This was a nice town, small and too windy and most of it needing a coat of paint it wouldn't get before winter came, but a nice town. He could see Oakpine Mountain obscured in the weather. His entire history was here; there was no other place he knew like this one. To the west, the sky was three big shipments of gray coming in. He knew it was raining over the rail yards and into the implacable North Platte and beyond out into the reservoirs and the backs of a million antelope that wouldn't mind this last warm rain. He didn't mind it. Now he had to climb down and change the buckets under these drips. When the sun came out, he'd be back with a tub of asphalt tar and get this old place right and tight.

At the hardware store, Craig Ralston always liked the rain, the lights in Ralston Hardware a kind of shelter from it. People came in for the tarps and the roof seal, both plastic and tar, and a lot of guys came in for reloading gear and gun-cleaning kits, and there would be those with basement projects the rain had brought to mind, some plumbing or some hobby stuff, the balsa wood and glue. Craig got lost in it, of course, and he took a real pride in knowing good gear from second-rate, though he carried both because people had to decide for themselves. He wasn't unhappy as he stood in the open doorway and felt the air edge of the rain, but he felt what? Kept.

In the Brands' garage, Jimmy slept, weaving his dreams into a long exhausting saga. He'd been worn out before being taken to the airport in New York, and he had flown in a dream west to his old home. The knowledge that underlined this capitulation was that he would die, and so every afternoon or morning, when he would waken to his mother's tray with tea and sandwiches and soup and her homemade cakes and Jell-O and lemonade, moving from one dream to the other, he was surprised to be alive. It all surprised him. He stayed in bed this way, heavy with his weary blood, for a week, leaning on things to get to the bathroom, and after a week of such rest, he woke one morning to see the perfect parallelogram of sunlight from the back window printed on the wall like a cartoon from his former life, and he thought, *I'm in the garage. I'm home in the garage.* And then he said it aloud to taste the words: "I'm home in the garage." He said again: "Home." His voice sounded like a radio in the other room, but the bright badge of light seemed to give him strength. When his mother came out with her towel-covered tray, he was sitting up, making some notes in his journal.

They talked. She sat on the bed and felt his forehead, and he sipped the coffee and had some toast. It was the first time they'd spoken without tears. "It's a beautiful day, isn't it?" he said.

"It is," she said. "Sunny and clear. How are you feeling?"

"I'm okay," he said. "I'm tired. You've done a nice job on the garage. Is this all for me?"

"I'm sorry you're not in the house with us," she said. "Your father just has too much on his mind with all of it."

"I understand that. Believe me. I didn't think I'd be back here causing you this trouble." He lifted his hand, the fingers. "I need to talk to you."

"It's not any—"

"It's trouble, Mom. I'm glad to see you, but it's trouble. I mismeasured it in New York, thinking my money would outlast me, but I couldn't sit there anymore. At the end I wasn't even with friends of friends. They had no way of handling, of dealing with—"

"We want you here," she said. "The garden's coming in."

"Thank you," he told her. "But I need you to see it all." Now he lifted both hands and pressed his fingers against his eyelids. "It's going to be a mess. I'm going to die out here. My insurance is gone. You're getting a tough deal. There's some Medicaid, but I'm going to leave you flat, holding the bag. You're going to have to call the mortuary, bury me."

His mother sat still. She took his hand. "Do you understand this?" he went on. "Do you see that is what is going to happen? If I had a choice, I'd help you somehow, but I'm all out. There'll be a little money next spring from my books, but still."

"I'm happy you're home," she said. "I can do what I need to do." They sat. He noticed the sunlight from the window had moved down, onto the floor.

"Are you going to have a ton of zucchini?"

"We already do. You want to see it?"

"Yeah," he said. "I'll get dressed in a while. I'd like to see the garden. Tomatoes?"

"Any minute," she answered.

"I wouldn't mind a tomato sandwich. I want to count a tomato sandwich in my future."

She stood and straightened the covers. "You heard me, right, Jimmy? I can do what I need to do. I'm your mother."

"Thank you," he said. "I heard it all."

On Tuesday every week, after football practice and dinner, Larry Ralston would meet Wade Nunley at the park, and they would run for an hour through the town. Saturday they'd hang out, sore from the game, and Sunday throw the ball a bit, and then Monday was school and practice, Tuesday the same, but their theory was that a long run Tuesday night made them strong. They'd be tired Wednesday but back by Thursday, and then there was nothing but to polish their helmets and put on their clean jerseys for the game on Friday or Saturday. No one asked them to do it, and no one else did it. What it was was, they were brimming, and they had plenty, and so they ran. Once they had done it for three weeks, they could not not run. They were full of life, and the nights were stunning in Oakpine in September. Larry could feel the torque of the earth pulling away from the sun, the air trying to chill, and they ran through it, crossing downtown with long steps, floating, alive. From there they ran out past the high school and up toward Oakpine Mountain, a route that if you described it to people would make them wonder at such length, the miles, loping like animals through the dark along the undermountain road. For Wade it was work, the last third, but his father was the coach, and Wade was a good soldier.

In the last mile or so, dropping back toward town, Larry grinned with happiness. His body disappeared and became the fresh night, the exhilarating air, the vanished limits of any world. His strides were longer than he was tall, and they were smooth, and soon he was lost to Wade, and happily lost to Wade. Alone, flying toward the park in the disembodied night, his high tenor breath sounded like laughter. He forced himself to wait there, in the park, for Wade, who would come jogging up a moment later. They'd slap five and head off in different directions for their homes, and Larry had trouble not running again. The world was pulling at him in a way he loved, but he did not understand. It took all his muscles not to run. He walked through the quiet streets. "You little town," he said aloud. "Turn off the TV, you town, and go to bed. I've run around you now, so sleep. And Wendy, tell Wade to go home. I'll see you in school." He opened and closed his hands. He lifted his chin and closed his eyes. He walked.

THREE

Houses

Mason Kirby was back in Oakpine to sell his parents' house. He said this to himself. He wasn't really on a mission, but it helped to say that as he drank coffee in the lobby of the little hotel. He'd been to his hometown five or six times in thirty years, and he wondered if this would be the last trip.

He went out into the surprising air, and it all fit again, the size of the sky, the emptiness north and south, and now the railroad and the river and across Main and Bank streets and the towering clusters of trees pulled him to Poplar Grove, and then slowed to a crawl, he turned onto Berry Street, his windows down and the morning as sweet as anything he'd known as a boy, the smell of the dew and the leaves whispering and holding the fresh light. He hadn't thought about this part, being alone on his old street. He hadn't planned it. Somehow he had hoped to finish his part with the property in one weekend, but as soon as he drove onto Berry Street, he felt the weight of the ages, and then he saw his house, and of course it was more real than any of the plans he had for Denver.

Standing on the cement porch, he could see there was more work than he could do in a week, and for some reason for which he had no explanation, he wanted the work. The place had claimed him, the shushing trees and their clashing shadows had claimed him, his old porch, the house. Hell, the drive up. He closed his eyes and stood still. The smell of the dew lifting from the old brick. He felt the wiring in his neck; he was tired, and he knew if he sat on the stoop, he'd be there all day. He hadn't stopped in thirty years, and he thought that and then dismissed it. "Thirty years," he said. And he knew it was true: he hadn't stopped.

He cuffed the keys from his jacket pocket and tried the door. The entire lock cylinder turned with the key, and he couldn't get it back out. Through the two large front windows, which were plated with grease and dust, he could see that the house was scattered with stuff, boxes, furniture, debris. His renters, the Gunnars, hadn't called him. When he didn't get July's rent, he tried to reach them. Their phone was disconnected in August. Mason had called an old classmate, Shirley Stiver, who handled real estate, and had her go by the place. Even after her report that the house was abandoned, it had taken him until now, mid-September, to drive back up from Denver. The Gunnars were history. Mason Kirby looked at his watch. Shirley would be over in an hour.

This was the house he grew up in, and though it looked like a ruined artifact, he knew it hadn't changed. The sunlight on the red bricks and the smell of the trees and the gardens in the early fall altered his breathing as he kicked through the high grass into the backyard. There was a metal clip and a cord on the clothesline as well as a worn oval in the shaggy lawn; the Gunnars must have had a dog. He was history too. The back porch door was open two inches, and he remembered: it was never fully closed. The door was always a bad fit, but now it wouldn't open either. He bumped it with his hip. It had swollen and chafed against the planking of the floor. He grabbed the handle and remembered the noise. It made a sweet little ring for some reason, something loose for decades. He nudged the door again with his hip, and the old sheet of plate glass popped, and a crack ran diagonal across the pane.

He was able to pry open the two old hinged garage doors, and daylight was visible between many of the planks. The dark space was mounded with dank trash dating back, he supposed, through the Gunnars and their six years in the house, through old Mr. Jared, who died there after nine or ten years as tenant, all the way back to his parents, who had raised Mason and his sister in the place. They'd been gone for almost twenty years now. It had not been in his plans to visit the cemetery, but as he looked around at the stained boxes sitting in the gloom, he knew his plans had changed.

The voices of children drew him back out into the open air, and he saw the kids shuffling along, a loose gaggle coming down the street for school. Six or seven ten-year-olds with their little backpacks. Three boys marched in a line, their arms out on the shoulders of the boy ahead of them, trying not to stumble, a boy machine. Two girls stopped and got on their hands and knees by one of the large poplars on Berry Street, examining something in the raised gray bark. They looked like children at the foot of an elephant. A little boy came along behind them all, shuffling thoughtfully. He'd lift his palms away from his ears and stop walking. Then he'd cover his ears and walk a few steps. Mason stood in his old weedy driveway, the two-track of cement utterly overgrown, and watched the boy traverse the whole street. The smell in the shade of the house was familiar, weeds and oil. He scanned the open backyards down the block, and he realized that this—in all the world—was the place he knew best. He was a little dizzy. Down by the Brands he could see old man Brand's boat under a bright new tarp beside the garage. Mason stood still and made sure. *My god, the old boat.* It was shocking to see it really, and he remembered Matt Brand drunk at the reservoir the day after graduation. And Matt Brand's body found that night. Mason put his hands over his ears, and listening to that high distant roar, his body working, he made the decision to stay and clean this place and fix it up. He felt light being out of Denver, and he wanted this dirty work. He couldn't make anything that mattered in his life happen, but he could make this happen.

Ten minutes later Shirley Stiver pulled up in her white Town Car. She was still vaguely blond after all these years and polished with a fine coat of realtor's makeup. "Looks like you've got a day of it," Mason said to his old friend. "Nice suit." He stood out of the passenger seat of his Mercedes, where he'd been on the phone with his office.

Shirley smiled and kissed his cheek. "Same old, but we've got some big new places up on the mountain."

"You know this country's about done when they start building trophy homes in Oakpine."

"You be nice, Mason Kirby. Oakpine's a good place. You'd be smart to take a look around. The big city has got a genuine hold on you."

"Oh Christ," he said, taking her arm and walking over to the sidewalk in front of his house. "I didn't mean anything. It's everywhere you go. I'm glad to be here. Did you know the Gunnars?"

"I had heard they were gone, probably back to her folks in South Dakota. He worked at the high school, maintenance, painting, something."

"That's what I got here: some maintenance, painting, plenty of something."

"I figured it was a mess. Did they owe you much?"

"No, not really. Three months. Four."

"Do you want me to hire it done and call you?" she said. "It looks like there's some roofing. We can get it patched up and on the market." She moved to the side and was looking it all over. "We've had a week of rain."

"When I called, I thought I was going to flip you the keys and blow town, but now I don't know. There's some volunteer zucchini out back, and a lot of this work looks like I ought to do it."

"You got a month?" She'd come over, and they were standing by his car. Both turned to view the house. "Two months?"

"It's wide open. I've got as much time as I want. But I'm thinking that I need this job."

"And how is Elizabeth?"

"Elizabeth is better than she's been for a while. She's getting on with her new life."

"I'm sorry to hear that."

"It was inevitable. She did the right thing. How would you like being married to an asshole?"

"Mason, I can answer that question with real authority. I'm still sorry."

"It's okay. You're looking at the king of the type A's. I've always only done one thing: drive hard for the hoop. And the lesson is that I never really understood the game. Listen to me. Listen to me talk to Shirley Stiver, the tallest blonde in Catchett County. Anyway, dear, I'm going back to Denver today and come back in a week or sooner. Can you call and get the power back on here? The water's still connected. Who do you guys hire for help?"

"Call Craig. Craig Ralston, down at the hardware. He likes a project, and his boy is a good worker too. If there's nothing structural, they'll be good."

"You remember that?" Mason asked his old friend, pointing down three houses to the red boat.

"What is it?

"It's that boat Matt was driving after graduation."

"That was too bad. That whole deal."

"Were you out at the reservoir?"

"Oh yeah. I think Jimmy's back."

"Jimmy Brand?"

"I heard he's back home. He's sick."

Mason Kirby walked in a little circle shaking his head, and then he escorted Shirley over and held her car door. "This place wants to get to me, Shirley. How can it smell the same?"

"I know," she said. "It's your hometown. It's how a hometown works. It doesn't always sell a house, but you can't ignore it."

"Thanks for coming out," he told her. "I'll get it fixed up, and then you sell it to some homesick soul."

The next afternoon Jimmy Brand sat in a lawn chair in the backyard. He'd had some toast and tea, and his headache was almost nil, the buzzing gone. It was just noon on a warm day in late September, and though the sun was already well south, he could feel it on the back of his head like some small pleasure. His mother was working before him in the garden, showing it off: "We've already had two crops of carrots, and this one could come out any time." She parsed the lacy tops with her fingers and pulled one of the bright orange carrots from the ground.

"I'll eat that right now," he said. He started to push himself up, but she came over, stopping to wash it in the trickle that ran from the garden hose. She'd been watering her tomatoes. There were thick green clusters on the eight tall plants, hanging heavily, a few already red.

"How do you feel?"

"I'm eating the best carrot in the world in Oakpine, Wyoming," he said. "Who would have thought?"

She stood beside him, her hand on his chair.

"You'll have plenty of tomatoes, Ma."

"Plenty of everything. Every year it all gets a little bigger. It's something about me. We need less and less, and I'm planting bushels." She had rows of peas and green peppers looking polished, three rows of corn, and then the wild section of squash and pumpkin, the vines in cascades, spilling out in every direction across the lawn.

Jimmy could smell the earth here, the high musk coming off all the plants. With the bees working through the garden, it felt as if you could see things growing. The carrot had been sweet. He stood, happy to be out of the rigid chair, and felt how dangerously tall he was for a moment, and then he walked carefully to the pooling squash vines. He bent with no dizziness and lifted the broad leaves so he could see the squash and melons in the lambent green shade. He walked around the perimeter and then into a short passage. "This one will be mine, right here." He knelt and tapped a zucchini for his mother to see. It was as big as a football. "It is going to be vast. This squash will outweigh me."

"They grow fast," she said. "I can hardly keep up. We'll come out next week and take a load down to the church."

He lifted his hands to his face and smelled them, the green world. "I know this is tough on you. And on Dad. If I can get my strength up, or if there's someplace else you can think of, I could—"

"No, you can't. We're doing this. I'm your mother, and you're home. Your father and I have our differences on this, and that also is simply the way it will be. Really, Jimmy, hear me. I'm glad you've come. We won't talk about the other. You're here. That's it."

With Jimmy home, Mr. Brand went out as much as he could. He went to the Elks twice a week for cards and coffee and an occasional Canadian whiskey, and he still had cronies at the district maintenance warehouse, and he could spend the day there fooling with somebody's truck and talking to the boys. He'd been chief there when he retired and had run a good shop.

Yesterday, the first day that Jimmy had felt good since his return, he sat with his mother in his guesthouse suite, as he called the garage with a smile. She had brought him a bowl of pears. All the caretaking had allowed them not to talk, and now things were sorting themselves out. Jimmy fumbled through his last bag and withdrew a copy of his new book and handed it to her. His mother took it in her hands and looked at the cover. The title *Blue Elements* was in dark blue lettering over a watercolor of a rainy city street. On the back she saw his photograph, his hair gone, his eyes bright, younger than the face.

"I sent you the others. You got the others, right?"

"I did. I have them, Jimmy."

"I wrote six books, Mom. And I wrote for the paper. It's how I made my living, mostly. This is the last, another novel."

"You're a good writer," she said.

He waited to respond because she'd startled him with this, and he wanted the words to last, to remember them. Your mother tells you that you're a good writer.

"This is the last," he said. "It's about Daniel before he was sick. It's about New York."

"You've got Oakpine in some of the books," she said.

"I do. It's my take on all of it, Mom. I know that wasn't any fun for you."

"Some was hard to read. It's all behind us now." She took the empty bowl, the spoon.

"Did Dad see the books?" Jimmy lay back on the bed.

"He didn't."

"Does he know that I was a writer?"

"I'm sure he does. He does. He's confused, Jimmy. But I know he's glad you're here. He can't say it."

"Has he ever said my name?"

"He has, at times. He has said it in his sleep."

Later that day Jimmy heard something that woke him, his father's raised voice in the house, and Jimmy stood by his door in time to see his father in the overalls he'd worn forever come onto the back porch and throw the blue book into the yard.

Saturday morning Larry Ralston delivered a television, a little Sony with a remote that Craig had pulled off a shelf in Ralston Hardware and offered Mrs. Brand as a loaner. Jimmy was reading in the old up-holstered wing chair in the small space when Larry knocked.

"You must be the guy that ordered a television," Larry said, back-ing through the small door with the appliance.

Jimmy watched the boy cut a distended silhouette in the rectangle of daylight, and the sudden sight shocked him, and he took a breath and decided to say what he saw, even the gambit of a joke: "It is with-out a doubt Craig Ralston Junior bringing it in."

Larry footed the gray milk crate around and placed the set on it. "Oh, please don't say that. I can't look like my father."

"Twins. You are twins." Jimmy put his book on the bed. "Thirty years between models. Haven't you ever seen the photographs? And I've heard your football exploits celebrated by an expert. I think, that rainy day, I might have seen you play. This was at some distance."

The door opened again, and another figure cut the light. A young woman stood there with a long cardboard box and an extension cord. "Hello!" she said, then quickly taking in the oddly bright room, she added, "This looks great."

Larry went to Jimmy in his chair and introduced himself and turned to the girl. "This is Wendy."

"Hi," she said. "Where do you want this?"

They spent ten minutes arranging things, adjusting the television, fooling with the rabbit-ear antenna, the girl sitting on the bed while Larry turned the ears, trying to get the PBS cooking show to come in clearly. The chef was making a clam sauce. Jimmy smiled at the two young people. He hadn't been lonely, but their association affected him, filled the room. They talked and moved in a way that told him unmistakably that they were falling in love, destined to, an orbit of innocents, but neither knew it yet. The garage was too small a space not to reveal all the unspoken things between them. It was a heady dance they did, and he smiled and smiled, saying, "Not to worry. I'm not going to be doing any cooking."

Wendy pointed at the screen from the bed: "You almost had it. Go back." Larry was on his knees in the corner.

"Is that static, or is he frying bacon?" Larry said.

"Both," Jimmy said. "And both is perfect."

Larry came around, and they all watched the chef bend and pull half a squash from his oven on a tray. He raised his fork, waving it once, and grinned at the camera. Then he raked the squash into spaghetti strands.

"Spaghetti squash with clam sauce," Wendy said. "We could do that."

"Looks good," Jimmy said.

"So are you Mr. Ralston's friend from New York?" the girl asked.

"I'm Mr. Ralston's friend from Oakpine. But I lived in New York for a long time."

"You're the writer." she said.

"I was," he said. "I wrote some books, reviews of plays."

He could feel her now looking at him. "It's pretty weird that you're out in the garage," she said.

Larry had opened the long box and was carefully assembling the tubular electric radiator. "Dad said this will heat the whole place," he said. He lifted the unit and secured it on a wheeled frame and plugged it in and rolled it over beside the wide garage door. "It heats the oil," Larry said. "There's no fire danger."

"We're not afraid of fire," Jimmy said.

Larry sat down on the bed beside Wendy. She had been looking at Jimmy again for a moment, and now he watched her lean forward and touch his knee, pat it with two fingers.

"Are you afraid?" Wendy said. She and Larry sat still, their faces without irony. Such young faces; they were at the edge of their lives. It was okay to envy the young. You knew all about them and you knew all about what was to come, and it was all right to envy them anyway.

"This is an unusual girl," Jimmy said to Larry. "Isn't she?"

Larry's face lifted at the setup. "She is an unusual girl. She'll say anything. It's all over this town about her unusual qualities."

"Yes, Wendy," he said. "I am afraid."

He saw Larry take her hand, and by her reaction Jimmy knew it was one of the first times such a thing had occurred. The sunlight came through the one window like a bright joke, and it fell across their shoulders. "Well," Larry said, standing. "Do you need anything else?"

It was so wonderful to talk about things to do. Jimmy had known it all his life and seen it keep things afloat a thousand times. It didn't move things forward, but it kept you from crashing. He could see Craig Ralston in Larry now, the tall young man standing there, his hands ready for the next thing.

"There's one thing." He leaned back. "I think there's something up there"—he pointed—"in the rafters that I'd like to get down." They all looked up through the translucent plastic into the dark space. "I may be hallucinating—no, I have been hallucinating—but besides that, I think I see my old case, a guitar."

Wendy scooted farther onto the bed and lay back. "I see it," she said, pointing. Larry lay back beside her. "Oh yeah." Jimmy looked at the two reclined figures. These kids were just the ticket. If he could keep them here, he'd last all year.

"Could we get it," Jimmy said, "without tearing up all this work? If it's too much trouble, let it go."

Larry retrieved the ladder from behind the garage and leaned it against one wall and began tenderly to pull the stapled plastic away.

"What did you write about?" Wendy asked.

"I wrote a book about being seventeen in Oakpine," he said. "About my life in the city. About someone I loved." They watched Larry lean onto a rafter and reach for the neck of the guitar case. "Be careful," Jimmy said.

The black case, printed with a grid of dirt, appeared through the plastic, and then Larry slowly slipped it down through the opening and handed it to Wendy. "Wow," she said, "what is it?" Larry stepped down and took the dusty case outside and batted it with a rag and then laid it on the grass and wiped it off. He returned and placed the case across the arms of the chair and opened it. He lifted the red and white electric guitar from the blue velvet and laid it in Jimmy's lap, and

Jimmy felt the hard plastic shell on his bones. It hurt. He couldn't even hold a guitar.

Larry said, "It's a Fender Stratocaster."

"Like its owner, this is an absolute antique." He was wiping at the dust with his handkerchief. He would ignore this pain. The strings were sprung, only one still in place. Larry took the ladder out and returned, saying, "We'll come back and restaple that plastic this afternoon." He saw Jimmy with the guitar.

"You guys actually had a band."

"For seven months some years ago, that is, for seven months several decades ago, we were *the* band in Oakpine."

Larry turned to Wendy: "I might as well tell you: my father was in a band."

"So cool," Wendy said. "What did he play?"

"Craig Ralston was the best drummer in Wyoming," Jimmy said. The ache in his legs had simply taken all his strength, and he sat very still.

"No way," Larry said. "This is science fiction." He opened the door for Wendy.

"Hey," Jimmy said, "thanks for all the gear." He was empty now. His leg was afire; the ache along his backbone was warm, and he could feel a pressure in his head. They all said goodbye, and then he added, "Wendy, there's a book of mine out back by the garden in the grass. You can take it if you'd like."

She disappeared for a moment and then came back with the book, looking surprised. "Thanks," she said. "I'll read it." And then she asked, "What was the name of your band?"

Jimmy felt pinned in the chair by the guitar, so heavy was it now. "Life on Earth," he said. "That was our final name." When they left, he couldn't get up. The guitar was like a bar holding him, and the pain beat in his legs and then crescendoed as he went into the kind of delirium he hated. His mind slipped and slipped again, the sensation was of sliding down a dark vortex, trying to stop, but unable to form a sentence or an image, grab hold, he just descended. There was no rest in it, a thousand spinning defeats, a terror.

Sometime later in the early dark, his mother came out and lifted the guitar from him, and he felt it in his tattered dreaming as a blow. He was then sick, and she helped him into the bathroom and then to bed. He couldn't eat the meatloaf, but even later, at nine or ten, she came back, and he had a bowl of applesauce while they watched a situation comedy on the television with the sound turned off.

The next morning, Sunday, Mason Kirby stood in front of his house again and shook hands with his old friend Craig Ralston. The Ralston Hardware van had been parked in front when Mason pulled up. He'd left Denver just before five and had felt charged and alive in the dawning day as he drove. He still had the backseat full of clothes and a ragtag box of whatever tools he could gather in the trunk of the Mercedes; some were his father's and he hadn't had them in his hands for twenty years. What he felt was young and old at the same time. Being up before dawn in the fall of the year like this meant he was going hunting with his father, coffee from a thermos, apples. But leaving Denver meant shifting clients, nothing life or death, but this was different. He remembered his father, who worked tech maintenance for Chevron in the fields, saying, as he'd arrive home at night, "The way the workday ends is that you leave. If you don't leave and go home, one thing will lead to another all night." Driving through the beautiful mesas in the strange first light as he crossed into Wyoming, Mason knew that was what he was after: a change, an end, some new chapter in this old life. He'd start with a month of work on an old house. He wasn't lost now. This was not an inquiry; this was a serious trip.

"The attorney comes to Oakpine," Craig said smiling. "Good to see you."

Mason took the other man's shoulder. "I need a little help here." They walked around the place and pulled open the garage. They forced the back door open and found the house full of bad news. The basement was dank with garbage. The old floors on the main floor were ruined, as was the ceiling, which was boiled up and peeling. The tub was cracked, and one toilet was shattered. There were two motorcycle wheels on the window seat of the bay window, and the rest of the motorcycle was in the kitchen. The fridge was gone, and a layer of gray furze covered everything. While Craig climbed his ladder to look into the attic space, Mason wandered the rooms. He could still see, of course, where the piano had been and his mother's plants and his father's chair. He went out on the front porch and sat on the ledge. It was a good house. The door sills were solid, and the wood trim inside, the mantel and ornate ceiling moldings, were restorable walnut.

Craig opened the large front door. The vintage diamond-shaped, beveled-glass courtesy window in the center was chipped, but the thick oak classic closed precisely and latched with a sound Mason remembered from his boyhood. "You're fine above the ceiling," Craig said. "The rafters are all solid, and there is no water damage, though you can see the sky in a couple places. You want to start with the roof?"

"You?"

"We want to beat the weather." Craig was happy to be starting this. "Let's get the roof," he said. That afternoon a truck delivered a huge blue dumpster bin, setting it alongside the house in the driveway, and they began.

Two weeks later Mason and Craig sat on the exposed planking of the roof of the old house in the benevolent October sun. The old boards were deep brown as if burned by their age. The men sat on the angled surface with their knees up. They'd torn off all the old shingles and tar paper along with two or three of the one-by-eight planks. The rusted rain gutter had fallen off voluntarily. Mason had gouged his left palm on a broken nail, and so he'd been to the clinic and now wore a padded bandage on that hand under his work gloves.

On the roof, his hand ached in a way that was all right. He'd hurt it; it would get better. The two high school boys Larry and Wade had joined Mason in cleaning the house, and they had emptied most of the debris from the interior and had shoveled trash and swept. Below the men now, the dumpster seemed a marker of some kind of accomplishment, almost full.

Craig had a thermos of coffee, and he poured two cups. They had their gear—lunches and jackets and extra tools—stored on a plank they'd tacked level near the roof peak. It had been better work than Mason had imagined, the teardown, removing the old shingles shelf by shelf, brittle things that had been facing the steady plains weather forty years, and they came off easily, almost neatly, nails and all, as if ready to quit. Mason was surprised not to be in worse shape. He regretted the hand because there were nails everywhere, and he'd been methodical, he thought, but he hadn't seen the stub protruding from the planking. He immediately lifted the torn palm as the blood welled up, and as it did and he looked for a place to wipe it, finally settling on his trouser leg, he realized he hadn't bled since he was here last, not even a good paper cut. There was something perverse in the way he watched it bleed as he thought: I'm going to get some good out of these hands yet.

He made a fist on a wadding of paper towel and drove over to Oakpine Clinic. The young medic had him sit on the papered examination table, and he scrubbed out the gouged flesh so they could decide on stitches or not, and suddenly Mason found his hand in the hands of a woman, her red hair curling in wisps at the corners of her forehead, and he almost started to see his old friend Kathleen Gunderson, and his second take was without question a flush of embarrassment as he waited while she examined his naked lawyer's hand.

"It's true," she said. "Here you are. What'd you do to yourself?"

"I became a lawyer," he said. "Can you do anything for me?" He was going to go on, say something about it, some small joke at the expense of his soft city hands, but she freed his hand then and folded her arms and smiled and said, "It's your call, Mason. We can put two little stitches in there, or tape will do if you're careful."

"Hello, Kathleen. I think I'm in a careful phase right now, despite my old house. Let's go with the tape."

She scrubbed his hand again, which glowed now, and pressed the gauze and tape into place. She gave him several packets of gauze and half a roll of the tape.

"Over on Berry Street?"

"Right," he said. They walked out into the nurses' station and spoke over the counter while she checked down an instruction sheet for him. "Craig Ralston is over helping me prepare to sell it."

Kathleen Gunderson now directed the clinic; she'd been a nurse for twenty-five years. They'd seen each other two or three times in the thirty years since the spring of graduation. "Are you having a small moment of déjà vu?" Mason asked.

"I don't think I held your injured hand at any time," she said.

"Must be the pain," he said. "I haven't had an injury for twenty years. I'm reassessing what I've been doing with my hands. I type. I unfold napkins."

"You do good work in the big city," she said. "And you talk the same bullshit you did in high school."

"Not exactly the same," he said.

"No stitches," she said.

"I'm going to fix that house up. I'm on vacation or something."

"I'll see you around, Mason. Be careful with your project. You look well," she said.

"I'm holding up. You look the very same."

"Did you see Frank?"

"I haven't, but I heard. Are you okay?"

"We've been coming apart for a long while. Everybody's okay."

"And business is booming," he said, nodding back at the waiting room.

She walked him to the glass doors and out into the angled sunlight. "We used to have a lot of drug-related work accidents," she told him. "Now it's more just drugs, sometimes a car."

"I'm here for a month."

"We'll get a coffee," she said.

"Maybe dinner with Marci and Craig. I've been staying there."

"Keep your hand dry," she said. "We'll see you."

Up on the roof at the center of the day, Mason said to Craig, "I've never been up here. I lived in the place seventeen years, and I was never on the roof. I was on the garage, and I was on top of Jimmy's house once, getting a football out of the rain gutter, and the two shoes we'd thrown at it, but this is a first, this week." They had laid three overlapping sheets of tarred roofing paper and had three to go, working their way up the planking. They wanted the paper down by nightfall; there was no more rain on the way, but still. Mason had hired a roofer for the green asphalt shingles, which stood on pallets in the side yard right now. Mason's shirt was soaked through and flecked with tar paper lint. He hadn't sweated through a shirt for twenty years, and it felt good. Tomorrow he and Craig would be downstairs working inside.

"When was it that Mr. Starkey fell off his roof?"

"Oh my god," Mason said. He ran his packing knife through the black paper and stapled both corners. "Mr. Starkey." He sat down next to Craig for a minute and pointed. "Where'd they live?"

"Behind the Millards." Craig raised his hand, wandering over the houses an alley away. "There, the blue one with the carport. It used to be green, but they sided it."

"I was in tenth grade," Mason said. "Virginia Starkey was in my class."

"She was a beauty."

"She was," Mason said. He was grinning, about to laugh, and he put his hand on Craig's shoulder. "And what was it? The old man was on the roof? Oh god, I'd forgotten this whole story. It's in one of Jimmy's books."

"Matt Brand saw it. One night Virginia was in there changing—I guess she never closed the curtains, and Matt was out back of his house over there, cleaning his football cleats with a stick." Craig pointed across the yards, each effulgent garden, and as he did, they saw Mrs. Brand come out of the garage with a tray and go into her house. "And he saw some guy lying head down on the roof, trying to hang over and look in on the girl, and then the guy screamed or yelled and fell off. Matt said he saw the guy fall and heard the thump. He said there was no way he didn't land on his head."

Mason was laughing, and Craig finished the story. "As it was, he broke his arm and had a wrist cast that summer. He worked for the board of education, a painter."

"And she closed her curtains."

"Right. She got curtains and started closing them."

"Virginia Starkey was a remarkable personage. Where'd she go?"

"California, I think. She married that kid whose dad owned the drugstore. He was a Lloyd, a couple of years older than us." Both men looked out over the houses. They could see Mrs. Brand's garden, the deep green of the large squash leaves in a jungle the way it had been when they were kids. It was three houses down and through the open backyards. "We had a lot of dinners there," Mason said.

"Yes we did. No band ate together more than we did. The food was much better than the music."

"I've been in every house all the way across Tribune Street," Mason said. He spread his hand out over the neighborhood. "All of them. Hardmans and Griffiths and Goodsells."

"Starkeys too?"

"I'm sure. Some cookout or Christmas party in grade school. We all had the same carpet. That guy came through here with his big carpet truck and did some good." Mason went on, "Yeah, Jimmy put that Starkey fall in one of the novels, though it wasn't the old man. It was the boyfriend. He changed a lot of things. I guess writers do."

Mrs. Brand appeared again with a thermos and went into the garage. "It's hard to believe the old man won't let him in the house."

"Brand was a strong guy, remember? He's a strong old guy, and he's using it all to keep a grudge."

"Is it because Jimmy's gay or because of what happened to Matt?"

"Who knows? By now it's just the cluster of hurt, the reasons all gone," Craig said. "But everything's years old. And none of it's worth this. You could lay out the case to him a, b, c, but some things don't get a fair trial. He got hurt when Matt died in that accident, and then Jimmy is who he is and left town, and it just hurts, and no facts can put it back in line." Craig stood and lifted the diminished roll of roofing paper, lined it up for Mason to staple, and began to run a layer down the roof. This paper would protect the house. It was such simple good work, and Mason was glad to have it.

The light seemed to last longer on the roof, because by the time they'd step off the ladder, it would be full dark, and they'd just drive up to the Ralstons. Mason wanted to get over to see Jimmy, visit his old friend, but every day they'd worked late.

That evening he and Craig saw Wade's beautiful black pickup drive onto the front lawn beneath them, and Larry and Wade jumped out. Young guys jump everywhere. In the bed of the truck, besides mops and buckets, was the frame and mattress of the futon Craig had arranged for him and a little square refrigerator and two tables and some chairs. Larry lifted the coffee table out of the truck and balanced it aloft on one leg. He waved at his father with his free hand and then tossed the table up and caught it with both hands. "I hate to see you move in here, Mr. Kirby. The few days you've stayed with us have been fabulous for Marci Ralston's teenage son. She has worn her robe every night."

"Don't pick on your mother when she's not here to give it back."

"I'm not, Dad. I'm proud of her. But Mr. Kirby, please be sure to compliment her on that robe. You must admit it is so robelike and so perfectly opaque."

"You talk," Wade said to Larry. "This kid is a case." Wade lowered the tailgate, and the boys hauled the bed frame to the porch and called, "Give us an hour, and this place will be home sweet home!"

Mason's actual plan had been to return to Oakpine and camp in the house; he'd been ready for something spartan. But the place had been too torn up and dirty. Marci and Craig had insisted, and so he'd been staying up in the guest room at their new house on Oakpine Mountain for five days, but he was moving down tomorrow. Marci had been in their class and was part of the circle of high school friends that centered on the old band. Mason and Craig were up early every day and gone before Marci came downstairs, but yesterday she caught them, and she and Mason had coffee while Craig readied the van.

"I'm sorry to hear about Elizabeth," she said. Marci moved about the kitchen, putting breakfast things away and loading the dishwasher. She wore a brown checked tweed jacket and a snug black skirt. Mason had been surprised by her appearance every time he'd seen her.

"Right," he said. "We were good for a while, and then we fell asleep at the wheel."

She looked at him questioningly. "There's a metaphor."

"And?" he said.

"As opposed to the truth."

"It was my fault. It still sounds like a metaphor. I don't have an answer for it except to know I won't be that guy again." When he went into this place in his thoughts, he shook his head, and he shook his head now. "I'm a success, you know. You get a couple of divorces with that."

She folded her arms and nodded.

Since they weren't playing games, he went ahead. "It hurts. I hurt some people. You don't start out to hurt anyone, but I evolved, we'll say. I felt bulletproof, which means arrogant and careless, and I lost true north and made my own personal mess. I'm glad to have this house to pound on."

"Well," she said. "I'm sorry. We met her at the wedding . . ."

"Seventeen years ago."

"She seemed nice."

"She is nice," he said. "And she's a success too. Denver's full of success."

"I'm going to rinse this pot. You want another cup?" She held up the glass carafe.

"I do." She poured the coffee. "You've got a fine character in Larry," Mason said. "He's brighter than we ever were."

"He's seventeen. You were a genius at seventeen too." She had lifted a white paper box of pamphlets for the museum show onto the counter and taped it shut.

"My dad, who was not a poet, said that part of us is always seventeen."

"Could be."

"I'll carry that down for you," Mason said, standing. "Larry says you're a ticket."

"Meaning?"

"I wouldn't know. Just a metaphor. I'd say you have the look of a successful person."

"Oh, for chrissakes, Mason. A woman wears a suit to work in a small town, and she's lost?"

"I wouldn't know," he said. "I'm just talking. You and I could always talk."

"We could," she said. And she was thinking that: *We could talk.* But it was a flat and hard surprise to her that this person before her, whom she had meant to offer shelter for a few days as he changed lives, was still that same seventeen-year-old, part of him. He'd been so confident and assertive yet never part of the mainstream in high school. He viewed it all from a distance, and the distance bothered her. Maybe he could see something. She was dressed for Stewart—and for part of herself; she wanted this life or the illusion of it. She liked being held, petted, in her good clothes, while he held her in his office and ran his hand up inside her jacket. She liked his dry aftershave, how lean he was, the clean office space. It was a rush, she knew, but a good rush, the rush she wanted. It gave the day a drive she wanted. And now here was Mason, from high school, telling her to be careful.

She picked up her purse and turned to go. She saw him examining her face. He said: "You have everything." It infuriated her. Outside, Wyoming spread brown and yellow to the west in the new sunshine, lines of chimney smoke drawing north over the old town.

"And who is taking inventory? You? The attorney from Colorado."

"I'm sorry," he said. He stood holding the box before him. "Something's happening to me, Marci. Honest to god, don't listen to me. I'm up here, and I climb right in, don't I? Something's got a hold of me, and something has tricked me into thinking it's all still here for me, that I fit in, that I know anything at all about this town, because I grew up here." He backed and pushed open the glass door onto the entry deck. They heard a concussion and saw Craig close the hood of the van and wave up for Mason to come along.

They went down the redwood steps, and Mason laid the packet into the backseat. He held her car door and said, "Really. Marci. I'm sorry.

I'm here because I finally know that I don't know a thing. It is real good to see you all again and to be here. That's all I meant. It's your life, not mine. I used mine up."

She looked at him. "Come down to the show," she said. "I'm proud of all of it. You haven't seen the museum. The opening's tomorrow. Bend down now and kiss me on the cheek and go to work." He did as instructed and went around to the van. If she hadn't said the last, he would have thought his notions about her were all wrong.

FOUR

1969

On a sunny Saturday afternoon in October 1969, Frank Gunderson, one of Oakpine High School's best halfbacks, swung right on a strong side sweep on a critical third down. He collected the football that floated out his way in the gentle lateral pitch from the quarterback, tucked the ball up under his folded arms, and sprinted, digging hard for the corner. It was the second game of a promising season for Oakpine, and the stands were crowded. They were full for every game. Football Saturdays always closed the town down. The play took a while to form, bellying back and gathering blockers. Craig Ralston, exactly two hundred pounds that year, pulled from his guard position and sprinted parallel to scrimmage. He loved these days, playing full out, throwing himself into football, literally, just throwing himself. He liked this wide play, the Single Sweep, because he got to run, lead the play if he could, and block downfield. They also had the Fake Sweep, where he started to pull and then blocked back as the quarterback faked the pitch and came back to his side on the draw. But now Frank had the ball tucked away and was coming from the backfield, swinging for the sideline, trying to beat the traffic, make the turn. He was going to graduate in May and go into the Marines and to Vietnam. He had a plan. When he got back, he'd join the sheriff's office. The turmoil of the war and its protest had not rattled Oakpine very much, and Frank thought of enlisting not as a good thing or a bad thing, though he resented the little he heard about the protesters. He simply thought of it as something he was going to do. The military had been a real and useful thing for his father and some of his older friends. He didn't want to go down to Laramie to college like so many kids did, and he didn't want to stay on and try to get into the oil fields, where his dad worked. He liked being a senior finally and having some sway. He had no steady girl, but he could see having one from the group of friends that was forming in the new school year. He was thinking about joining the band that Jimmy Brand was putting together. He and Craig Ralston and Matt Brand were going hunting tomorrow morning early; his truck was packed with camping gear and beer. Antelope season started at dawn. The sunlight now on the people in the bleachers and the smell of the turf as he ran made Frank exult. He had the ball and he had two and now three blockers, and they leaned forward together, his hand on Craig's back as they crossed the line of scrimmage. What he didn't see was the safety for Sheridan, who was among the fastest high school football players in the state and who would set a state track record that spring in the 220 and the 440, streaming down upon them all. This kid came across the front of Craig like a car racing a train and, diving, he met Frank Gunderson exactly in the left knee, way low, folding that leg out and under with a pop that they all, even as other bodies rained and tumbled around them, clearly heard.

Jimmy Brand put the sound, a simple crisp snap, in a book, saying that it was the one time he was sure to have witnessed the exact turning point in someone's life. This was in a novel, and the character was not exactly Frank Gunderson, and he was turned from other things than those that changed for Frank that afternoon. Frank missed the hunting trip, letting Craig and Matt take his truck way out to Yearbow, where they took two pronghorns the first day, some of which would be part of their many dinners at the Brands. Frank was prevented from joining the Marines because of his leg and the pin in it; in fact, all military service was beyond him now. Because of the attention he got in school that fall, a hero, the crutches, help with books, homework, he had to change, come out. Just deflecting all the attention caused him to develop a wry and quick sense of humor, so that he became a kind of entertainer. He started saying "Nothing, it's okay," standing there on his crutches, and the phrase tilted with understatement and became funny, as did his other phrases: "Thanks for the help. Just put my books there, Champ. See you after class." This was the first time he'd kidded with his classmates, talked to girls at all. It all gave him a kind of confidence, an understanding of how to deal with people that would become such an integral part of his career. When everyone went off to college or the war, he remained in Oakpine, hanging out, schmoozing with the locals, and in two years, when the economy faltered, he'd borrowed and bought three buildings, including the Antlers, and he was in business.

But the moment that everyone remembers was in the hospital, the day after Frank Gunderson broke his leg. Jimmy Brand and Mason Kirby had already talked to Frank about forming a band, but Frank had deferred because of football. Jimmy had been fooling around with his guitar for years. He'd received a red Fender for Christmas when he was sixteen. Mason played the rhythm guitar well, his father's Gibson, and they'd jammed together on the Brands' back porch, just idling, two guys who were not going to play football. They played together once at the Junior Talent Show, two songs, Mason singing the second, an up-tempo but not altogether wacky version of "Tom Dooley." Craig had said, "You need a drummer, guys. You made that song sound like he was going to be released, or at least escape." Jimmy and Mason walked into Frank's hospital room and made a campy presentation of the secondhand bass guitar, holding it out like the most honorable award, while they bowed their heads and hummed an ominous bass line from "Tom Dooley." Frank was drowsy but still run with adrenaline, and he took the guitar with a smile. Little Bobby Krause, in the next bed, a day after his appendectomy, watched the whole deal and said, "Cool."

Frank fingered the strings a moment and looked up. "I'm going to need something to do. I'm out for the season."

"And it fits," Mason pointed.

"Craig said he'd drum if you'll play bass," Jimmy said. He nodded at Mason. "We can play at the Fall Festival if we want. They're going to have some bands."

Frank snugged the instrument tighter under his arm and tested it again, thumping the strings in a slow rhythm.

"What do you say?"

There were three flower arrangements on the tables in the room. There would be a dozen by evening. Oakpine had won the game after his injury, using the unfortunate incident as a spur to make up a twenty-point deficit. The entire team had come by the night before on their way to the victory bonfire, but he'd been in surgery, and now flowers had been arriving all day.

"Does it hurt?" Mason said.

Frank shook his head without looking up from the guitar. "Naw. It will later."

"It sure made a noise," Jimmy said.

"I guess," Frank said.

"When is the Fall Festival?" Bobby Krause said from his bed by the window.

Frank Gunderson looked up at Jimmy and Mason. "When is it?"

"Two weeks," Jimmy said. "We'd only need two songs. We'd only need to work up two songs."

"And a name," Frank said. He was a little dizzy in the white room. "A band needs a name."

They had three names, in the first three weeks. They played the Fall Festival in the gym as the Rangemen, doing two Rolling Stones songs, "Lady Jane" and "Mother's Little Helper." Frank did in fact play bass, sitting against a high stool in his leg cast, Jimmy played lead guiitar, Mason sang (along with Jimmy) and played rhythm guitar, and Craig played drums. At rehearsal the night before the festival, Craig spray-painted the head of his bass drum cherry red and glued half a cup of sparkles to it. Their first performance came between the three Griffin sisters, who lip-synched "Itsy Bitsy Teenie Weenie Yellow Polka Dot Bikini," and the Four Sticks, a coed baton team. The Rangemen were a little raw, and they knew it. In fact, they were terrible, and they knew it. No two elements of their playing coincided correctly. Both their numbers sounded purposely discordant, as if in some thematic link with the lyrics, drug songs, and happy to be here. People in the gym milled about nervously during the eight minutes of punishing music, some stopped short by the sparkles drummed loose from Craig Ralston's drum kit, flecks that floated up in the little thermals present in the old wooden room.

But what stayed for the four boys—every one of them sweating to catch up to melodies, chords that raced ahead, every one of them certain of at least partial humiliation in this, the first real independent venture of their lives—was that from the first chords of Jimmy Brand's Fender and then the raucous drumbeat and visceral bass guitar under

Frank Gunderson's fingers, twenty, maybe thirty of their schoolmates, not just girls, came up to the plywood stage and stood in a crescent around the one AudioVox speaker, and these kids leaned there and took it. And when the Rangemen finished their set with the last three descending notes of "Mother's Little Helper," these twenty kids clapped and stayed after the applause and looked at the band, and a couple of them came up and helped Craig move his flaking drums. Three or four kids lingered at the side of the stage when Jimmy and Mason and Frank came down, and there was something there that had not existed nine minutes before, and now it was different. They'd gone up there four odd ducks in the early days of their senior year in high school, and they came down as a band. They didn't need to say it or clap hands or even go *oh wow*; it had happened, and though they had been so ruthlessly terrible, they were a band. They would get better. They were a band.

It was a great night, a night that Jimmy Brand put in a book, assigning the euphoria and confidence the four of them felt to other young people, kids at a party. He'd disguised it. But his feeling always had been that it was a great night, one of the top ten for him. The other great nights were mostly in New York, with Daniel, small victories that they shared. He'd been a writer, he realized early in his career, because he lived for loveliness and intensity but only if he could know about them, be aware, have the distance and the words that would make them ring and ring in him. He'd been self-conscious as a kid, and he knew that night that something had happened for them all that was beyond the ordinary, and at seventeen he loved the knowing.

Without really plotting it or planning, they started rehearsing every afternoon in Jimmy Brand's garage. Craig's drums were already there, and Mason lived three houses down. After football practice, Craig would pick up Frank, who would be in a full leg cast until December, and they'd pull into the Brands' driveway. The garage door was open, and Jimmy and Mason were in there tuning up. They learned their instruments a song at a time. Craig had taken drum lessons and had the basics, and Mason had had some guitar, but it was uphill for everyone. They'd pick a song and learn it line by line, so that the neighbors that year got used to hearing random electric noises suddenly galvanize into ten or fifteen seconds of "Help Me, Rhonda," or "I Get Around." Leaves from the giant poplars and cottonwoods fell across the mouth of the open garage and scattered red and yellow as if urged by the music.

At some point in the session, Matt Brand would get home and wander around to the garage. There were always six or seven neighborhood kids sitting and standing around the open door. They gave Matt way, as everyone did. He was the kind of kid that came around once a generation in a place like Oakpine, the single apple of the town's eye that year. It was the football and his strength, of course, but it was his confidence and youth mostly. He would live forever. He was moving through, moving on to bigger things, and everyone he knew was proud of this polite and energetic kid. His black hair and straight broad shoulders drew people toward him, and after the kids moved aside so Matt could lean against the doorframe, they came back up and stood near him.

"Rock 'n' roll," he said. "My brother is Mick Jagger."

"Your brother is Jimmy Brand," Jimmy said back. Then to the guys, "You ready: one, two, three . . ." And a clashing bangfest of "Barbara Ann" exploded for five seconds, then ebbed.

Matt pointed at Craig on drums. "Don't hurt your ears, big boy."

"What?" Craig said. "I can't hear you. I recognize you, but I can't hear you."

"He can hear you fine if your hands are at his butt and you're saying, 'Hut four, five-four, hut'!" Frank said.

"Again," Jimmy said. "Barbara Ann. When you have a song named after a girl, she's cute and unobtainable. When you have a song named after a man, he's on death row or about to be hanged in some lonesome valley. Ready: one, two, three . . ." They blasted into two or three bars of the song and then unspooled and stopped.

"You guys," Matt said to the band. "You've got a future. I can say I knew you when." He stood now and cuffed playfully at the kids orbiting around him. "I'm going to eat and head out."

"Say hello to Kathleen for us," Frank said. "If you can remember."

"Not a chance," Matt said from the driveway. "I say one thing about this band—"

"The Rangemen," Jimmy told him.

"I say one thing about the band knowing her name, and she'll be out the door and over here, and I won't get any homework done."

"You won't get any homework done anyway, Champ," Frank called back. Matt was in the back door now. He would eat a quick dinner and go over to his girlfriend's house for some homework and television.

Mr. Brand would arrive while the band was rehearsing, park on the driveway beside the house, and come to the open garage door. He liked these boys and the loud simple music they attempted. There always was the possibility of politics when rock 'n' roll was played, but this wasn't any of that. "Generation gap"—the phrase was only a few years old, and it did not apply. The Democratic Convention in Chicago a year before had seemed, like all television, remote and unrelated to life in this village. The images of people, young people in the streets protesting, seemed theatrical and bizarre. Mr. Brand listened to two or three of their four-bar explosions and kidded with them about when he would again get to park his precious truck in the garage.

They were blessed days for Louise Brand, all the teenage traffic in her house, the time in a person's life when everything has a use, the garage, the porch, the kitchen, and her skill as a cook, life at the limit, as full and delicious as a world gets. Her boys were both still in the house, and when she heard the concussive music from the garage, she cleaned the kitchen and prepared dinner with a sense of well-being so complete she couldn't have described it. She always loaded her oven with squash, which was coming in faster than she could bake it, and when Edgar came in and went to wash, she'd wait for his word, and it came every night: "Invite them in—let's feed these musical prodigies."

"They're going to be good, Dad," Matt said, finishing his meal, placing his plate on the counter.

"And you're off to Lady Kathleen's?" his father said.

"Yes, sir. I'll be back when my homework's done."

"Will Mrs. Pullman be home?" Louise Brand asked her son. She asked him every night.

"She will, Mom."

"He's got homework, Mother," Edgar spoke to his wife. He looked at his son. "And he remembers to honor the family name."

"Whatever that means," she said.

"It's as close as we're getting to the birds and the bees, Mother," Matt said to her. "And it's close enough. You've raised a good boy who minds his manners." He went to the door. "And does his trigonometry with his girlfriend. I'll see you in a while. After the Beatles have eaten."

When he left, she put her husband's dinner on the table, a steak and baked potato with a steaming slab of butternut squash. They didn't speak because they didn't need to. She hummed a little. A moment later he might say, "Trigonometry," and they'd smile, two people. The spirited periodic cacophony would close down for the night in fifteen minutes, and the boys, Frank, Mason, Craig, and Jimmy, would stumble into the house for the dinner she'd prepared.

These nights were the very center of her life. Her kitchen brimmed with these boys, how they could fit, all talking, reaching for the platters of food, assembling three-story burgers and buttering the squash. There was an ongoing wrangle about which songs to learn, and it was a real debate because none of the four had any clear favorite; this was all new to them. Jimmy loved Buddy Holly but was open and ready to hear more. They were lined up on the mainstream, some Beatles and the Beach Boys, a few songs, and the Rolling Stones. They were divided about whether to try some Kingston Trio; Mason liked them but knew it was too slow and years old. They trashed bubblegum and the conversation grew loud, Craig mocking "Yummy Yummy Yummy," and then they joked further, laughing and singing parts of "White Rabbit," which was not anywhere near their style. "We grow our hair long like Al Price and take drugs!" Frank called. "We change our name to Wyoming Acid Trip."

"You won't get the right girls with that move," Mason said. "Shawnee Despain will go out with you right now and save us the time of learning any music."

" 'Shawnee' would be a good title for a song."

"Not really, she's attainable. But she is cute."

"Watch your language at the table."

"Sorry, but I have it from a good source that she's been attained."

"I'm not in it for the girls," Frank said, and he was hooted down. Craig whined a few lines of "Big Girls Don't Cry," and there was an appreciation of the Four Seasons, but it wasn't their style. After they'd spun through a dozen bands and twenty songs, Jimmy brought them back to the Beach Boys, where there were ten songs they wanted.

" 'Let Him Run Wild,' " Jimmy said. "It's made for us. It's got all the stuff." The table was an empty ruin now, the serving trays decimated, the last roll pulled from the basket. Craig started a rhythmic *bom bom bom*, the four-four beat of "Let Him Run Wild," and the boys waited and picked it up, humming and tapping the song, the table rocking faintly as they built and focused. Mason sang the lyric, and Jimmy came along in harmony. Craig rapped his fingertips on the edge of the table, and Frank mouthed the bass line. Louise Brand turned from where she'd cut the pumpkin pie and watched them, how serious they were about the fun they were having.

Edgar Brand came back to the kitchen door. "Louise, hold the pie until the boys in the band have heard something that will change their minds for good." He hoisted his beautiful black and white accordion to his chest and began a slow version of "Little Brown Jug" that filled the room with sound. They all knew he played, and he had the instrument out every Christmas back to the edge of memory, playing any of the dozen polkas he knew. The tune grew faster and faster as it progressed, and when he finished the last bar and called, "Hey!" the boys clapped and cried out. "Now there's a song that will get the girls, men," he said, pulling the straps from his shoulders. There was no room on the table for another thing, not a glass, and yet the pie was distributed and those plates found places, and the pie was devoured.

"Thank you, Mrs. Brand, Mr. Brand," Mason said, standing up. "I better get home for supper." They all laughed. "I'll see you guys to-morrow."

"You're welcome, Mason," Louise said. "Say hello to your folks for us." And suddenly the dishes were clattering again in their transit to the drainboard, the boys clearing up, cleaning up, and departing. Outside it was fresh now, almost cold, and Craig helped Frank down the porch in the new dark, holding his crutches while he hopped to Craig's old truck for the ride home.

Jimmy stood as was his custom; he would walk Mason halfway home. On the narrow sidewalk, they strolled with their hands in their pockets and had a joke of bumping shoulders to jostle each other out of stride. It was always quiet on the old street, their ears worked over from the practice session. One night in the fall, a week before homecoming, where they would play at the party, they stopped, and for some reason Mason took Jimmy's arm. "What's going to happen to everybody, Jimmy?" Their faces were very close, so strange, and they just looked at each other. Mason let Jimmy's arm go and stepped back and then put his hand on Jimmy's shoulder and then let that go too and made a little wave, and silently the boys turned and walked to their homes.

One week later they played for the homecoming bonfire as Wildfire, a name that not only didn't last, it barely existed. Matt, as captain of the football team, had volunteered them for the late-night party on Oakpine Mountain, and he had forgotten their real name and told Kathleen Pullman, his girlfriend, to put Wildfire on the flyer. She inked in the letters, making them look like flames, and she ran off a couple hundred mimeographed sheets that were circulated in the stands at the homecoming game against Cody.

Bear Meadow Bonfire after our Victory over Cody. Kegger, bonfire, and the rocking tunes of Wildfire!
Bring a friend, two logs, five bucks, and an attitude.

Go Cougars!

Craig kept some of the flyers for a scrapbook, but no one ever said the word aloud: *Wildfire.*

Edgar Brand arranged for a gas generator and let them use his truck to take their gear up the mountain in return for a promise that they wouldn't drink. They set up in the aspen grove about halfway up on Oakpine Mountain, where the bonfire had been for every homecoming sixty years running, from when the high school had been in the wooden building that was now used for storage by the railroad. It was exhilarating for the three of them to be in the hills like this, alone with the tower of ruined lumber that the spirit committee and some of the industrial arts guys had been delivering all week. Jimmy and Mason set up the generator and ran the power cable to the little platform stage that Frank had constructed by bolting plywood sheets to milk crates. He hopped on one foot at times, used his crutches at others.

They'd had to leave the game early with the score tied ten to ten, but as the fall twilight swallowed the meadow, Frank looked up and said, "Listen." For hours the only sound had been whippoorwills and the banging noise of the setting up. The three boys stood still in the mountain air, and after a moment they could hear the bleating of distant car horns, the concussion of approaching vehicles. "We won," Frank said.

"Must be," Mason said.

"Oh yeah," Frank continued. He held up his two hands, listening. "By two touchdowns. This is going to be a party."

A few minutes later the first four cars packed with kids circled into the meadow, easing over the grassy, uneven ground, all of them parking nose in toward the pile of lumber. Ross Hubbard, who was spirit leader, one of the boys who would go to Vietnam and never return or be found and would be Missing in Action, jumped out of his rusty Datsun and started waving the others away as kids piled out of every door.

He walked along in front of gathering vehicles. "No, no!" he yelled. "Back up. Back, back! Do you understand? This is going to be a fire! Davis, you want to burn up your father's car and have him kick your ass once more? Back it up! Move these or lose these!" he pounded on the hoods of the cars. "Back! Move it back!" He swept his arm. "Park back by the trees!" Immediately a kind of controlled chaos set in, boys and girls everywhere, some diving straight for the trees to relieve themselves, some throwing more wood on the pile, calling greetings, screaming out fiercely, joyously, for no apparent reason other than that they were young people out of town under the sky in this little random village in the woods. "Leeper!" Ross Hubbard yelled at one boy who was standing on the hood of a car. "Move this heap unless you want to burn it up!"

"My dad wouldn't appreciate that!" Leeper said, dropping to the ground.

"I don't think he'll like those footprints either."

"It doesn't matter," Leeper said from the driver's seat. "We kicked Cody's ass!" He laid on the horn, and two other horns jumped to join the noise.

The two boys, Doug Leeper and Ross Hubbard, started hauling and restacking the assemblage of lumber, making a cross-hatch chimney of four great logs and then filling the center with the hundreds of ruined four-by-fours they'd gathered last fall when the railroad dismantled the huge shed for the train roundhouse. Hubbard showed a group of boys how to interleaf the dozens of pallets they had so that they wouldn't fall over. After half an hour the two leaders were standing atop the structure, which looked like a huge wooden soldier with a square head. Someone threw Ross Hubbard a rope, and with some effort he hauled up five gallons of kerosene and drizzled it down through all the vertical timbers while Doug Leeper walked the circle calling out, "No matches, no flames!" They hauled another five gallons, and Ross spilled it happily. Then there was the problem of getting him down. "It's all right," he called. "Burn me with it. It's worth it, the way we beat Cody. Just a sacrifice, small but sincere."

"Stop screwing around," Janice Day said. "You're not funny, big man. Somebody get him off there."

"Move back," Ross said, making as if to jump. Then he tied the rope to the top beam and shimmied down. Though they wrangled with the rope for ten minutes, the knot would not be jogged off the post. Doug Leeper cut it as high as he could.

"That," Ross told him, "is my father's anchor rope for the boat he loves more than his firstborn son."

"Will he know it's thirty feet short?"

"I'll ask him as he drifts away," Ross said. "It's a sixty-dollar rope. Let's get a donation." And then there was a call for "Rope fund! Rope fund!" And Doug Leeper went in two big circles around the encampment with his football helmet out for cash, counting as he received each bill and coin, returning with forty-one dollars and fifty-five cents.

"Why do you have your helmet?"

"It goes everywhere with me," Leeper said. "We've got a special arrangement."

Two dozen cars lined the edge of the clearing when Craig Ralston arrived in his old blue Ford pickup. It was full dark. Kathleen Pullman and Matt Brand were with him in the cab, and in the bed of the vehicle were four bright kegs of beer. He orbited the bonfire pile slowly three times as kids jumped on and off the back of his truck. His hair was still wet from the showers.

Jimmy Brand and Mason and Frank had all the instruments set

and watched the wild parade from the band's little platform. "The heroes have arrived," Frank said.

"You ever want to play football, Mason?" Jimmy asked him.

"I played last year, remember? But not really," Mason said. "I had other plans for my youth. Did you want to?"

Jimmy watched the antic parade. "It would have been fun. We were in high school—it's part of it."

"Right. This is high school, boys. Wake up." Frank said. "And what were your plans for your youth, Mason?"

"Play guitar in the mountains a couple times. Not break my leg. Get out of Oakpine in one piece."

"Lose your virginity to one of our fine groupies?"

"Any girl who loves music is a friend of mine."

"Any girl who loves our music is disturbed," Frank said.

"Better," Mason said. "She'd go for me just fine."

"Next year," Frank said, "you going to Wyoming?"

"I'm going where I get in," Mason said. "I wouldn't mind Laramie." Mason Kirby took in the dark meadow, expectancy rife in the place. He took Jimmy Brand's arm; it was his habit to take Jimmy's arm. "Are these our people, Jimmy?" It was the way they talked.

"They are, Mason." He looked at his friend in this deepening year. "Whether they like it or not." He pointed at his brother. Across the open space they could see Craig Ralston and Matt Brand wrestling with one of the kegs on the tailgate of Craig's truck. A crowd was gathered around them, and suddenly a cheer went up, and Matt stood up and raised a glass of beer.

"They got her tapped," Frank said.

Craig came through the crowd in his Oakpine sweatshirt. His hair had dried in a wild nest. "Gentlemen," Craig said. He stopped and drank off his cup of beer and threw it into the air. He stepped up and rattled his drum kit, checking left to right each wing nut.

"For you," Frank said, producing two sets of drumsticks from behind his back.

"Always a pleasure," Craig said, taking them. He was consumed with happiness, the open air, the night to come.

"Mr. Ralston," Mason said, "I hear we kicked their asses."

Craig shook the snare assembly one last time and, finding it sound, stood and looked at the other three. "We won the game," he said. "But everybody, including your drummer, got his ass kicked. I don't want to play that game over even in my mind." He climbed in, sat down, and played a riff on each of the drums. He smiled at them. "This is more like it. Music. Let's play some soothing music."

A group of football players grabbed Matt Brand from his perch on the truck and carried him around the space on their shoulders. He'd been on other boys' shoulders a dozen times in the past two years. He held his beer cup aloft, slopping some over the sides as the gang lurched toward the precise and twisted obelisk of lumber. Jimmy could see Kathleen leaning against the back of one of the cars, arms folded in the dark. They were referred to as Matt-and-Kathleen, a compound noun now, coupled and permanent in that high school way.

Ross Hubbard came running and jumped onto the low band platform. "As fire marshal—"

"I thought you were Fire Wizard," Frank said.

"Thank you, Frank Gunderson. I am, but I didn't want to intimidate you. But as fire wizard, I must advise you that you are in what we in the profession call the circle of big fire. That is, you guys are going to get a little toasted here, do you think?" he said, measuring the distance to the pyramid of wood.

"You're toasted right now," Mason told him. "We'll be all right. It'll be hot for a while, but Ross, we're tough. We're from Oakpine."

Saying the word *Oakpine* sent Ross into the Oakpine cheer, a martial chant that was picked up in the meadow and carried to its whooping conclusion. When the calls had subsided, Ross shook Mason's hand. "Okay, sounds good. Just so you're fireproof." Ross went on. "Gimme a drumroll, and we'll get this party under way."

Craig started with a low simmer, which he built up in a blur, which he threw to his bass drum and then held up again in a floating snare. The drums quickened the night, and the circle of a hundred boys and girls with their cups of beer tightened around the site. Craig now ran a classic drumroll, and Frank plucked the first dozen notes of the theme to *The Twilight Zone*.

"All right, Oakpine!" Ross yelled to the crowd.

"All right, Oakpine," Frank deadpanned into the mike.

"Oh, there's a mike," Ross said, turning. He spoke into it then: "All right, Oakpine. Let's have Matt Brand, Matt Three-Touchdown Brand, start what we call the official fucking fire! We won, and we won't leave without a conflagration!" Ross jumped forward and ran to Matt, pressing a book of matches into his hand.

"Quite the speech," Mason said.

"Get ready, guys," Jimmy said. "The Rangemen are about to play their second American date."

"Wildfire," Frank said.

"Whatever," Mason said. "I am ready."

Matt Brand, obviously full of beer, held the matches aloft and then dropped them to great laughter. Then, resupplied and with another flourish, he struck one. He stepped forward and threw it at the lumber, falling as he did. Ross and Doug Leeper pulled him back, standing him braced against Kathleen. Then Ross rolled a tube from one of the paper flyers and lit it, and when it flared, he went forward and thrust it into the thatched stack of wood. Instantly a bright yellow spearpoint of fire arose and slipped through the mass, rising until inside of a minute there was a four-story blaze standing in the meadow. The kids backed and then backed again as the heat registered, their faces two-dimensional in the strange moment.

In the sudden light flashing against the side of everyone, Jimmy Brand said, "My friends: one, two, three . . ." and the band kicked into "Be True to Your School," a song they were shaky on, but it was simple and loud enough to carry. The speaker and the amplifier filled the mountain with ten tons of sound, enough to go with the ghastly fire, and the figures in the firelight pulsed to the hard beat, their shadows dancing distorted and gargantuan on the wall of trees in Bear Meadow. The party had begun.

The band knew nine songs well, four fairly well, and two were rocky possibilities, and so their plan was to play each with an extra chorus or two. They were worried about running out of stuff, but there was no need to worry. Before they were halfway through the third song, "Let Him Run Wild," that Beach Boys tune, the night had fallen into an easy pattern for which the band was a steady background. They worked at furnishing each room in all the songs completely, overdoing it, taking all the corners wide and coming together in the performance better than they'd ever done in the garage. They'd never had this much room, and they'd never let go like this, played so loud. It seemed to Jimmy that they were playing slowly, but it was right on tempo. The meadow teemed with kids, a circle around the fire as it flared and collapsed once and then rose again as a real fire, not a temporary tower. A lot of the young people lined the stage, some dancing, though only a few, and the rest coming and going from the woods and the cars and the groups of four or five in letter jackets, and smaller groups in conspiracies of mischief and affection.

The band worked, rising above themselves, into the music. After the first few songs they felt no longer like the center of attention, and it was all like a big open rehearsal, fun. They didn't pay any attention to the party, because it seemed that the party was out there, remote. Even the half-dozen kids dancing seemed to be part of something else. Between songs they could hear kids calling for more, clapping, whooping for this song or that, as if taking requests were even a possibility. From where he stood, Jimmy watched it all, and Mason saw him take it in. Jimmy had words for things and Mason could see his friend formulating his overview. When they looked at each other, pounding out "Wendy," the look sparked, and Mason's faced closed up in a smile, and Jimmy came across and hugged his friend with an arm around the neck, brushing faces. The moment, the happiness, was choking.

Kathleen Pullman came up to the band, her arms folded in her jacket, and smiled at them. She nodded at Jimmy and rolled her eyes at him, a thing she did sometimes that always meant: *Matt*. He could see his brother way back sitting in the center of a group of boys on the hood of a car. Matt was drunk. It was his right as a hero, and he took it. In the flashing firelight the black and white scene seemed to Jimmy a tableau from the *Iliad*. Matt gestured with his arms, telling stories, and the boys laughed.

Their classmates stumbled around the fire, spilling beer, sometimes coming to the edge of the musicians' platform and toasting them, "You guys are fucking great!" All night long guys and girls came up to Frank and signed his cast, many with bits of charcoal from the fire, initials in black, and smiling faces, until he was smudged thoroughly. Elsewhere in the meadow some couples had paired off, only a few surprises, retiring to the cars as the evening grew late and the fire tumbled into itself every once in a while, sending a thick flock of red cinders pooling briefly into the chilly air.

Between "Satisfaction" and "The House of the Rising Sun," Mason stepped over to Jimmy and now said, "You're a little old man at the kids' picnic."

Jimmy looked at his friend. They both were tuning their guitars.

"I'm afraid you're right. I don't know what that's about, but I keep looking at the stars, the woods. It's nine miles to Oakpine, and then what?"

"Let's do one more and take a break," Craig said from behind them.

"You got it," Jimmy said.

"This is good, right, the band?" Mason asked him. "There's something more to all this than just the music. Let me know if you find out what it is."

"This is real," Jimmy said. "This is the best." His eyes shone. He turned to Frank and Craig. "This is the best."

"We are rocking," Frank said. "And I finally know all the lyrics to these songs. That's really the hard part. And now we are absolutely rocking."

To no one, he said, "We have a year of this." And then he turned to his friends and said, "My friends, at the ready! One, two, three . . ."

They did almost four sets of the music they knew, as well as some extended jamming. They played until the fire was a heap of pulsing orange embers and the generator had to be regassed. They played until there were only three cars left in Bear Meadow. Craig Ralston threw his drumsticks onto the glowing coals, and they flamed briefly, white-yellow ciphers in the deep red. He loaded Matt, who was passed out, into his truck and hauled him home. Jimmy, Mason, and Frank put on fresh, dry shirts and jackets and broke down the gear, and they loaded up with the help of four or five of the band's new followers, including Kathleen Pullman and her girlfriend Marci Engle. Marci came over and put her arms around Jimmy. "You don't know," she said to Frank and Mason, looking on, "he might be my boyfriend." When they were packed up in Mr. Brand's truck and Kathleen's car, the boys shoveled a short berm around the ten-foot firepit and then tossed a layer of dirt over the whole pile until it was dark and reduced to two or three steaming streams of smoke.

Mason walked over and rapped on the trunk of Dougie Shelton's Plymouth to wake Dougie and Yvonne, who weren't exactly asleep. "Honeymoon is over," Mason called to them. "Don't be the last couple on the mountain." The dark empty space made it feel very late on the mountain, and a kind of seriousness had assumed the lonely place. Jimmy started his truck, and Mason got in. Frank Gunderson climbed into Kathleen's car with Marci, between them in the front seat, Mason noted.

Marci rolled her window down and called toward Dougie's car, "Come on, you two bunnies! Three times is enough for any bonfire! You're going to freeze your parts off!" She laughed, and Kathleen honked. The dark car started, and the lights came on, and Doug called, "That's a good band you guys have got going." He backed out and eased tenderly out of the clearing. A moment later Kathleen followed down the mountain. When all the cars were gone, Jimmy stepped out of the idling vehicle. "I've got to take a leak." The two boys stood out behind the vehicle, one facing north and one south, a million worlds within their view. The wheel of stars had broken and turned, and the Big Dipper was a only a handle now, rising from the trees.

When they climbed back into the truck, Jimmy said, "Just this." And he leaned and took Mason's shoulder. "Life on Earth," Jimmy said into the windshield of stars. And the band had its third and final name.

FIVE

High School

Marci was together. That had been the word for her in high school. She was organized and looked organized, wearing her smart dark-brown hair in a part around her pretty face. She had been elected class historian and then did all the work for Matt Brand, who was president of everything. In the fall of her senior year, she dated Jimmy Brand because he was the first focused boy she'd met, and he was kind and solicitous and gave her some of his writing. She was impatient with being sixteen and then seventeen; she'd read about it, adolescence, and stood outside of it, waiting for herself. They would kiss on her front porch like a couple out of yesteryear, and then she'd find flowers in pop bottles there in the morning. His mother's gerbera daisies. He talked to her, laid out his plans; he loved drama, reading the plays. He spent the night at her house twice that last spring, but only on the couch after close sessions kissing. A couple times she'd whispered, "You can," moving his hand under her shirt, and he had lifted his palm to hold her as if in measurement so that the light touch burned her, but he wouldn't press, and she was confused by the ache—was it affection? His mouth against hers, she remembered him saying, "High school." And she could feel both of their mouths smile. She knew then, years ago, but she didn't ask him or say. It was okay, and it was okay now.

Then at year's end Matt Brand was killed, and a week later Jimmy Brand left Oakpine. The funeral was tough, and when Jimmy left, Marci knew that something real, something not high school had happened. She received two letters from Jimmy, one that summer and one later the next fall when she was starting to see Craig Ralston. They both were full of thanks and affection, and in the last he said, "Thank you for kissing me," and they were both signed "With love." She still had them somewhere. Then her life unfolded a week at a time: with Craig and their travels and return to town, work in the community and getting the store going, and then Larry as a baby and the new house and their plans and comforts and what. And now Marci was still together, the organizing force at the museum, and known for it, but with Mason back in town, the high school wise man, and Jimmy back in town to die, Marci felt the old adrenaline, threads of it. Here we are, she thought. It's all high school. Everything is everlastingly high school. Marci thought it first when she was fourteen and about to enter Oakpine High in the ninth grade and somebody had broken up with someone (she could remember the names), and for a week it was a federal case, a walking tragedy, and then somebody else got a necklace with a little Woolworth's ring, and all the talking went marching off in another direction. And every day she dressed for school, she felt like a chapter from a book, knowing what would be said about her by Kathleen or the other girls in the old lunchroom, every half hour had its half hour telling. And her studies were all a federal case, the emergency run-up to the chemistry test, the aching essays for Mr. Lanniton in history, worse than a job. And not dating was a federal case, and then dating was a federal case, the only boy she kissed, really kissed was Jimmy Brand because he was the only interesting kid in the place, or so she said, *interesting* being her word. And her crush on him, and the way he looked out for her and gave her the few poems and the surprise flowers in pop bottles on her porch some mornings, was a federal case.

To think about him at times was to start or say stupidly and unbidden, "Oh my," and even her husband, Craig, knew now what it was after thirty years. Every two years or so Marci would start and shake her head or say those words, and Craig's hand would come to her shoulder, perhaps the only thing in the freaking world that is not high school, that understanding. And raising Larry, year after year, in a village of folks who knew him, a whole town like a high school. A day running errands, the grocer, the cleaners, stopping by the hardware for Larry to say hi to daddy was like walking the halls, class, class, locker, locker, did you hear this? Or this? And somebody's pregnant, like high school, and someone gets a new car, all the way from Casper, or a parent is dead and those two are breaking up, my god, oh high school, old Oakpine, the Oakpine Cougars, red and black, and underneath an entire nation of activity the old school song, "Our memories linger after, sing the praise and voices raise to Oakpine . . ."

She didn't know what to do with this thinking; it seemed so rueful and wrong, a big game. Even when Kathleen and Frank separated two years ago, it felt like something achieved along a row of lockers opposite the office, and now her play with Stewart at the museum was exactly stolen kisses behind a closed door, one eye open. Behind his office door she had stood and taken him in her hand and pushed him to stillness with a long kiss, the clenched hand still and still until she felt him shudder. There was adrenaline in it, in every new sentence in the high school story, but Marci felt something else too. Was it a game? Was she just out for sport? Craig had hauled the drum kit out to the Brands, and Larry now was practicing guitar when he wasn't being lord of his life, an omniscient agent in their house, sometime traveler. This season wouldn't last. High school. She could think that far and then no further. She was married to someone she had met in study hall when she was fifteen; they had a new house, and it was fall again. There'd be new babies in town and a fall after that, grandchildren on the football team, as strange as life gets. Or normal. She knew all about it, outside herself again, and even Kathleen would point at her over coffee and say it: "You are so together," when in fact it was Kathleen for whatever reason who had become the adult.

The Oakpine Museum still smelled new. Three years ago they had finished refurbishing the old train station: they'd knocked out some walls and scoured all the original brick and block walls and carpeted the two galleries. As a last touch, Craig had come out with a ladder scaffold and enameled all the wrought-iron scrollwork in the eight arches engine black. The first show had been the "The Age of Aquarius." Stewart, the curator, had gotten two large but minor Peter Max paintings and some original album art from Cream and Big Brother and the Holding Company, as well as a mongrel assortment of psychedelic art from San Francisco and New York. That show had been Marci's first assignment there, writing copy for the poster art, and she'd won the day by noting that "the museum had hung this crazy show, but it would be off the wall." They had piped in elevator versions of acid rock, and the retrospective, parts of it, received campy reviews all around the country. Stewart, who was from Milwaukee, lost a little of his big-city mystique with his overenthusiastic response to Marci's program puns.

There was such an edge in all of this for her. There had been a part-time slot, and it became a full-time administrative assistant, her new job. It gave her a jolt, having an office and a big window looking across to the high school and the hospital and the rooftops beyond. She guessed it was pride when she tried to tell her mother about her work, her mother who had lived forever ten blocks from the museum. The expectation was museum equals oil paintings of red flowers in a blue bowl. That was the way Stewart had put it. And that was finally all Marci would give her mother on the phone: it's not all red flowers in a blue bowl, which would send Mrs. Engle over the edge. She'd say back to her daughter, "Marci, you need to give me a little credit here." Marci would invoke Stewart, the curator, and talk about how all he was trying to do for Oakpine was introduce their old town to such new ideas. "Marci," her mother would say, "We've taken *Time* magazine for forty years, and I'd love to see a new idea."

Regardless, Marci found the pressure of hanging a new show a puzzle, assessing the aesthetic and trying to describe and explain the thing in a way that would draw people to the show. She was on the inside here, a member of the steering committee, and with Larry in high school, she gave it all of her attention. This new "Terrain" display would get written up in Cheyenne if not in Denver.

It also rushed her that Stewart wanted her to go to Chicago after Thanksgiving, on museum business, for the National Museum Society. They'd be in the same hotel. That was the way he had said what he said: We'll be in the same hotel. December first loomed for her, drew her forward through the fall. In the meantime, she closed the museum every Tuesday night, and he was often there. She watched him make work to stay around, always there to give her a look, pat her hand, put his arm around her waist, sweet and sort of fun, and sometimes both arms, a quick embrace stolen in the hall, mock dramatic, pretending to pin her against the wall and then pinning her against the wall. It was high school certainly, but she liked the feel of his suits, and she liked how angular he was, so utterly different from Craig. But mainly she liked his smell, so dry and sweet, and how smooth his face was. It was nice to feel sought. She played it that way. She loved the moment after she'd turned off the lights in the display areas and turned on the security lights, when he'd come out of his office and meet her in the hall. It was the meeting that started her heart, his taking her, the kiss, the way he put her against the wall. There was a rush in this, but also a limit. She'd dressed for all of this so far, but also she'd dressed to keep him out: layers. Now, however, she was going in a few weeks on business to Chicago.

The night before the opening of the geologic show, Marci held a gala preview for museum patrons and friends. She closed the building at two in the afternoon, did a last walk-through, and waited for the caterers. These were the nicest rooms in Oakpine. In two hours they would be full of Oakpine's finest. The show was bright and lively, large plates of stone and realistic landscapes and surreal landscapes, mountains and plains. She straightened again the show guides on the oak tables in the glassed lobby. Stewart was waiting for her in their hall, and they fell together easily, familiarly. She felt his hands on the back of her skirt, and he pressed her against the wall, kissing her with more urgency than she'd expected. "You're going to wrinkle me all up."

"Good," he said. "With an hour, we can do a good job of that."

"Stewart."

He was at her neck now, his mouth. "I want this," he said. He ran his hand up under her blouse. His hand on the fabric quickened the moment, but while they were still kissing, she pulled his arm down and away. She thought of what Mason had said to her the week before. A metaphor. The back of his neck was clean to her touch. He'd been to the barber this afternoon. "But we've got the caterers. Let's meet after."

"Afterward you'll start to act awkward and then run off. You won't stay and let me drive you."

She felt smart in all of it, smart and desired, but the truth was that she was confused. There was a taste of danger in it, but they had gone slowly, inching along all year. Stewart had been considerate, and they'd left so many moments unfinished with a kind of promise over it all, an infatuation that she found delicious.

She was about to say, "In fifty-nine minutes Tip Top Bakery will be buzzing at the back door with all their goodies." In fact, she thought the words, preparing the sentence. But before she could say it, Wendy Ingram came around the corner carrying a cardboard box of labeling materials. Marci looked Wendy in the face, and before she could shrug Stewart off or make him aware of what was going on, Wendy passed them, without a word, and was gone toward the workroom way in the back.

"What?" Stewart said. "Please."

Marci took his face in both her hands and looked at him. "No. Not now. We need to be careful. Wait." She kissed him and set him back away from her. She liked the way he looked at her now; some of this was so sweet, so much fun. "Wendy's still here. She saw us. At some point tonight, let her know that you'd grabbed me in a moment of joy at a job well done, something like that."

"Not a problem," he said. He was already putting on his game face. "Excellent."

She watched him go and then folded her arms and leaned against the wall. High school. Three years ago, when Craig had unrolled the plans for the new house on their old kitchen table, he'd said, "Let's do this. It's something we've always wanted. But if we're going to be un-happy, let's do that now and not wait until we're in the new house." Why did he think to say that? The remark wasn't like him at all.

In making deliveries for the hardware store, Larry Ralston always double-parked the truck and then ran to the end of whatever block he was on and turned, taking serpentine steps and sometimes running backward down to the other end of the block as if on his toes and then back to the truck, where he would open the back gates and grab what-ever he was delivering and take it to the door. People were used to see-ing him running. Now he loped down Berry Street and back, and then he reached in the truck for the envelopes, which weighed five ounces, and he skipped back to Jimmy Brand's garage and knocked on the door. There was no answer, but sometimes, Jimmy Brand did not answer. It was a sunny October Friday afternoon.

"What is it?" Edgar Brand had come out onto the back porch and was addressing the boy.

"Hello," Larry said. "I was just going to see Mr. Brand. Jimmy. He asked me to come over to check on his—" Before he could finish the sentence with the word *guitar*, which came out as an offbeat after-thought, Edgar had stepped back inside and the door shut. Larry pushed into the garage and peeked in. "Yo, Jimmy?" In the gloom, Larry could see the form of Jimmy's body under the covers. He laid the paper packet of guitar strings on the dresser and slipped out.

He started his truck, pulled an easy U-turn on the street, and slowly drove three doors to Mason Kirby's house, where three men worked along the crest of the new roof. The yard was littered with bits of torn shingle and other carpentry debris. Mason and Craig worked along the side of the house on a low scaffold, securing the new aluminum rain gutters. His dad had lost weight in the month's work, and he looked at home tacking the stripping in the eaves. Mason had moved back into the old house and had kidded with Larry about crashing anytime at his bachelor pad. "Of course," Mason had added, "you've got the same problem I have. No date." Larry liked Mason, having him in town. The time he'd stayed with them had been fun, his father looser and more with it than Larry could remember. It was obvious that his dad enjoyed working on the old Kirby place. They'd talked into the night, going through the old yearbooks with his mother, talking about Mason's divorce, which had taken two years or something.

"Larry!" his dad called. "You want to get some lunch?"

"Naw, you guys go on. I've got four more stops, including all this Romex for those guys building the duplex in Rosepark."

"You run those blocks, every stop?" Mason asked the young man.

"I do." Larry grinned. "It's mine for the taking, Mason. My legs want every block. It's a way to put the charm on this sleepy town."

"Nice game, I hear," Mason said.

"Strike early, stay ahead," Larry said. "And be real fast and real lucky. We've got Jackson Hole this week—the city kids will be a test." Larry pointed at Mason. "How is that hand?"

"Cured. Stronger than ever. I just wear the bandage for show. I see you down at the Brands. What's up with Jimmy?" Mason put down a section of gutter and hopped to the ground, coming over to Larry's window. "How's he doing?"

"Sleeping. Yesterday he said he'd like to see you."

"Come back later if you can," Mason said. "We'll take him down some dinner."

The roofers gathered up their tools and fastened their two extension ladders to the top of their truck rack in full dark. Two of them walked the yard picking up the old shingles and throwing them into a large cardboard box they dragged around the whole house. Mason wrote them a check on the hood of the vehicle and shook all three men's hands. When they'd driven off, Craig came from around back, where he'd been putting his own tools on the porch. "Okay," he said. "Let it rain. Tomorrow we can go inside and start spackling and test some of the wiring and replace the cracked switchboxes."

"You like this, don't you?" Mason asked his friend.

"It's good work, don't you think?"

"I believe it is," Mason said. "It beats kissing ass around a conference table."

They had walked across, and Craig got in his truck. "It beats pricing tubes of caulk. You want to come in tomorrow, pick out the paint."

"No, just bring it out. We'll go with that sky white. It's workable and leaves the new owners plenty of options."

"Good with me." Craig began to back his truck out the drive.

"And bring some of that caulk," Mason said. "Bring plenty."

When his friend had left, Mason went in and showered, holding his injured hand above the spray. It was healing fast. He was utterly at sea, and he welcomed being lost and had no haste about emerging. He liked his new little Spartan life in the back of this old house. He had the kitchen and his parents' old bedroom and the tiny bath that adjoined it.

His suitcase was open on the hardwood floor, and it pleased him to open the closet and see five shirts and two pairs of pants hanging in the empty space. He dressed, put on the one sport coat he'd brought, a brown tweed that was almost twenty years old, and sat back down on the little futon Craig had loaned him. He couldn't quite think, gather his life up yet, but it was coming.

He was openly surprised by how quickly his bright notion of his own life had rusted in the open air of Oakpine. In Denver he was his reputation in the workplace, and he was feared in the way that comes to be called respect. He wasn't liked, but people didn't speak badly of him. Now his knees ached, and it was that feeling, along with the burn in his upper arms, that he wanted to know about. His footing was slipping and then gone, and he didn't want it back. Success. It wasn't so simple, the chase and the money. He could feel something coming. He hadn't cried in his life, not even under a bicycle as a child.

Though unchanged except for five or six coats of paint in the last thirty years, the room felt radically different to Mason, strange and new. His parents had had wallpaper in here, in much of the house, a dreary vertical floral pattern, mauve and gray, that made them seem even then only old, made the house seem meant for adults, something from another era. Certainly it would have been papered on before the war. There had been a crucifix on the wall opposite the bed, Christ on a gold cross that must have been a foot tall. His sister must have that out in Portland. And there had been a gilt-framed mirror over the bureau to one side. His parents' bed had a little cabinet headboard on which there had been a maroon runner embroidered with gilt thread and a wooden shelled radio and a shiny black porcelain panther his father had brought back from Manila after World War II, when he was in the navy. Mason lay back on the bed. The original light fixture was still in place, a milky glass bowl hung on the old brass chain, and he remembered it. Now he saw it was the same type as the one in *Lost Weekend* in which Ray Milland hid a bottle of whiskey. This one was too small for that, but he could put a minibottle in there if things got real bad. Mason rubbed his eyes. Where was he? What was he doing? He had the urge to call Elizabeth in Denver and tell her he was confused; she'd take it as a sign of humanity.

His love for her was full of airy spaces, he saw now. As a driven man who had made his life around driven men and never known it, he was off balance in the quiet house. If he'd only found this silence ten years ago, she would not have gone away. It was the first still part, the first quiet part of his life. He could feel it pressing.

What he did was sit up and then stand up. In the kitchen he clipped the ends from two potatoes and put them in the oven. He had two folding chairs and the Formica table the Gunnars had left behind. Leaving the lights on, he went out the back door and walked down three houses to the Brands.

He didn't walk anywhere now. He hadn't walked for years. In Denver he parked his car in the basement of his office and walked to the elevators; he parked in the basement of his condominium and walked to the elevators. There were two places in his office building where he could get lunch, one up and one down, and to get to them, he walked to the elevators. He was never out of doors. It didn't happen. He took an inventory now quickly and saw it was true. He walked fifty feet on painted concrete to the elevator and then upstairs, though the entry to his offices, and down the hallway on carpet. He would live the rest of his life and never wear out a pair of shoes. And now in the dark that smelled like turning leaves, he walked up to Jimmy Brand's garage, a walk he'd taken a thousand times years and years ago. Sometimes he'd run. The sidewalk on Berry Street had been buckled by the poplars and cottonwoods, repoured, and buckled again. He'd been in some of these trees. The air was at his neck, not cold, but sweet and sharp. He couldn't quite get the right stride, walking this route, and he felt exposed out in the old world, and this feeling too was part of his confusion. He felt strange and exposed tonight. He didn't know what to do with his arms. It would have been ridiculous to drive. *I'm so highly evolved that I can't even walk*, he thought.

He hadn't seen Jimmy Brand for thirty years. He didn't need to do the math. He had the morning in his head like a photograph. The days they'd spent in the Trail's End Motel and after their encounter, Mason had twisted in a way he thought would certainly kill him, and then Jimmy let him off with a hand on the side of his face, that touch, and saying, "Let us get over ourselves. It's okay. It's over. The year. My life here." He had smiled. "And that band is over with. Mason, I have to leave. Ten reasons, and you are not among them. I will see you again." It was a morning in June, and the birds were crazy in the trees, calling, and Mason retrieved the car, and Jimmy came out of the room with his duffel. They drove without a word to the Greyhound station, which was an anteroom on Front Street by the tracks, and the bus was there idling. It had come and gone all his life, and Mason had never seen the bus before. Jimmy got out of the car and leaned back to say, "Don't be an idiot. You were kind to me. Don't look back. I'll see you." He shut the car door and went into the bus. A minute later the bus door closed, and it eased onto Front Street headed east. Mason turned off the car and got out and stood and looked across the street at the Antlers, bright from its new coat of paint, but still a dive. Two men sat on the sidewalk against the facade of the building, rolled blankets in their laps. If they got up and crossed the street, they could sit in the sun. The town was a plain little place before him, his home, and it felt now empty and without one mystery of its own.

Now he moved down the sidewalk on Berry Street stiffly, new at this game. He'd walked at first. He'd beat the streets for two years when he first came to Denver. Every time he'd hear of a firm with an opening, he was there. It was an era of close calls but no callbacks. Everybody liked him, and everybody knew him, but by the time there was a bona fide position ready for him, his own business had taken off. He'd started alone, taking what he could, some corporate spillover from the big companies. An old associate, on hearing that Mason did wills, trusts, and divorces, sent him some work. He wrote deeds. Mason did DUI's for friends of friends only. He made a lot of money in a wrongful death suit on behalf of a family run down in a movie line by a drunk driver. Then the year he was thirty a big case fell on his desk. Fourteen people had been injured in one of the city's softball complexes when the aluminum seating failed. Two would never walk again, and a child had perished. They had had representation by a firm in his building that hurried the deal and started talking money at the initial strategy session. The plaintiffs were hurt and shocked. Mason literally met them in the elevator, the five people from the three families that were suing the city. It was an accident, but he knew who they were. His first words when they got into the car and he assessed their faces were "You want a glass of water?"

He didn't say it was a ploy, but it was a ploy. They talked two hours that first day, and he learned to listen, to try to grasp the weight of the damage. It was as close to empathy as he could get, and he learned that it helped him know how to talk to them.

He moved the case slowly, as the plaintiffs wanted, and he went step by step. He never talked money with them, even when the city's attorney tried again and again to cut a deal. Mason already knew what a life meant in a settlement, but the city attorney told him again anyway: $2.6 million. Mason told the woman that that wasn't the issue. His clients wanted a trial. They wanted to tell what happened, be heard, be seen. Their lives were changed. By now Mason knew his life would be made of stories. And so it went to trial, and because Mason was methodical and quiet and obviously thorough and in no hurry, and because he used the three weeks in court to display and listen to the stories of all the victims, then the bleacher company, an aluminum girder expert, another engineer and a metallurgist, and the comptroller from the City of Denver budget department, the plaintiffs won the award of $41 million dollars. He got almost eight, the agreed percentage.

He moved the office to an old building downtown, which he bought, and took in two partners, one of them a woman he would marry some years later, Elizabeth. His evolution was begun. The case made him a hotshot but a strange one. He was respected, but he had few friends. He hired two serious attorneys. Kirby, Rothman, and Phelps began to turn work away.

Mason knocked on the Brands' front door. Up and down the block he could see lights on in the living rooms, televisions, families. The storm door rattled, and Mrs. Brand appeared in the glass. She pushed the door open to him. "Mrs. Brand," he said. "It's Mason Kirby. Do you remember me, Hilda and Ted's boy?"

"I knew it was you, Mason. Come on in. I've seen you down there at the house."

He stepped into the small carpeted front room. Mr. Brand stood from his big red recliner and shook Mason's hand. He wore a blue plaid shirt and a pair of clean overalls, and he looked the same to Mason: a large man in working clothes. "What are you doing? Selling the place?"

"Good to see you, sir," Mason said. "Yeah. I've been proven to be an ineffective landlord, and my sister has no interest in returning to Wyoming."

"Where is Linda?" Mrs. Brand said. "She was a sharp one."

Mr. Brand sat back down and motioned for Mason to take a seat on the couch. He turned the television down with the remote.

"She's out in California, which was always her goal. Her two kids are almost in high school, married a guy who is something in UPS, middle management. She's doing well."

"And you're a lawyer," Mrs. Brand said. "Craig told me that you've done well too."

"Is there much work in it?" Edgar Brand said. "All you hear now is lawyer this, lawyer that."

"There're plenty of lawyers," Mason said. He sat on the edge of the couch with his elbows on his knees. "There's some work in it. You meet with people who are pretty torn up, and you try to figure how to help. It's been interesting. I've had some luck, and mostly I think I've been on the side of the good guys, but that's my opinion. I am a lawyer." He opened his hands and shrugged. "I'm having more fun fixing up the old place than I ever have in Denver."

The little room with its carpet felt terrifically close to Mason, especially after all the air and stars and leaves. *They've lived their lives in these rooms,* he thought. He didn't know anybody anymore who lived in one place. There were several family photos framed on the wall, and he picked out Matt Brand in his football uniform and a studio portrait of all four Brands taken when the kids must have been eight and nine. The muted television was on to an evening news program, *20/20* or *Primetime* or such, but the room itself was decades removed from Mason's world.

"We didn't see much of your last renters." Mr. Brand said. "They had a daughter, and the old man drove an El Camino, which is a vehicle I never did understand. Light blue."

"They had some problems," Mason said. "I think the bottle had him by the neck. It happens. Listen, I understand Jimmy's here"—Mr. Brand's face changed in the lamplight, went blank—"and I came down to see if I—"

"Come in the kitchen, Mason," Mrs. Brand said, holding the door open for him. Mason stood and followed her into the bright back room. As the door closed behind them, he could hear the television resume. Mrs. Brand moved about the kitchen for a minute, preparing two cups of tea for them, and then she sat opposite him at the gray swirls of the Formica table, which swam suddenly into his memory.

"This table's served me more than once," Mason said.

"We had fun here."

"But you've changed the room."

"Yes, we did. We moved the fridge and changed the back door. Remember, you used to come in here by the basement stairs?" She showed him the arrangement.

"And you put a little deck over the back porch."

"Right. Edgar built that sometime ago."

"It's tough for him to have Jimmy home."

"Edgar's all right. He can do what he can do. He's a good man, but this all is beyond him. He got hurt real good a long time ago, and this is just a heartache."

"I know that." Mason laid his hands on the old table. "Forgive me, Mrs. Brand, but I've had clients lose children, and I don't think people get over it. And I'm not even sure they should. Matt was a remarkable kid. And now Jimmy's pretty sick."

"Thank you, Mason." Her face was a slate. "I think he is."

"Well, I came down to see what I might do." Mason assessed the woman, and she seemed ready to talk. "Should Jimmy be in hospice there at the clinic? I think we know where this is going."

"Jimmy says he knows, and yes, I know. It's not surprise we're after. I'm so glad he's home. That's all. We've talked about it all, Mason."

Mason reached past the teacups and took her hand. "I can help with any of the expenses. Absolutely."

She patted his hand. "I want him here. If it gets too bad for him, we'll go from there."

"Has anyone from the clinic been out? Has he seen the doctor?"

"That's next."

"Look. Let me call Kathleen Gunderson down there and have her come out. There may be some things they can do for him. She's the head of the clinic."

"I see her around town once or twice a year."

"May I call her?"

Mrs. Brand's eyes closed for a moment, and she nodded. "It won't hurt."

Mason stood and leaned into the front room, "Nice to see you, Mr. Brand. Take care. I'm going to slip out the back."

"Mason," the older man said as farewell, without looking up.

On the back deck Mason asked Mrs. Brand, "How's your garden? I can smell the squash growing."

"Come back tomorrow, and I'll load you up."

"That's a deal. Goodnight. Thanks for the tea."

"Goodnight. Thank you, Mason." She stepped back inside and closed the door.

In the chilly silent night under the ancient trees, Mason scanned the neighborhood. It was confusing how so many pieces of this old map fit. Lights were going out; half the houses were dim. The garage in which Jimmy Brand slept his sleep looked like a cottage in a fairy tale in which children were in danger. Mason walked backward out the Brands' driveway. He wasn't dizzy, but it was strange to be here, strange to walk. He'd let it get too late again and he had wanted to see Jimmy.

The books had affected Mason, and he had read them all. The first novel, *Reservoir*, was the story of that last week, the accident, the long day. He'd read it when he was a struggling attorney, and he wanted to tell Jimmy about reading it in his one-bedroom condominium in Denver, because it was the only book that had ever made him gasp and hurl it across a room, breaking the glass on a framed Weston Grimes print that hung above his old leather couch. The first nice piece of art he bought. He had then gone over and picked the book from the glass and reread the section about the party at the reservoir aloud, making sure, and then he had thrown the book again, this time into the corner where all it could do was gash the wall. Jimmy had gotten the scene just right, the wind in the ancient dry cottonwoods, the sound the car tires made easing over the river rock by the old boat ramp, the powdery white dust puffing from every footfall.

Mason saw himself in the whole novel as Mark, the responsible one, the sardonic one. In the last third of the book, the day at the reservoir, Jimmy had changed one thing. He'd changed what happened so that now when the angel boy, who was Matt, named Zeke in the book, full of beer and sorrow, as drunk really as Mason had ever seen any-one, takes the boat out into the reservoir, somebody goes with him. The somebody was Jimmy, whose name in the book is Cameron, and the two of them fight in the book, and Zeke does not return. Zeke, like Matt, never returns. Mason knew how to read such a scene in such a book; he knew what fiction is and what nonfiction is, and he also knew it was just a book, a story. And still when he finally picked it up again two days later and cut himself on a little triangle of glass caught in the cover, he was filled with the great urge to throw it again. That day had been the best and worst day of his life, and he'd been full of the sense of the day as a pinnacle. His whole life had been coming together for seventeen years, and he knew it was a false feeling, but he gloried in it that day at the reservoir, and knowing what had happened was impor-tant to him, essential to him. It rankled him to have Jimmy make it fiction, but he loved that the book glowed with the feeling of the day. It rankled him more to be such a callow reader.

Now Mason wasn't dizzy, but it was unearthly to walk on the dark driveway, to be in the past this way, deeply in the old days. He turned in a circle, taking in the Brands' house, the whole night world, his old world, blades of light flared at the edge of things. He drifted toward the street watching the little garage, and the quiet shelter seemed to float in the familiar dark.

Wendy Ingram rode her blue bicycle one-handed up the uneven center of Berry Street and halfway up the driveway of the Brands' house the next afternoon. The sunlight caught in the great loads of heavy yellow leaves gathered and waiting in the old trees, and she stood and looked up; the whole street felt like a glowing cavern. She carried three books and walked back along the driveway to the garage, where she knocked lightly on the side door and then peeked in. "Hello?"

"Come in," Jimmy Brand said. He was sitting on the bed in a white dress shirt and a pair of corduroys typing on his laptop. There was a pillow under it.

"You're writing," Wendy said, coming in a step. "I'll come back later. Do you remember when I was over with Larry? I'm Wendy. I got your book." She held it up, along with the two others in her hand. "I got another. I read them. I'll come back when you're not working."

"Don't come later." Jimmy smiled and tipped his head back. "Come in the door right now. How's the weather?"

"I love the fall," she said. "The leaves are just turning and it's still pretty warm out, but it's all so . . ."

"Sad," he said.

"Some," she said. "I guess. But it's a beautiful day. You want me to open the door? It's not cold."

"Let's do that, Wendy," he said. She opened the door, and a plank of white light fell onto the floor, and light took all the upper corners of the odd room, reflecting off the plastic sheeting stapled there. "Well," Jimmy said. "Hello. That's better. It is a day. With the leaves, you can be sad or get ready with your rake. In the old days we made some leaf piles like haystacks."

"We still do it, but everybody has a blower."

"Of course they do."

She sat down, the books in her lap. Now she was uneasy and unsure of what to say, why she had come. "How are you?" she asked. "Can I get you anything?"

"I'm fine. I've got everybody hopping, and my mother is taking remarkable care. How's your Larry?"

"Larry's great. He's always been great. But he's not my Larry."

"Oh?"

"I go with Wade. Did you meet him? We've been going out about a year."

"A marriage," Jimmy said.

"How's that?"

"Nothing. I'm teasing, but I'm not very good at it."

She pointed at his notebook. "Are you writing? What are you writing?"

"I'm just paddling around, taking notes. Do you keep a journal?"

She looked at him seriously, and he saw that this was what she'd come to talk about. "I do. It's just something I do. I'm not sure of it. What should it be?"

"What is it?"

She shook her head and smiled. "It's everything, a mess. It's what I see and what I do and sometimes what I feel."

"And sometimes all three."

"Yes."

"Like three guys trying to get through a door?"

"That's it," she said. "Except five and in a rush." She met his smile and asked, "What do I do about that?"

"Take your time. Don't push. Let each idea enter the room and find a chair. Give them half a page and then a page. Can you do it? Am I making sense? We're really talking here."

"I know what you mean, and I can do it sometimes. But what I get is nothing like what you write." She lifted one of his novels in both of her hands. "It's not like this. It's not clear like this."

"You read the books?"

"I loved these books. It's like something I've never read before."

She sat back, embarrassed to have spoken so freely, and then she looked up again. "I never read a book about Oakpine before. I knew a lot of the places. The mountain, the reservoir, the town. It hasn't changed very much."

"Right, sometimes a book about a familiar place can seem—"

"No." She stopped him. "I know what you're going to say. I don't mean that. It's not the town. Because I feel the same way about this." She held up the second book. "And this." She held up the third. "And I've never been to New York. I don't know what it is. That's why I've come over. I didn't tell Larry or Wade or anyone, but I wanted to talk to you." She had come forward in her chair, her face a serious thing. Jimmy felt as awake as he had since returning. "How do you know what I'm feeling?" she said. "How'd you write it?"

He'd had a thousand discussions about writing with people, at conferences and on the radio, some on television, so many in person after dinner somewhere with Daniel, and Jimmy had been appreciated, celebrated at times for his work, but he'd never had someone ask him this way about what he'd done. He'd had all the workaday questions, and the social impact questions, and the courage questions and the risk questions and the syntactical questions, and he'd worked at answering them all with true honesty, but that wasn't this. He'd never really taught, though he had spoken at seminars on fiction and on reviewing, and there he'd met students who were always earnest and smart, but their questions were practical in the main, not really artistic, not really personal. Now he felt relocated, found, and he saw Wendy's questions as real things, his heart suddenly thudding in his wrists as he took the questions on the way you might lift a load, a book, or a box of personal effects. The sunlight rocketing around the room pleased him, and he looked at this young woman, her hair edged with the white

light and measured his words. His vision was going, and he knew he
would be sleeping in minutes.

"I apologize," she said, "for my stupid questions. I know I have a lot
to learn, and you've already—"

"Don't say that," he said. "I want you here, asking me these things.
These are the only questions. We can talk and talk. Why do you keep
your journal?"

"Because there's too much," she whispered. "There's too much,
and it wants to come out. My heart, whatever it is, maybe not my
heart, but it feels like my heart is full, and I write it down. I have to
write it down."

"What is it like when you read it later?"

Wendy sat back in the chair and folded her arms. "It's not the same.
I mean I'm glad I wrote it down, but it doesn't have the feeling. Like
when I read about Cameron. That's you, right?"

"I guess," Jimmy Brand said. He decided not to stand on a lesson;
this was a new place long past where a lesson about point of view or
persona or anything but the true writing would suffice. She was a
shape now, a silhouette in the shimmering gray light.

"Where Cameron goes back to the reservoir that night into the
cottonwoods and everybody's gone, and he goes to the campsite on the
shore where they'd parked the boat. The wind is warm, remember, and
he finds Mark's knife by the campfire stones, and he puts it in his
pocket. When I read that scene and then reread it, it pulls me apart. He
wants to go back and have the day over again and prevent the accident,
but he wants to go on, leave town, leave for the future. No one will
know, ever"—here Wendy leaned toward him, her hands woven
together—"ever know"—and she dropped her voice—"what is in his
heart. Sometimes I want to leave so badly."

Jimmy sat still in the bed. It was a blurred waking dream, and he had both worlds in his heart, what had happened so long ago and what he had written, and both were alive to him.

"How did you write that?"

He was whispering, "What do you want to write?"

She stood and said, "I'll go and let you rest. Thank you for speaking to me."

"What," he said again quietly, "do you want to write?"

"I don't know, but I know I do. More than anything."

"More than being with Wade?"

"Yes."

"Are you sure about that?"

"Yes, I know I'm sure. I went to Dallas last summer, a month ago, for the Spirit Club convention. It's our service group. And the whole time I felt something calling me, not calling but something that wouldn't let me sleep. I went to the roof of the hotel in the middle of the night and looked at the city, and the day we left I went up there in the afternoon, and I was all alone and no one knew where I was, my folks, Wade, no one, and then I thought, no one knows my heart, what's in it. Not even me." She stood up, frowned, sat down. "You think I'm a schoolgirl."

"I don't know what to think."

"It's a good heart, Mr. Brand. There's stuff in it. I want to write. I'm sure people who read your books have said they feel like they know you, because that's the way I feel. But I came over today because I feel that you know me. The wind at the reservoir and Cameron's decision. The New York stories."

"You read them."

"I read them all. I'm sorry for your loss."

"Thank you," Jimmy Brand said. He closed his notebook and leaned back into his pillows. He could feel the familiar friction in his eyes building to a headache. "Do you want to write a story?"

"I want to write a story," she said, "and have you read it."

Jimmy thought about it all, ran the good and the harm of such an enterprise, and then made a decision in a minute, like all things he did now, which was based on the way he was living this last fall. "I'll read it, Wendy, but you must have it here tomorrow. Is that going—"

"I'll bring it by at four o'clock." She stood up. She placed his books on the little table. "Thank you so much. You can't know what this means to me."

"If you miss the deadline," he said, "the deal's off, and you'll have to marry Wade and have his fourteen children."

"I don't know what will happen with any of that, but I'll be here tomorrow." She crossed to the door, and then as her shadow in that rare sunlight reached onto the bed, she waved, a little crazy wave that could only be sincere.

SIX

The Wind

The next afternoon in a light skirling wind, Mason Kirby parked his Mercedes in front of the old Antlers, a bar he'd help paint thirty years before. Mason stepped into the wide empty street, avoiding the puddles. He scanned the old funky skyline of his hometown: the brick buildings, all two, three, and four stories from this end of the street, made a kind of child's drawing. The clouds were now broken and sailing, and deep shadows came across the village, gliding up onto Oakpine Mountain and beyond to the horizon. He could smell the dry diesel of the railroad yards, and the air was neither cold nor warm. It was odd not to be focused, in a hurry, and the old street charmed him as he finally remembered how it had changed. The far side was curbed and guttered where they'd parked and smoked, sitting on the fenders of Frank's car, and the ratty Chinese elms that made the dead end a leafy warren were gone. The bus stop had been near the far corner. It had never been marked; the bus just stopped there and a gaggle of the busworn would walk across the street carrying their packs and cases into the Antlers for a drink. There had been a smoke shop and a little liquor store, almost a closet, but later when Mason was away at college, there had been a shooting, the owner had killed a drunk robber, and he'd closed up and moved towns. You would. The facade had been re-bricked pale yellow, and the two big windows were lined DUNN-ARMOR ATTORNEYS AT LAW in black letters with gilt edges.

A dirty white Suburban drove by him, and he watched it park against the train fence. The vehicle hadn't been washed in its history. A woman got out and hurried to the back doors and began to wrestle with her big folded stroller. Mason stepped over quickly to help her lift it up so it could clear the backseat. The wheels were big as plates. He'd never, in the twenty that had come his way, taken a stroller case. The ones that appeared in his office had been made out of the wrong materials from the wrong design. Every metal hinge caught, and the wheels, until five years ago, had been like toys. Mason swung the big blue device free and turned and set it on the ground, where it unfolded neatly, and he snapped each crossbar into place. He checked each jointed rivet and saw the plastic finger guards. Good for them. He hoped it was just planning and not the result of lawsuits. It was well made. The woman now came around with the baby, an infant giant, thirty pounds and eyes roving like a soldier; he fixed on Mason and started to grin.

"Wrong guy," Mason said, rubbing his knuckles on the kid's cheek.

"Thank you, sir," the young woman said.

"He's going to be a fullback," Mason said. "Look at this guy." The baby was now situated in the stroller, and all through his installation he had stayed on Mason's face.

"Oh, don't say it," the woman said.

Mason immediately knelt and put a finger under the wide face of the child. "Don't you bump heads with anyone," he said. "It's okay to watch the game and talk to the girls. Can I say that?" He smiled at the woman. "It's what I did. All my buddies were on the team at Oakpine."

"One million years ago," Frank Gunderson said, crossing the

street. "Lorna," he said, "this is the front man for my band, the Range-men, other names, then Life on Earth, Mason Kirby."

"Nice to meet you," she said. Mason could still see Frank's high school face underneath the goatee and the gray streaks in the sides of his hair and the smokers' wrinkles and weather.

"And this is Lorna and Roger Beckstead, who are related to the approaching railroad engineer. Roger is just now one year old."

"Fourteen months," the woman said.

"Oh?" Mason said.

"Come, come," Frank said, steering the stroller now toward the steel train fence. "It is so good to see you, Mason."

They walked in the flat sunlight, and Mason could see the woman listening, and then he heard the old friction himself. He shook his head. "Trains." Now he could see the boy was aware of the air changing. "I need more trains in my life."

"Let's hold him up for Darrell," Frank said, bending to the child. Frank lifted Roger and straightened the little blanket and handed him back to Lorna. He was a heavy baby, but she held him up easily as the locomotive rose along the fence line and passed in a rush. A moment later with the train gone, she tucked the boy into the stroller and walked up around the block for the little coffee shop.

"Lucky kid to have a dad work the railroad." The two men shook hands. "How are you, Frank?"

"Still on plan A, but keeping my options open."

"That's what Kathleen said," Mason said.

"That's what Kathleen would say," Frank said. "Come on in. I heard you were in town."

They walked back into Frank's bar and talked business for an hour, surface stuff, Mason's firm, his plans, a lawsuit that he'd helped Frank with fifteen years before. Frank had five buildings now, four of them nicely leased. "I don't know. I've paid attention to business," Frank said. "For the first time I'm kind of stepping back and taking a look. I mean, I've worried about money all my life, and now the whole package is about right. It could carry me. I kind of wish I'd gone to college or got out real good for a while. Even Craig got out for a while. I mean I'm having fun, I guess, but there's something working at me." Frank drank his beer and poured them both another glass from the pitcher. The two men were silent. "You got any of that going on?"

"Plenty," Mason said. "But I'm not thinking about it these days. My thinking might be faulty. I'm into renovation, carpentry, plumbing, electrical, another month of it here before I have to start thinking again."

"Have you seen Jimmy yet?"

"I haven't. I saw his folks. I'm going to wait until I hear from Kathleen about it. She said she'd go over there tomorrow morning." Mason leaned back and put his hands on the table. "I don't know why I haven't been down there. I guess I'm scared or something like it."

"He's dying, Craig says."

"I believe he is," Mason said.

The two men sat in the quiet bar. Suddenly the light dimmed again under a cloud, and it was a moment that went out on them, through the big plate-glass window across the gray street and up above the town in a moment, reaching past the last house and the few bad roads newly bladed into the prairie and the antelope in clusters on green-gray hillsides beyond that and then hovering beyond and beyond, the world, their lives, the full gravid sense of afternoon. There was nothing to do or say except ride this part of the day together there, both men feeling the weight register, the men they'd become. It was a beery afternoon in their hometown.

The second time Kathleen Gunderson went to see Jimmy Brand in his little garage room, the same young man answered the door, Larry Ralston, and again he had his Martin guitar in his hand. She thought she'd heard the rippling intro to an old song, "Help Me, Rhonda," as she walked up the driveway.

"Kathleen," Jimmy said. "You're right on time." She'd come the week before and spoken to Jimmy and gotten his signature for his medical records in New York. At that time Larry Ralston had been wiring new strings on the red Fender, which now lay across Jimmy's lap on a pillow.

"How are you feeling?" she asked, setting down her tote and her briefcase and taking the chair by the bed.

He waited to catch her eye and then said quietly to her, "Good. We're good."

She took his blood pressure and temperature. "You're starting a band?"

"Anything's possible," he said. "Right, Larry?"

"He's teaching me a few new riffs," Larry said.

"Old riffs," Jimmy said. "Ancient secrets from the Pleistocene era of rock 'n' roll."

Kathleen set two big bottles of prescription medicine on the bed-side table. "There are two more we'll get next week that go with these," she said. "Now I want to get some blood."

"Kathleen," Jimmy said.

She snapped the rubber gloves on, then stopped. "What?"

"Larry," Jimmy said, "could you kindly check with my mother about the availability of some of her cinnamon tea?" The young man put his guitar on his chair and went out.

Jimmy took Kathleen's wrist. "My dear old friend. We were in a cappella together."

"I remember," she said. "We were in *The Nutcracker* together in fourth grade with Mrs. Weyerhauser."

"I used to detest *The Nutcracker*," Jimmy said.

"You were horrible," Kathleen said. "You called him 'that little wooden fascist.'" She laughed. "Jimmy, we were children."

"I got over it. He was misunderstood, like everyone else." He waved at the room. "But here, with this. With me back here like this. We're not going to trouble with any program. My dear, I know what this is, and you know what is going to happen." He waited. "Right?"

"I do," she said. "I've seen it."

"Then don't worry," he said. "And you don't have to bring anything around." He gestured at the bottles of medicine. "I'm thinking I would want something later on." He looked at her. "Morphine, whenever. It's what helped Daniel."

"Your friend in New York."

"My friend in New York."

"I can see to that," she said. "And in the meantime this stuff will actually help. It's powerful, and it works." She helped him take two of the pills with a glass of water.

"I was sorry to hear about you and Frank."

"Not at all," Kathleen said. "Frank recently made a stimulating decision. Not so recently really—everybody knew this was coming for a while now. We divorced and he has a new friend." She saw the concern on Jimmy's face and changed tone. "It's not a big deal to me. Once he realized he was successful, he got scared. I don't think he was bored, but he had to have something new. We've been through it. It was a good marriage. He worked hard, and so did I. I'm a little surprised we didn't have kids, but everything was fragile. We were always scrambling up the mountain. It's going to hurt when he has babies with this new girl though. Mister Jimmy Brand, that is going to hurt."

The plastic on the ceiling billowed and the door opened as Larry and Mrs. Brand came in with a tea tray. Jimmy noted his mother's face when she saw the nurse, and regretted the hope he saw there. Human beings. There was always hope.

Mrs. Brand disappeared for a moment and came back with a grocery bag full of zucchini for Kathleen, and then they all had a tea in the little room, and then Larry lifted his guitar, and he and Jimmy played the rippling opening of "Help Me, Rhonda" three or four times, almost getting it right.

The nights cooled down, and Larry and Wade continued to run. Larry loved it, striding through the tangible air. After he was warmed up, jogging through the streets of his hometown, he felt something fill him, something he couldn't have explained to anyone. He was changing, and he liked it. Wade wanted to walk certain stretches and give Larry advice. Wade was indiscreet about what his father said about other players on the team and repeated these things. Guys were screwups or lard asses. Larry deflected the remarks, defending his teammates when he could. Wade's behavior was a surprise to Larry and it dismayed him. It was odd to have a friend act this way.

On the team, Larry had made his clear mark and was the undisputed starting defensive end and he rotated every other play on offense. Wade told him that his father had said that he'd wished he'd made Larry co-captain, and though Larry deflected this also, it got through and surprised and steadied him. He'd been heavily celebrated after the Rawlins game, guys clapping him on the back and talking about him making all state. He'd lost himself in the game. Here, halfway through the season, he knew his position well, and his body had caught up and was ready for all of it. He'd made eleven tackles and he took it all, the running and the diving and all the knocking about, as a kind of pleasure, rising from the grassy field with new energy after each play. There was still more in him when the game ended, and it was apparent to everyone. He was tall and strong, and as he pulled his helmet off and left the field that day, he said, "I'm tall and strong." It was strange and thrilling to hear. He'd loved being a boy, but he wasn't a boy anymore. He was the next thing.

They'd showered at Rawlins, and when they came out of the gym, it was nearly ten o'clock, and the wind had come up with its cold edge. On the bus all the way home, he'd ridden with the corner of his forehead against the window and watched the Wyoming night and felt apart from everything in his life. He watched the miles become a hundred miles, and he knew he could have run it. The boys on the bus, the game he'd just played, his home on Oakpine Mountain. He thought about his mother and father, their lives, and he knew what they had done for him, and he knew they loved him, but he felt separate from them now. His mother was a bright woman who was trying to make some kind of mark. He saw that.

He saw that she was different from the people she worked with at the museum, wanting something different. Thought opened now, and he could see her as the girl she had been, like girls he knew, and if that was true, then she lived in a kind of danger every day; she wasn't finished at all. This broke his sense of safety, and he blinked and put his head back against the window. *Good*, he thought, *good*. He said it: "Good." His father was happy these days with Mason Kirby's house.

His father wanted to build the world. In the dark bus, Larry wondered what people lived for; his parents—what did they want now?

He had a bruise above his left knee, and he squeezed it and saw again in his eyelids the tackle when he'd earned it, and then he pressed it with his fist again, and he saw the play, smelled the grass again. What was he living for, in this body, except these small surprises? Larry Ralston rode the bus. He had the clear sensation that it was going the wrong direction, taking him to a place he'd never been before. Around him, the team had settled down, quieted. Several boys were asleep. He put his lips against the cold glass and whispered, "I'm tall and strong," and it misted on the window.

Now, running with Wade, he felt a pull at his sleeve. Wade had stopped, wanted to walk. "It's a run," Larry told him. "Not a walk."

"Just a block or two," Wade said. Larry pulled up, and they fell in step. "What did Barnes say?"

"Barnes is on," Larry said. They'd already been over this. He'd asked Stephanie Barnes to the homecoming dance, which was a week from Saturday, and they were doubling with Wade and Wendy. Wade was going to drive. They were going to dinner afterward at the Tropical, the only Hawaiian Chinese restaurant in the county.

"She's cool," Wade said. "She's going to UCLA." Wade had said this before also, and the chatter and the walking made Larry impatient. He skipped sideways.

"Let's go," he said.

"You still taking guitar with the fag?"

Larry stopped, and Wade walked by him on the dark street.

"What?" Wade said. He was ten steps ahead. "Are you? You must be getting pretty good."

Larry stood still in the center of the pavement.

Wade stopped and turned around, threw his arms out. "Come on," he said. "I didn't mean anything by it. The guy's a fag, right?"

Larry was amazed that Wade had turned out to be an idiot. He'd known him all these years, every year, and now within two weeks Wade shook out as an absolute dunce. Larry looked at his old friend, his silhouette on the dark street. He breathed in and out; he was impatient to run again.

"Let's go," Larry said, drifting into a jog. "Let's get some good out of this."

"Hey, wait," Wade said. "I'm going to stop by at Wendy's for a while—come with."

Larry was now twenty yards beyond his friend, and he loped back and stood before him. "You go ahead," he said.

These were crazy days, he thought. He wondered consciously what he was going to say next. A few days before, he would have just run home, and now he was up for some kind of confrontation. Everybody was shaking out, it seemed, even him. Who would he be?

He smiled. "Wade." He touched Wade on the shoulder. "I'm going to give you one more chance, okay? About Jimmy Brand. Don't call him a fag. It makes you look stupid. Are you stupid?" Larry heard himself say this, and he didn't shrug or duck or laugh. He'd said it, and he'd meant it. He was surprised but happy with that. He was likely to say anything.

"Wendy said he was a fag."

"No, she didn't. She didn't say that."

"She goes to see him," Wade says. "It's sick."

"Let's run."

" 'One more chance'?" Wade said. "What does that mean?"

"I'll see you tomorrow," Larry said. "Tell Wendy hi for me." And now he turned and filled his lungs with air and plunged away, starting fast and staying there, striding powerfully down the street, each step a flight, faster than he'd ever taken such a distance. As the motion adjusted itself and he settled into the pattern, pushing and reaching, pushing and reaching, he knew that his heart was good for all of it. There wasn't enough road for this heart. There was no way he would slow down before he flew into the park.

"Wendy," he said as he ran and again, "Wendy, watch out, my dear, for stupid Wade approaches." *Oh god*, he thought, and he heard the words as they came from his mouth, "Who am I now? Who am I now?"

Painting the Kirby house went very well. Frank Gunderson came by and joined Mason and Craig for the job. The three men did prep for two days, taping and sanding, and then they struck the entire interior with an airless sprayer in one long day, working with two lamps as the fall twilight fell and doubled. "I'm a get-it-done painter," Frank told them as they masked the light fixtures and doorframes. "We paint the men's room five times a year at the Antlers. I'm not really into your fine work."

"How many times have you painted the front since we did it that summer?" Mason asked him.

"Twice, I guess. Maybe three times. Every ten years, if it needs it or not."

"What did old Wattington pay us?"

"Four days." Mason said, calculating. "I think he gave us sixty bucks apiece." He had finished papering the two large front windows. "Jimmy would know."

"It was the money we used for the reservoir remember? Somebody went with me to the Bargain Basket, and we filled two carts, piled it up, steaks, watermelon, tons." Frank looked at Mason, and his smile dimmed.

"We'd played at Snyder's up in Gillette that weekend and were already flush. Life on Earth. A four-hour drive, a two-hour gig, and four hours back in the dark," Mason added. "What were we, nuts? What'd we get for that?"

"I know it was two hundred dollars," Craig said. "It was a record for us."

They'd all stopped working. The taping was finished. The sanding was done.

Frank spoke. "I didn't know what was going to happen."

"Nobody did. We'd been out there before," Mason said. "There'd been worse parties."

"No, I mean in general. I thought, I guess, that we'd just be a band for a few years, something. But we go to the reservoir, Matt drowns, and everybody vanishes. It was like time broke in two, and then we've had the rest."

"He got cut to pieces," Craig said.

Frank uncoiled the hoses on the airless paint sprayer. "Who's painting?"

"I am," Craig said. "Tomorrow."

The three men, dusted like ghosts, went out onto the front porch in the deep gloaming. Frank had brought a cooler with bottles of his new beer, and they cracked these open and sat on the steps. It was dark earlier now, and as they sat brushing dust off their arms and the tops of their shoes, they could hear men and women call for children from time to time.

"Old man Brand could call," Mason said.

"God, could he. 'Ma . . . att! Jim . . . my!' He had a quarter-mile radius. We heard him one time when we were on the railroad bridge," Craig said. "Matt and I were down there spitting on a freight train."

"Now it's cell phones and beepers," Mason said.

They heard a voice call, "Dav-ey! Time for dinner."

"Let's go over there," Mason said, "see what they're having."

"What else you got on this place?" Frank said.

"Clean up, polish the floors."

"You want to put in a dishwasher?" Craig asked.

"We'll probably do the kitchen," Mason said. "Cabinets. That lighting."

"No hurry, sounds like."

"I need this job to last a couple years," Mason said. "Until I get my head on straight. Until I find my head and get it on straight. Oh, just my head. Forget straight." He lobbed his beer bottle out onto the thick front lawn. "Good beer, Frank," he said, taking another. "But we'll probably finish up and hand it over to Shirley Stiver in a couple weeks."

A white Land Rover pulled up in front and a young man got out and came up the walk. "Mr. Ralston?"

"Yes, sir," Craig said, standing up.

"I spoke to you about a remodel up on the mountain?"

"Right," Craig said, and walked the man back to his car, where they talked for several minutes, looking at a short roll of papers the man handed Craig. Behind them on the street, four kids stepped by arm in arm, girls, their baggy white sweatshirts floating like their voices in the dark.

"You know, Jimmy put that day at the reservoir in one of his books," Mason told Frank.

"He did?"

"Yeah, but he turned it all around. He put himself in the boat with Matt. The names were all different, but you can see what he did."

"Right, Matt took off. Hell, I could write that day and put it in a book. Matt was fucked up."

"Was Kathleen with him?" Mason asked.

"Kathleen never said word one about Matt Brand. But Matt was out alone, and he was as drunk as you get to be."

Mason pointed down the block. "The reason Jimmy Brand is bunking in the garage is that Old Edgar thinks that thirty years ago he was in the boat. He thinks Jimmy could have done something. I'm sure of it."

"Jesus. How is Jimmy? Now I hear he's feeling better?"

"Kathleen—you know I spoke to Kathleen?"

"Right."

"Kathleen says he's a little better. She arranged some medicine. He can get out of bed every day now. You want to go down there this week?"

Craig shook hands with the man at the car, and the man drove away.

"I think I will," Frank said.

"Is that another job?" Mason asked Craig.

Craig sat down on the steps and took a fresh beer from Frank. "Absolutely. My life is just beginning."

"And this is simply the weirdest season in my fucking life," Mason said. "If I didn't know better, I'd think I was happy. Sand the walls, sweat, drink beer."

"Lawyers," Frank said.

"That goddamned boat," Mason said.

Another car pulled up, Frank's Explorer, and the window slid down. "Come on over a minute," Frank said to Sonny, who was driving. "Meet my old friend Mason."

Many days that fall after school Wendy came early and helped Mrs. Brand prepare a tray for Jimmy. Whenever she arrived to talk, Wendy stood by the little door in the side of the garage and looked across at the kitchen window, and if she saw the older woman moving in there, she'd go and knock. Wendy was already a fair cook, but in those weeks Mrs. Brand led her through the construction of a huge apple pie with a cross-hatch crust. A pie they made one day while Jimmy napped. Mrs. Brand was glad for the company, and the young woman helped her go deeper into the cooking than she would have alone, sometimes making snacks for Jimmy, tea sandwiches and canapés of all kinds, a kind of flourish, and sometimes, if Jimmy was sleeping, they'd plow ahead and make dishes with the garden's riches, great pans of layered zucchini lasagna, and stuffed peppers with wild rice and sausage, and late in the season two golden pumpkin pies. The first two or three sessions were a little stiff, with Mrs. Brand pointing and suggesting, and they moved carefully, to not bump into each other in the little space, but then they simply fell in, and Wendy knew where the bowls were and the shallow pans and such, and they talked or didn't talk. Had Mrs. Brand known that Jimmy would be a writer?

"I don't know," she said, laying out rashers of bacon on a broiling pan. They were going to make bacon crumble to sprinkle on top of a pan of fettucine. "He was a skinny little kid, much smaller even into high school than his brother, Matt, and he was bookish, I guess, and the teachers said he had an imagination. He skipped a grade, and we didn't know if that was good or bad." Mrs. Brand laughed. "We knew it was good. Then he got involved with the music and the band for the year before he left, but I knew he was writing. Like you, he had notebooks."

There were narrow pages of pasta laid out on waxed paper on the counter, and Wendy began to construct the layers in the glass pan. "It must have been hard to read some of his books, the ones about Oakpine."

"It was only for a minute, and then I saw that it was his way of sorting it out, making a kind of sense of the terrible accident, and I could read them. I read all of them."

"That's amazing."

"And now you're talking to him about writing?"

"I am." Wendy looked down at their huge creation. It was always like this. They made ten times more food than Jimmy would ever eat. If a dish had an extra feature or the possibility of one, they included it. Mrs. Brand's fridge was full.

"I feel lucky about this fall, Mrs. Brand. I've never learned so much."

"I'm glad he's here too," Jimmy's mother said.

The garage at Mason's house was in mean shape, great deep stains in the concrete floor, and the walls were bare splintered wood, also for some reason lathered with oil spills, the whole room dark as if burned in a fire, and the two old doors sprung on the ruined steel plate hinges. Mason retrieved the ladder and went up into the garage rafters and pulled down long sheets of aluminum siding and a dozen ruined bicycle tires and twenty greasy fan belts stretched and cracking and coils of wire nailed to the rafters and four old cardboard cases of empty cans, rusted through, and the cracked plastic windshield of a motorcycle. As the pile grew in the center of the floor, Mason got more and more committed to his plan. He knifed the windowpanes so they could be reglazed, and he tied his kerchief around his nose and mouth and used the broom to brush the walls, and then he swept up the floor using the old snow shovel as a dustpan, and he threw all the junk into the Dumpster. It was only noon. He could feel the backs of his legs burning a little from toeing that ladder; it felt good. He came out into the fall day and again took in the gigantic trees on the old street. He could hear the motor of the paint sprayer in the house. Something moved between the trees, and Mason stepped clear so he could see. It was two great lines of sandhill cranes in long V's flying south. They were silent in the distance, as if something observed on a remote screen. There was a motion out front of the house, and the hardware van crossed onto the driveway and parked in front of the Dumpster. "Lunch!" Larry Ralston called, jumping from the driver's seat with a white paper bag.

Mason waved at the boy to come over.

"You're gutting the place," Larry said.

Craig came out the back door, pulling off his paper-painting mask. "I see reinforcements are here," he said.

"Not really," the boy said. "You're still on your own. I'm off to other deliveries, and then my life as a teenager. Perhaps you remember that era, then again, perhaps not."

"Enough!" Craig said, looking into the bag and extracting a beautiful baguette. "Are there drinks?"

"As ordered," Larry said, running back to the vehicle and returning with two huge paper cups of soda. "See you soon."

Mason said, "Larry, bring me back a mop and charcoal lighter. Any." And as the boy waved and departed, Mason stepped over and sat on the grass in the dappled shade, and Craig joined him. "I'm halfway inside, and I will say it is white, but not too white."

The baguettes were Muenster and chicken salad with Chinese mustard. Mason tore off half and took a bite and said, "My god, we're rescued."

"I love it when we eat like lawyers," Craig said. "These are from Edelman's just to show we have some capable luncheries in Oakpine."

Mason, still chewing, pointed at the open garage with his sandwich and said, "What do you think, old friend, of our band's new rehearsal hall?"

"Okay," Craig said. "Good, good. But what is our name? Did we have a name?"

Mason said quietly, "Life on Earth. We were mainly called 'Those four guys from Oakpine,' which is kind of truth in advertising, but I remember Jimmy wanting 'Life on Earth.'" They were talking and chewing and gesturing with their paper cups of pop.

"Whatever fits on the flyer," Craig said.

"How much paint have you got?"

"Plenty," Craig said. "Do you want to paint this?" He indicated the garage.

"I do. Tomorrow afternoon. I'd like to spray it like the enemy and move in."

Craig sat still, unnerved to be happy this way, his old friend in town, all this old new stuff ringing his ears. "Done," Craig said. "I'll finish in the morning and bring out the gear."

They were silent for a while after eating, old friends, and the day ticked in them, leaves falling along the street and the sun rolling away, weaker every day. "Okay," Craig said finally. "I'll finish upstairs by six or so, and then we can make plans for tomorrow." They'd talked like that the whole time, measuring the steps.

After lunch Mason found the little brass pressure nozzle for the hose and hooked it up. When he turned on the water, the old green rubber hose snared and bulged and then shot a sharp narrow stream twenty feet. Mason grabbed two loops of hose and marched into the open garage, shooting his avenging water into the upper corners of the little building and then back and forth along the walls, as scraps and splinters and dirt and spider webs flew free in the powerful wash. He was having fun. The place would blow-dry overnight and he could spray it tomorrow, but when he turned to the back wall, the jet of water caught the window and two panes blew out, and as he moved the spray to the sidewall to assess the damage, the pressure slapped two planks loose, and so he gave the entire room the careful once-over, loosening ten or twelve wallboards, smiling, thinking, I'm going to wash this house down.

Having found a project he hadn't anticipated, Mason climbed into it with both feet. He bought a dozen fresh one-by-eights and laid them on sawhorses the next day before the doorless garage shell. He could see light between the planks in many places. He was able to cinch about half the loosened boards, running two screws into each end. Then he pried off the five or six that were worn and weathered beyond reclaiming and threw them in the dumpster. He measured each missing slot and cut his new lumber with Craig's bright circular saw, tapping them into the wall with his hammer, each piece snug as a puzzle. The golden sawdust misted up into the afternoon sunlight, and he was happy to have a good day. At one point he was on his knees behind the building, laying in a bright new board along the base of the foundation, and he caught a motion in the corner of his eye: Jimmy Brand waving from his chair just outside the Brands' garage.

"Be careful!" Jimmy called.

"I know you!" Mason shouted back. He stood and waved his drill motor. "The new clubhouse. The band is going to sound real good at this distance. When I get cleaned up, I'll come down for a drink." Again, standing in the weak pure light looking down through the gardens of the backyards and calling to his friend rushed Mason with a vertigo that he couldn't understand, a gravity, a recognition. It wasn't déjà vu. He waved and smiled. Waving a drill—it was a wonder.

He brushed the new spots and the rough spots inside and out with gray wood primer, and then he cleaned the doorframe of the old hinges and plugged the old screw holes with split shims and mashed them flush with the head of his hammer, and then he measured the aperture twice and wrote down the numbers on a card in his pocket. He'd install a new door, a lift door on tracks. Craig would know how.

SEVEN

Kathleen

The next day by noon, Mason had run one more spray of house-white exterior latex along the bottom plate of the wooden garage. He'd given a good coat to the inside and the outside, and he backed out of the space looking right and left for any streaky holidays. The backs of his legs were pinging, and his eyebrows were dusted white. Craig was geared to go with the airless sprayer, and as he began painting the interior with the first of twelve gallons of Navajo white, which he would use by nightfall, Mason went out and cleaned the yard once again and then cut the front lawn. The day rose and held on the fulcrum of the ripe summer morning, then tipped without a breeze or a weighty cloud into a fall afternoon, the yellow light now an ounce removed and shadows drawn from the old book, unmistakable; the season had capitulated. Mason edged the front walk with a shovel, realizing he was just hanging out. He washed the shovel and leaned it inside the bright garage with his rake and broom. The old cracked cement inside the garage was clean; he'd scrubbed it with the charcoal lighter, a solvent. From the house he could hear the periodic hissing of the airless. His furniture, such as it was, was all covered with tarpaulins, and he'd spend tonight up with Craig and Marci while the paint dried. For a moment he lifted the rake and thought about pulling through the lawn one more time, the satisfaction, but he put it back. Mason walked down the old block to the Brands and stood at the end of the driveway for a moment. He approached Mr. Brand's boat and put a hand on it, a boat he hadn't touched in thirty years, and as he did he heard voices, a female voice, and by the cadence he could hear that a woman was reading. By the open side door he stood and listened for a minute, the words coming steady in a young woman's voice. Mrs. Brand's garden had stepped out of its bed. Several pumpkins showed their orange shoulders in the dusty green growth. The voice stopped, and Mason considered knocking, calling hello, and then he heard Jimmy Brand's voice, the same voice in a tenor whisper. Jimmy was remarking on whatever she had read, and Mason heard only parts: "No, it's going to tell you where to go now. It'll take all your attention, but you're in. Well done."

Before Mason could move, the young woman came past him, her face flushed, agitated and glorious, smiling, and she said, "Excuse me," and settled her papers into a folder as she grabbed up her bicycle and wheeled toward the street.

"Hello, Jimmy?" Mason called into the dim garage as he entered.

"Mason, for chrissakes."

"Something like that," Mason said. Jimmy stood from where'd been sitting on the bed. Mason hugged his old friend. He said quietly, "You're sick then."

Jimmy smiled, rolling his head back in the pillow. "I've been slightly worse. Kathleen Gunderson got me on some killer drugs. She told me you were back in town."

"We're neighbors again, big boy. We're going to be seeing each other." Mason sat in the armchair at the foot of Jimmy's bed. "What I mean is, Jimmy, I'm sorry I haven't been down here sooner." As he said the sentence, it felt inane to him and it hurt, but he claimed it and continued: "I came back to this weird planet, and that was one kind of tough, and I didn't know you'd be here, and all the days in these years I wanted to call you, how many, hundreds, they suddenly stacked up and . . ."

"Got heavy," Jimmy said. "Don't let them. I am glad to see you, mister. You were kind to me, and I knew you were all right or doing all right, and I also knew that I'd see you again. I always knew it, but I didn't know it would be like this, with this."

Mason sat and looked at Jimmy and felt again his heart beating the seconds away. It felt unreal to be in the same room again. "Thirty years," he said. "What is that?"

"Minutes," Jimmy said. "Yes? Is it still you?"

"I see now that it could be," Mason said. "I like your place." He leaned forward and put his hand on the bed. "You got my letter, my one letter."

"I did, and you got mine."

"I didn't say it all right in there."

"That book upset you."

"It did, but I loved it. I didn't want you to blur what had happened. It was all simple to me: Matt was at fault."

"It was a novel," Jimmy said. "I know what you're saying."

"No, it's a good book," Mason said. "I think I was angry because I didn't write it."

"And you know I didn't really have a choice," Jimmy said.

"I know. There were many days when I wanted to talk to you about the books, all of them."

Mason had read all of Jimmy Brand's books and had some of his feature writing printed off the Internet in his office. He'd followed

Jimmy's career, at first because he had the same vague ache to write that all lawyers have, but then simply to see which way Jimmy was going to use the moments they'd shared in his stories. They were good books, and Mason had noted the reviews and awards, but he hadn't read the books the way America had. He'd read them to see Jimmy's take on the life they'd known. Only two of the books, both novels, centered on their hometown. One was actually set in New York and had flashbacks to a little town in Montana, which Mason knew to be Oakpine. The other was a rites-of-passage book, Jimmy's first novel, and it used street names and places, and it captured and delivered a feeling of growing up in Oakpine like nothing Mason had ever known before.

"They're all good books," Mason told his friend. "More than books to me."

"Thanks, Mason."

"*Reservoir* taught me an important lesson."

"Uh-oh."

"It did. It showed me that I didn't know how to read. That book made me crazy, because you—"

"Because it's a novel."

"Exactly. It's a novel and I was there, and I got pulled into a story I know pretty well, and when it turned, it threw me out on my ear. I know exactly what you were doing."

"Maybe you do know how to read. I'm glad to see you. How have you been?

Mason let the question rise and fall. "I don't know," he said. "Being honest, I don't know."

"Good," Jimmy said. "It's no help knowing. I can still see your real face in the years."

"That old face," Mason said. "And I can see you. It feels like I saw you last week."

"I still owe you for the Trail's End, the room rate."

"I've been worried about the money."

"Last week," Jimmy said. "That must be what thirty years is. I am so glad to see you again."

Mason stayed at the Ralstons' house on Oakpine Mountain for two nights while the paint at his place dried, and the second night in the thick early dusk, Kathleen Gunderson took him down to the care center. He'd been having a drink with Craig and Marci in their glassy kitchen, watching the lights of the town come on below them. Craig and Mason had already laid out their new campaign: treat and seal the floors, rebuild the basement stairs, install a banister and seven new windows, refurbish the fireplace, check the boiler. Mason rattled the ice in his scotch, gratified to have these things before him.

"You're going to make it so nice, you'll have to stay," Marci said. She'd come in while they were making their strategy, listing tools, materials, inventory. "Start a new life."

"I just want to stay until it snows." Mason turned to her, as she rolled the sleeves of a white shirt. After work, she wore a big shirt and Levi's. "Get some good out of that new roof. Until the snow falls, I'm just a sidekick to Handy here."

Marci crossed the room with her glass of merlot and sat at the butcher-block table with the two men. "Well, I want to get everybody up here once before that, a dinner or something. Could Jimmy come?"

"There are days," Mason said. "Kathleen told me he could go out." They watched a car turn up from the street, its lights now coming up the long drive. "There's Kathleen," Marci said. "She's giving you the tour."

"It's a date," Craig Ralston said.

"It's my hometown," Mason said, standing up.

"What should I do about Frank and Kathleen?" Marci asked.

Craig shrugged and said, "Invite them both. They're big kids. It's been long enough. I'll tell Frank not to bring the girl. It'll just be the old-timers."

They saw Kathleen stand out of her blue Volvo and wave. "It'd be good to get everybody together," Mason said. "Let's do it. I'll bring the keg and my tambourine."

"Don't joke," Craig said. "We'll fire up the drums at least."

"I'm gone," Mason said. "You two behave. I'll be home by ten."

"Touch-up tomorrow," Craig said. "And I'll rent that sander for the floors."

In Kathleen's automobile they talked about Jimmy. Mason had made arrangements to pay for the medications, but Kathleen had filed under the state Medicaid plan. "I'll just get it all," he had told her.

"He's indigent," she said. "It's covered."

"We want more than just the standard stuff," he told her. "I know there are levels of these things."

"There are. And we're getting him the best. I know you've got money, Mason. It doesn't exactly work like that. I know what's available as it comes available. I've always gone to the top drawer for all our patients. Jimmy Brand is not the first person with AIDS in Oakpine."

The speech was a scolding, and Mason took it as such. He'd seen

Kathleen a couple times since his return, and he understood she was smarting still or something, maybe it was that she was pinched by the embarrassment of Frank's decision; she was stiffer than he'd known her. He had felt familiar with the woman until that moment, and now he saw what it was.

Lights were on in the gigantic new homes well back in the thick scrub oak on Oakpine Mountain—these huge yellow plates printed the branchy imbroglio as Kathleen drove them down. He was a stranger come to town, lording it over everybody. He wondered if he'd been too bossy with Craig as well.

"I'm sorry," he said. "I know you know what to do. If I can help, I will. But don't let me—"

"I won't." She drove down the mountain road.

After a minute of silence, which then folded and magnified, Mason said, "You want to talk this out, or should we just carry on? I'm real good with the latter. I can do it for years. Correct that: did it for years." Kathleen turned and made a serious face at him, and the way the lost light fell on her cheekbones, Mason could see her freckles, the shadow of them. Didn't freckles fade?

"There's nothing to talk out, Mason. Please. I'm glad you could get out. Mr. Sturges will be very pleased to see you." She spoke as if she were reading something she didn't like, and Mason knew she was angry, but he wasn't sure it was all for him.

"I was eighteen. If he remembers me, he gets the prize."

"He's only eighty. He remembers."

"Why's he in the center?"

"Had a stroke. Lost his wife."

"Was she the—"

"Chorus teacher. Were you in a cappella?"

"I only sang in the band. You were in a cappella. Red dress. Hair like this, a bun?"

"It was a hairpiece." She put her hand on top of her head. "Something we did."

Mason looked at her until she turned from the road. "You look good," he said. "You always looked good."

"I'm fifty. Three years ago my husband found a girlfriend. It's the oldest story in the world. So watch what you say about how I look."

Mason wasn't going to say it, but he was sick of being judicious and silent, and so he spoke: "I met her."

"I have too."

"I meant: whatever it is, this old story, it is not a beauty contest. She's a tall woman, but she's not in your league."

"Mason, leave it."

"Kathleen, I don't believe I will. I believe I'll go right on here." They were at a light downtown, crossing toward the medical complex. Kathleen Gunderson sat at the wheel looking straight ahead. Mason shifted, the way a person does before launching into an explanation. "Frank's deal is not with you or about it. It's a disappointment and, in my opinion a mistake, a common and a large mistake, but it is about Frank and nothing about you."

"Divorce is divorce, as you well know."

"I know the legalities and nothing of the rest. I'm learning, but poorly."

"But you'll feel free to speak to them anyway."

With the light they crossed the intersection and began following State Street. "Again, old friend," he said, "I'm sorry."

The Gables Care Center was adjacent to the four-story hospital, both structures unfamiliar to Mason, and lit in the new night. Kathleen parked, but Mason stopped her before they went inside to see their old teacher. The care center was more a sprawling house with a shake roof; there was something pagodalike about it. When he took her arm, she turned to him, the hospital bright behind her. She spoke: "Jimmy's going to die, Mason. Regardless of who does what. These are powerful drugs right now, but they can't beat it. He won't see Christmas this year, so get ready or leave town or whatever, because you can't stop this train."

He dropped his hand and said, "I thought so, but I appreciate your saying it."

"It must be strange for you to be back," she said, a conciliation.

"I'm strange," Mason said. "This town is the town, but I'm a little tilted."

She took his arm and led him toward the care center. They were walking slowly, as if waiting for words to find them.

"It's weird that you and Jimmy are both here. The band."

"The years," Mason said.

Kathleen said, "You guys were tight as tight and then gone."

"I know all about it," he said. "But sometimes I wonder if anyone else does."

"Frank does. The band was big for him, maybe the biggest thing. You know when he started in on it? When he was drunk. He'd get drunk and start on the various gigs. The road trip back from . . ."

"Cheyenne, when the blizzard crossed us north of Ardmoor and we stayed at that place—" Mason stopped and dropped his chin to think.

"The dude ranch and their last customers in the lodge."

"The Wooden Star, it was." He looked at her. "It was not a small place—buffalo heads, a stone chimney three stories. That ranch is still there. God, what a night. We had about four times like that—when the world seemed like it was just made for four kids from Oakpine." He smiled at her.

"You never talked to Frank about it when you were up doing paperwork, those deeds or whatever?"

"We're men—we don't talk. We did the deals Frank needed. I never talked in my life, really. I did some business, and I've got a vocabulary for my work, but I have never, ever talked."

Mr. Sturges had all his hair, and he was dressed in a dark blue robe over a set of light blue pajamas. He had lived in Wyoming all his life, yet he had always radiated a sense that he was visiting from a larger world, come to civilize the children of the frontier. He had called the students mister and miss, and all through his forty-one-year teaching career, he had worn ties with white shirts and tweed sport coats.

"Mrs. Gunderson," he said, standing from the easy chair in his room. "Mr. Kirby. How kind of you to come. Sit down." Two folding chairs had been set up for the occasion, and as Kathleen and Mason sat, a nurse appeared at the door and greeted them.

"Tea all around?" Mr. Sturges said.

"Perfect," Mason said, and the nurse disappeared.

"Well," the older man continued. "How goes the profession of the law?"

"Just as the papers have it," Mason responded. "Stalled by self-serving sycophants, such as myself. Justice held hostage."

Mr. Sturges laughed. His smile when it came showed the small s of stroke on the right side. "That's not what I've heard, but you tell me. Which law do you practice?"

"I started a small firm in Denver, and we're primarily doing industrial claims."

"And he's selective," Kathleen added.

"I'm sure he is."

"If you mean I don't advertise on television," Mason joked. The nurse returned with a tray, and Mason poured three cups of tea, stirring sugar into Kathleen's. "But I think we've been able to help some people. I still harbor the sense that we are doing the right thing." He examined his cup and toasted his old teacher. "Real china," he said.

"This is a civilized place for keeping the likes of me," Mr. Sturges said. "I'm glad to hear that, Mason," he said. "You were a bright light that year."

"Who do you think had the hardest time doing the right thing?" Mason asked. "From history."

Mr. Sturges sipped his tea. "They're easy to spot in the history books. Anybody killed in his prime. We made it easy to kill people in this country. There's no cure for it, except mediocrity." He smiled again, and his lip fell down. "Listen to me. I sound like I'm eighty again."

"You were a good teacher," Mason told him.

"I appreciate that. I enjoyed the career. Now tell me a story or two about your cases. Tell me one where the people in the right were duly rewarded."

"I know a couple like that," Mason said. "If you can tolerate my opinion." Mr. Sturges nodded, and Mason leaned forward and began to talk. The two visitors stayed another twenty minutes until Mr. Sturges's face began to fade. They said goodbye and stood to leave.

Mason and Kathleen drove down to Oakpine High School. "You want to walk out to where Frank broke his leg?" Mason said. Immediately upon opening the car door, they could hear music across the green.

"I don't think so."

"New scoreboard."

"New track, all weather, and new bleachers, and new gym." She pointed each out. "A little walk?" she said.

"Walking," he said. "You pioneers. But yes."

The two sets of double doors in the new gymnasium were open and lighted, and they could see boys and girls coming and going with streamers and sheets of paper. "The homecoming dance is Saturday."

"Want to go? I came home." He quickly pointed to the white cupola of the old gym. "What's in there?"

"Learning center for second language, dyslexia, computers." They walked across the corner of the football field and sat on the stone steps of the main building.

"I ate my mother's sandwiches here two hundred times."

"Have you really enjoyed the law?"

"I have. I became what I expected, I guess. There's no surprise in me. Thirty years later, and there's no surprise in me. What would Matt have been if he'd lived?"

"He'd be dead," Kathleen said. "He would have played football somewhere, that's for sure, probably Laramie. He had a scholarship. Then he would have come back here to town and relived the glory days for ten years and passed out under a train."

"You guys were in love," Mason said.

"Whatever that means," she said.

"We know what it means, but let's talk about something else."

"No," Kathleen whispered. She took his arm in both her hands. "It's nice to talk to somebody. Besides, none of it's a secret."

"It is if you want it to be."

"Matt was killed in an accident, and I went down to Denver that summer and started my career in nursing, I guess, by having an abortion. You knew that."

"I did and I didn't. I never heard it spoken of, but I knew you were gone, and your folks acted funny the time I went to see them."

"They were freaked out. Absolutely. They loved him more than I did. We were married in their eyes."

"You've always been a serious person."

"It's a liability," she said.

Four kids ran out the side door of the new gymnasium calling, four girls in cowboy hats, and behind them came four boys in chase. They were after their hats. Kathleen sat up and let go of Mason's arm. The girls screamed and ran and separated, laughing, as they'd been caught. One girl threw the big black hat at the boy as he grabbed her, but he ignored it and swept her up in a hug from behind. "Oh, no!" he called. "You're not getting off like that! You're getting the Chinese water torture. Brad, come on!" Another of the boys came over to the squirming girl and began tapping her forehead. "Noooo!" she screamed. The other kids came over, the girls tame now, the boys snugging their hats on. "Doo-on't!" the captured girl laughed. "Don't. No. Oh no!!" "You better not," another girl said, "she'll wet her pants." At that the boys sprang away from her, shaking their hands as if to throw off water. "Yuck! Darlys, you learn some manners. We'll tell Chuck about your bladder, and then we'll see if he still takes you to the damn dance." "Chuck knows about her bladder," one girl called. "Shut up!" Darlys cried back. She was still laughing.

"I'll take you back up to the Ralston's," Kathleen said.

"Good deal," Mason said, "But let's go by the Mountain View and get a shake from the carhops."

"We can get a shake, but the carhops stop after Labor Day."

"Still, let's. You got time?"

They opened the car and stood talking over the roof. "Oh sure."

"It's sweet being tired in this way. I like it. I like this."

"Mason, who'd you take to homecoming?"

"I just asked you."

"Did I answer?"

"Not yet. Who'd you take?"

"You don't know, do you?"

"No, I don't remember you with anybody." She drove them down Main Street to the blue lights of the Mountain View drive-in. "I was over at Brands' garage, picking guitar with Jimmy. We'd played the bonfire the night before, remember, and he and I were fully dedicated to our lives as musicians and to learning some new songs."

EIGHT

The Window

Two days later the wind came up across Wyoming and entered Oakpine, an invasion, a steady warm layer of all the air that had been
heated by the high plains, odd and unseasonal at first, then with an
edge of chill and bucking waves. Mason had heard the wind in the
trees early in the morning, a sound he knew from his youth. His
mother didn't like them, the windy days, and she would get quiet and
move slowly about the house until the storm broke and passed. There
were so many winds. Mason had the large wooden kitchen window
frame on the floor of the torn-up room. It had been there for two days
waiting for glass, and now the wind did what it wanted with the sawdust in the room, seizing and dropping in gusts through the four-foot
cavity. The fall days had been so benign that he'd thought the window
could wait while he refaced the cabinets. There was something about
having the window out of the wall that he liked. Of course, in his office in Denver, you couldn't open a window with a crowbar; he'd been
sealed in for twenty years.

As the wind blew into the mouth of the vacant window, the doors
in the house creaked and banged, the old latches worn round. The window was three rectangular panes, and he'd been an hour in the windy

room doing the satisfying work of knifing the old grout from the wooden crossbars, and now he laid the stickered new glass sheets that he'd ordered carefully into each section. He smiled: fixing a window in the weather. He stapled five diamond-shaped galvanized keepers along each side and stood the window vertical on the floor to see if the panes rattled, and they did not. Craig had helped him take it out, and now he tested to see that he could lift it alone. He turned to the sash with his chisel and ran it around the perimeter, smoothing the lintel and the inside frame; the slivers and dried caulk crumbs blew against his shirt.

Outside the trees rolled and shuddered—they were full of the wild air, and he could see Mrs. Brand's garden, the great thick tangle of zucchini vines billowing as if crawling with demons, and every wire fence banked a cache of leaves, and more leaves fled steadily across the hairy fall lawns. Over everything in the West, the sky was purple at the horizon, blowing up to gray. It was a comic book version of a storm, approaching like a creature, and he was the only character in Oakpine with a window out in this western wind. He could lift it. If he could set it in place and refasten the frame, he could caulk it tomorrow. He'd been removing the original pressed-wood doors from the cupboards, which were all ruined with age, and his pockets were full of the little saved brass screws. The new oak cabinet facings had been delivered last night and were on the porch in two cardboard cartons.

Each job in the old house offered a different satisfaction. You could replace six screws, and a new cabinet door looked like a party. This old window was a workhorse, and it was simply needed. When Mason lifted it up onto the sink, he felt it take the pressure of the wind, and he set the bottom along the windowsill and pushed it up, the old wooden frame and sash binding together as they met again. He had made a mistake. He couldn't reach to seat the thing from here; he'd need to climb knees up onto the counter. He pressed his cheek against the center pane and nudged it tighter. The wind was cut off and he felt his face suddenly warm in the closed room. Then with a neat push, the window snugged into place, fitting like a jewel, and he saw that Shirley Stiver, his old classmate, had come up into the noisy room and pressed the side frame.

"Well, thank you very much."

"The door was open, and the realtor's here," she said. "The doors and the windows."

"And the glazier's at home," he said. "One moment." Mason aligned the facing piece of quarter round along the top and tapped it secure with four finishing nails. He did the two sides the same and then took an extra minute pushing the bottom solid and then nailing it. "That window was last replaced when Hoover was in the White House, and now it needs new caulk and a little paint. Quite an upgrade, right?" Mason ran the flat of his hand around the surface of the window. "And no leaks." Outside the trees pulsed and the hedges flared, and it felt very still in the kitchen. Mason turned the lights on against the dimming day.

Shirley Stiver was wearing dress jeans and a kelly green blazer. "It is a fact that you can sell a house in this country where the windows don't close. Well, about half the time, there are windows broken. We try to find all the doors though. You're doing a good job. I like the new paint out front. This place is a gem."

"And we've got all the doors, even the one downstairs, which is still pockmarked from antiquity, a door into which I threw a thousand darts competing with Frank Gunderson and Jimmy Brand." Her briefcase was on the wooden kitchen table, and she stood above it and removed two blue folders.

"You want some coffee?" Mason asked the woman. He was washing his hands and considered the kitchen. "I'm not making coffee here. Let's go downtown and do your paperwork."

Outside the wind had the day in its grip, everything pulling and bobbing, wanting to go east. In her car she asked, "What's your schedule?"

"I'm seriously not sure," he told her. "I've lost my clock. I'm going to stay for a while. I know that."

She gave him a short look, but enough for him to show her both his hands and say, "It's not a crisis. I'm not big enough for a crisis. I want to do this house right, and Jimmy Brand is back this fall. I'm not recovering anything. I'm covering, perhaps. I like these fall days. Every time I say I like them, I like them more."

They drove downtown, and Shirley parked in front of Oakpine Java, a block from Frank's bar. "This was what?" Mason said, looking at the new glass facade.

"It was Maryanne's," Shirley Stiver said. "Hair salon. Didn't you ever walk by and get a whiff of permanent solution? This whole block smelled like burning hair." Inside they got a bag of chicken salad croissants and two tall lattes. "No Starbucks, yet," Mason said to the young guy who made their coffee.

"Yeah, there is. Inside the Food King by the deli. That right there is the best coffee in town though," the kid said.

Mason stood again in the street as the air streamed by, and Shirley joined him. They heard the train in the track yard jostle and jerk into slow motion. "Shirley, you ever eat in your beautiful car? Could we just take a drive?"

"I'm yours until three," she said, giving him the keys. "And the rain won't hurt the car, when it comes. Just don't spill your coffee."

Mason drove them back along Main Street, turning past Craig Ralston's hardware store, the front doors closed in the wind. He followed First Street to the small highway, then went west there past the little airport, a one-story building on the vast plain, the wind sock at high alert standing on the roof. He loved small airports, the ticket agent also working security, then handling the bags. A moment later he turned right on the road to the cemetery. The way was paved for two hundred yards, and then came bladed gravel, a quarter mile up the sage hill to Oakpine Memorial Gardens, which every one just called Memory. Here the old pfitzer hedge had gone wild and grown into great hands surrounding the graveyard; the fingers were deep green and shot with yellow aspen leaves and plunging around today in the unreliable air. Mason parked by the gate. The maples were red, and a few had limbs down in the long grass. The two sat in the quiet car feeling the bump of the wind from time to time and sorted out the napkins and the coffee, and they ate looking at the gray sky bladed by clouds crossing over the town below.

The cemetery itself was two acres, fenced with wrought iron and the hedge ran along two sides. There were ten old oaks still standing in the graveyard among the other trees, most of their leaves gone now. Shirley pointed, "Miller Trumble and his boy mow it all summer and haul the branches way back behind for the bonfire in February, remember? But they may be done for the year. If you want to go over, go ahead. I'll wait here."

Mason opened the car door carefully against the wind and stood in the weather. He walked through the old arbor gate and out to where his folks were buried. The wind was at his pant legs while he stood and read their names. He felt it would have been strange to speak, but then he was talking to them for a while, saying he was okay and the house looked good and he'd replaced the kitchen window and it was another windy day and he'd been in trouble but was going to work through it and he missed them and loved them. The air took each word away. The circumstance of being in the graveyard standing over where his parents were buried seemed impossible. Where were they, really? Below, a freight train slowed going into town, and he listened for its call, but there was no call. When he moved again, he felt he'd been there a long time. Had he been asleep? You spoke in such places, but you never finally said the right thing, the thing that helped. Okay, he said, and turned for the car.

It was warm in the car in the gray day, and Mason said, "Let's drive out to the reservoir. Just to see it. I'm on a break from home repair, and the owner's paying me by the hour anyway." He drove down the dirt lane into the wind and turned onto the highway out of town, looking back up the hill. "Miller Trumble played varsity football as a sophomore, and he ran like a rat, and his nickname was Rat. We loved that no one could tackle him, and we called him Rat. I'm glad you said his name, because if I saw him in town, I would have trouble finding the Miller. He's done a good job with the cemetery."

They continued out across the ten-mile plain. The same abandoned houses stood every mile or two, back from the highway, only half of them boarded up, the same car rusting the yard as when Mason had been a boy. Looking at the lonely places, it was difficult to believe anyone had survived there even part of a good year. There were some drill sites and clusters of antelope against the foothills, standing confidently, rumps to the wind, the way Mason's dad had always noted, saying they knew it wasn't hunting season quite yet.

"Slow, slow," Shirley said, and Mason braked, but still he'd missed the turnoff. There wasn't another car in sight, and he eased a U-turn and went back. "The sign is down," Shirley said.

"It's not that. What is this? Where are the trees? You'd always see the cottonwoods."

"Right there." Shirley pointed ahead to the small cluster of great cottonwoods, and Mason eased the car along the smooth but uneven white stone road.

"There were hundreds, right? There, there, and there." Now he could see the blue water white-capped all along the mile-long dish of the broad desert reservoir. He pulled the car into the bladed turn-around overlooking the broken boat ramp. The boat dock and little marina building weren't there anymore. The concrete boat ramp was cracked in plates and grown with weeds. "This was the place, right?" Mason said.

"It was. Doogan pulled his dock farther west, and the state poured a new ramp there closer to the highway." She pointed. "He's got a gas station and bait shop down there. It barely goes. This section is multiple use, and I've leased it out four times, and no one can make it go. You know, there's a pretty marina up at the mountain lake now, a log cabin with a big wooden dock, and it's full all summer. There are probably people there today. People like a lake in the trees."

"Where do the kids party after graduation?"

"San Diego. They don't come out here anymore. At all." The dark blue expanse of the reservoir looked serious. "It is not pretty."

Mason wanted to say, Except in an end-of-the-world way, but he opened his door and excused himself with "It shouldn't take me long to look at nothing. This isn't even the same place." He stood now in a heavier wind and stepped up onto the ancient cement sheet of the boat ramp. He walked down to the water's edge, staying well back with the wind. Now it was strange for him, this place, where he'd never returned since an afternoon thirty years before. There'd been twenty boats and banners in the trees and fifty trees that weren't even here now, and the water had been brimming blue, ten feet higher than it was today. And young Doogan had been on the dock lifting coolers into the boats and calling out. Now the gray wind crushed everything; it would be cold tonight.

They'd water-skied a little in Mr. Brand's new boat, and then Matt had dropped Mason and Marci and Craig off here. Matt was drunk, and there had been a scene at the dock. Jimmy had argued with him, tried to climb onto the boat. The boat was idling. Mason remembered Kathleen's face as she waited in the back of the boat to see what was going to happen. Matt's good nature was all used up; he was mean. He'd proved a brittle drunk, always charging into it with high spirits and always fighting or passing out. Mason had known many alcoholics through his career, most of them quieter, all that vodka, finally all the vodka alone, but he always remembered Matt, how the alcohol had him stamped by the time he was eighteen. In talking about it, someone always said, "He could pound them down," and that was what he did, pound them. Mason wondered why people want pounding. It was so common, not just the drinking but the trouble, wanting to be pounded. Mason was a pounder and played to feel the register of his work. He was being dreamy today, he knew, but this terrible windy shithole reservoir had him by the throat, and he could see Matt, without blurring any of it, on that sunny day three decades before.

Matt Brand had by any measure been the best athlete in this half of Wyoming. You could watch him run without looking at any of his astonishing statistics and know by the fact that you could not look away. He flew. And when he drank, it was always a fierce, one-way descent. That day he was done with high school, and the engines that would carry him full-ride off to golden days at the University of Wyoming were two months away, and he wanted to be alone with Kathleen, and he wouldn't listen to anyone nor answer a question. Jimmy pleaded, but Matt struggled with his brother, finally backing him with hard palms-open pushes, until Jimmy tumbled back into the water. Before Jimmy swam ashore, Matt gunned it and turned sharply for the open reservoir, throwing a violent wake in the wakeless bay.

Mason had helped Jimmy up. Tears cupped his eyes, and his lip split. A moment later they heard the boat return, still not slowing as it passed the warning buoys, and approach the dock. Matt stopped short, or tried to, and scraped the dock hard. Kathleen jumped out nimbly, barefoot, onto the wooden planks, her towel around her neck, and Matt again spun and sped away, as the other boaters cursed him.

"We were one of the last classes to have a deal out here at all," Shirley Stiver said, walking down to meet him, pushed by the wind. "After Matt Brand, parents got wary. Don't forget this was a new lake then: six, eight years old. It was just finally full that year." She looked at the wasteland, the water. "Even two hundred kids and sunshine couldn't get it back. It's just a lonely place."

The wind flagged their clothing, her jacket flying, until she turned her back to the weather and clutched the front together. "You were here, right?" She looked at him. "I came out for the party, but if you want the god's truth, I was up in the bulrushes on the other side of the parking lot." She pointed. "That hill or that hill. With Ricky Leeper. He'd waited all year, and we were up there awhile. I remember later seeing you and Jimmy and those guys camped under the trees, but I didn't come down because I knew you could read my face like a book. You would have been a good lawyer in high school."

"Don't say that," Mason said. "Well. Ricky Leeper. His dad ran the Sears Outlet those years."

"Yes, sir. Rick's over in Chadron, Nebraska. Coaches something at the high school."

"You lost your virginity right back up there." He smiled at her.

"In all the world, that's the place. It was more like the Garden of Eden in the old days."

"Every place was."

"What about you? You were taking your time, I noticed."

"I waited all year and then some. I went up to college in Mankato and got drunk enough at a party to take some girl back to my dorm. To my shame, I do not know her name because I never knew it. Isn't that terrible?"

"I wouldn't know terrible," Shirley said. "Life goes fast. There're some bumps." She was still looking into the hills. "Yep. Right over there." The wind was steady and uninteresting, a noise that didn't build, didn't fade. The light channeled darker and lighter as the layers of cloud cover shifted in their approach to Oakpine Mountain. He stood in the lonely place with the woman. Too much sky. Mason had thought this would be some other place, that there would be something here instead of nothing, and his foolishness hurt him.

"If life is lived between two points," he said, "this is one of the points. I'm still looking for the other." The leaves, yellow and brown, came across their feet, and behind them the smoky shadow of Oakpine Mountain, low and dark in the distance.

"Matt came back and got her," Shirley said. "From the other side." She pointed over the rise. "The cove there. Kathleen was in the boat with him."

"He was drunk," Mason said. "It was an accident."

"Oh, I know it was. I'm just saying from where we were, I saw him come back."

"Nobody could have changed a minute of it. Matt had the drinking from antiquity, his dad and his granddad. I remember when old man Brand stopped drinking; it was a weird thing to do in the day. The only reason Jimmy didn't get it is because of what happened that day." Mason turned to Shirley Stiver and shook his hands in the windy air. "Shall we go back?" he said.

"What else, Mason? Go on. It was the day Jimmy left, right?"

Mason looked at the woman and nodded. "He did. Or a day or two later."

"It was a confusing afternoon."

"When we heard, we came down here." Mason said. "We'd been up under the trees with the guitars, and we heard about the accident, and then somebody said they were bringing the body back, and I think we saw the boat or somebody's boat coming around there, the point, and . . ."

"Jimmy never even saw the body."

"Right." Mason said. "Right. He just left."

Shirley took Mason's arm and turned him for the car. "Did you drive him?"

"I did."

"What did he do? How did he leave?"

"He took the bus," Mason said. "I put him on the bus a few days later. If he'd have gone home and told the story, he'd be in the house today. In all these years there are five or six sentences that haven't been said, and now it is too late to say them. It was Matt's fault. Jimmy tried." Mason stopped again in the everlasting wind and tucked his hands under his arms.

Shirley stood still on the bleached concrete ramp, her jacket flapping. "Edgar lost a son, and he looks like a tough man, but he isn't. Some guy works for the railroad for years on end, you think he can't get a broken heart. He did. He never came back from it."

"I know. You never come back," Mason said. "And maybe you shouldn't."

"Come on," Shirley said. She took his elbow. "What about another coffee then? In town. And we'll go over the paperwork."

Frank Gunderson drove up slowly and parked his big Ford double cab on Berry Street in the late afternoon, the sky scrubbed to a dark iron, and carried a wooden case of beer up the driveway to the Brands' garage. He could hear the stuttering guitars start and run a line or two, then stop and blink and start again. He stood at the door and listened for a minute, then tapped the door with the toe of his cowboy boot. Larry Ralston, his hand on the neck of his Martin six-string, opened the door. Jimmy sat in the chair with the red Fender braced above his lap on the arms. Frank could see his face now, narrow, and the angular chin and the bones in his shoulders through his shirt. Frank pushed by his first remark about his altered friend and said, "It is the older version of Frank Gunderson, stopping by with the fruits of his labors."

"Frank," Jimmy said. "It is good to see you."

"Hi, Jimmy. I don't know if you can have this or not, but it's just full of good nourishment and no preservatives and about two hundred calories a bottle. You can squander it on your company if need be. I'm sorry I haven't been over sooner. What is this, a lesson?"

"We're just playing," Jimmy said. "This kid goes door to door doing charity work."

"I do not," Larry said. "Hi, Frank. I don't have any friends my own age."

Frank stepped to Jimmy and took his hand, "You look good."

"I do not," Jimmy said. "But I'm sitting up and trying to achieve a few chords that aren't too murky. You want to play some?"

"I do, and I see by your attitude that we're going to get the band back together one way or another. Jimmy, I'll come by tomorrow with my bass. It'll take two weeks to tune." Mrs. Brand appeared at the door and came in.

"Do it," Jimmy said, "and we'll find a drummer."

"I know one," Larry said.

"Frank," Mrs. Brand said, "I'm glad it's you. I've got a job for you." Frank pointed at Jimmy and said goodbye. He went out, and Mrs. Brand gave him two shopping bags full of zucchini off the back porch. "Put them on the bar and see if they walk away," she said.

"They will," Frank said. "We need a festive touch at that old place."

The little white garage on Berry Street saw more comings and goings in October than it had in all the thirty years before. Many times there were vehicles parked across the street, Mason's Mercedes or Frank's truck and the hardware store van three times a week and Wendy's bicycle leaning against the wooden wall. And these people, carrying bags of croissants or coffee or bottles of beer or musical instruments or books and folders, walked up the driveway in the gray weather or the slanted autumn sunlight as it washed against the Brands' old house, rinsed of its warmth, but light anyway. And often the visitor would glance up and catch a ghosted face in the kitchen window, perhaps, as Mr. Brand wandered his house and watched the desultory cavalcade of pilgrims and friends who came to see his son. Once a week all the guys showed up, and they played music, the drums set in the doorway so that Craig Ralston had to sit in the open door on a milk crate. They didn't play long, never quite an hour, but they played, and it was disjointed but full hearted, and there were moments when they'd round into the chorus and it fused and took off. The favorites became the

Beach Boys and the simple Beatles songs, with Larry fingering the intros and Mason taking Jimmy's guitar after a song or two and leading them through "I Get Around." Larry showed them how to roll forward into "Don't Worry Baby" and then mute it still rolling, holding his left hand out flat, quiet boys, so that Jimmy could sing, his voice a tenor whisper, his eyes closed, and this soft refrain made everyone lean closer. They played the song with careful measure. Jimmy's singing that way, sitting in his bed, made them a band again. Behind where Craig sat in the doorway, the neighborhood kids, four or five of them, would stand listening, trying to see into the garage.

Jimmy Brand came to know the bump of Wendy's bicycle handlebar as she'd lean the three-speed Raleigh against the building and then knock on the door, two and then two more, before she turned the knob and leaned her face in, saying quietly, "Hello, are you awake? Am I too early?" It was amazing to see the face of someone who was writing, see that she'd been off in her own dark, writing stories. The writing tutorials went well. Wendy met every deadline, keeping a pressure on herself that she embraced. She wrote two stories for every assignment, printed them out, and then let Jimmy Brand pick one, left hand or right. She made him smile with that, and he was cheered and humbled to see her commitment. It was the way you did it, a page at a time, steadily, until the pages began to assemble themselves and want their own way. Pages and pages. He'd known a hundred writers, and most binged and floated.

Jimmy Brand had Wendy come over twice a week for the half hour before the musicians arrived. With her, he always had twenty good, lucid minutes, more if she did the talking, before he felt the first erosion, his energy dimming, sliding away. The friction in his blood seemed to gather, and by the time Mason and the other guys arrived for a short practice session, his arms and legs ached. Speaking with her and then sitting with his old friends as they practiced was a test, but one he savored, and at the end of an hour he was blissed out and burning. The crowded garage became hallucinogenic, a rolling cartoon some days. He smiled at it, but the smile hurt. He'd wake, and Larry Ralston would be playing the guitar. How did he learn to play the guitar? When?

As the band dipped and plunged through rocky versions of "I Get Around" or "Tell Her No" by the Zombies, Jimmy Brand could see the percussion on the inside of his eyelids, and then the silence when his musician friends stopped was a roaring vacuum that made him gasp. It was all physical. The medicines helped, but he could feel the half-life of each ticking within. Some days he was certain he could feel the crumbs of calcium bleeding out of his bones. His arms were useless. Other days those forces abated, and he could sit and see clearly, and talking was the pleasure it had always been.

Wendy's fifth story was a long one that crossed territories for her. There was dry anger in it: a girl being pressured for sex. When she handed the story to Jimmy, she had asked if she could request from him a favor. She sat on the edge of the easy chair at the corner of his bed and asked if he could be careful with the story when he fell asleep. She knew the musicians would be arriving. "If it's no trouble and you can remember."

"No one is going to read this story except me. And I am going to read it. You're worried that I'll pass out and somebody we know will come by and find this manuscript and read your work."

She looked at him unable to speak because he had spoken her fear.

"I will guard your work with all of my armies, my dear. I promise."

"I did what you said," she whispered. "I went for it. I wrote into something that matters to me."

"I'm alerted and on guard," Jimmy said.

She'd tried hard with the story, she said, and then apologized for asking such a favor, and she said, "I know you'll be careful—you've been so kind." And then Wendy sat back in the chair, and without moving at all, not a shoulder, she began to cry. Her crying was a strange thing to watch, and Jimmy Brand knew he was seeing something primal. She might have been singing. Things were still happening on this far edge of his life. At such moments he felt his chest open up and fill with air, and it was as if he were young again, the beautiful hurt. Her story was heavy on his lap. Finally Wendy lifted her chin and pressed the back of her wrist against her eyes and came out blinking. She wiped her eyes again and reached for her story. Jimmy now had it in his hand too, and when she tugged, he felt the pleasure of holding on. He looked at her. "I'll be utterly vigilant," he said. "I give you my word." They both still held the manuscript. "We're in a project here, right? You've done a lot of work. We're going onward. I want to read this." He let it go. "But I won't unless you want me to."

"Oh, I do." Wendy held the story in both hands before her and looked at him and said something he knew she believed, something he vaguely felt he'd heard long ago, some faded déjà vu: "It's no good. I'm not sure it's any good."

"Well," he said, "you look like a writer." He gave her his smile and counted on two fingers: "You look like you were up late typing and that you have recently been crying." Those were the two unmistakable tells.

Now she opened her face to him, and her eyes glistened with an intention he hadn't seen anywhere in years. He knew they were in it now, no quitting, just the work, words and lives, as they talked of her stories. It's a real thing, something to live for, he thought, but I'm not going to live for it.

Later he would tell her something he'd said in conferences when he'd taught in them: that you're not really started until someone has cried. He had said it to lighten tough moments, but everyone knew it was true.

Then Jimmy asked her if they could change the routine and not talk about the story she'd given him three days before, but instead read the manuscript on her lap, the one she was wrinkling in her grip.

She began quietly steady and measured without inflection, word for word reading as if presenting each sentence for inspection. In the story, the two young people are deliriously happy and exchange strange presents as their courtship ascends. She named them Steve and Eve and stopped the first time she'd read that and pointed at Jimmy Brand sitting in the bed. "I did that on purpose," she said. "If it's stupid, I'll change it later, okay?"

Jimmy said, "It's fine. It's like the words 'woman' and 'man.' They're not stupid."

Eve runs a roadside bait stand, selling night crawlers for two dollars a dozen. She gathers them at night from the city parks and from the four acres of sod behind the house where she lives with her mother. There is a good deal of night crawler lore—Eve has developed a knowledge and skills about gathering the creatures. Steve, who lives in town, has less patience for her work, even though he understands it is going to pay her way to college. The summer before, she made thousands of dollars. Eve has plans to go to the University of Hawaii and study oceanography. Steve wants to use her hours to neck in his pickup, but she soon learns that if she goes out after midnight, she has less success, and she doesn't get enough sleep. Eve's mother likes Steve. Everybody likes Steve. Eve likes Steve, but there is wear and tear in their relationship. It is impossible to go so far in his pickup. Eve wants college—she's wanted it all her life, but Steve is right there in her face. After he gets her shirt off, he wants her pants. Without her shirt, in his truck, she feels as if she cannot breathe. All the final scenes are about her pants. She isn't giving them up. Steve says that she can have his. "I don't want your pants off," she says.

While Wendy read, there was a noise outside and then a knock. She started and put her pages in the folder before answering the door. It was a kid Wendy knew from school, Michael Ganelli, who delivered for Walgreens. "Hey, Wendy," he said, coming into the small room. "Mr. Brand?"

"Yes?"

"They said the garage."

"This is it."

The boy stepped out and returned with a folded walker, bright blue aluminum with wheels. He opened it and secured the little basket on the handle and stood it by the television. "From Mrs. Gunderson at the clinic," he said.

"It's Christmas," Jimmy said.

"Sir?"

"Presents," Jimmy said to the boy.

"Can you sign?" Michael Ganelli held out his clipboard, and Jimmy Brand initialed it. "Thanks. See you, Wendy." The boy closed the door and went out along the driveway.

"That's cool," Wendy said. Her eyes were sad now, in the story.

"Sit down," Jimmy said to her. "I'll go for a stroll later. Please, let's read. That's how you know you're doing it, Wendy. Someone gets a present in the middle of your story, and he still wants the rest of the story. I'm serious." She resumed the story of Eve and Steve. She was reading faster now but soon slowed as the story unfolded. Steve is pressing Eve for sex, and every night they go out becomes a kind of skirmish. They twist tighter into this corner, until it becomes apparent one night that Steve is going to go ahead with his plans for her, over her wishes. In the struggle he cuffs her, and they stop. He is standing in the open pickup door above her, and they are contesting her pants, which are now at her knees, where he has pulled them. There is one moment when he might apologize, but he lets it pass. They both hear the unmarked silence. He's hit her on the cheekbone, and it was a surprise to both of them. "Let go," she whispers. The blow has hurt her head and changed something in her. Steve cannot let go. Her pants and underpants are fisted in his hands. He tugs again. "No," she says. He is looking at what he is doing and avoids her eyes. "No," she repeats. Steve now has the clothing bunched at her ankles. Suddenly she stops and says, "Okay." This causes him to look up. He's already thrown one of her shoes behind him onto the gravel shoulder. "Okay," she says. "Steve, Okay." He makes an odd smile, his eyes narrow.

Wendy stopped reading in the old garage. The story carried perfectly well, and Jimmy was alert in it. "There's one more half page," she said.

"Go on," Jimmy said.

"Is it sick?" Wendy said.

"Not at all," Jimmy said. "If I understand what you mean."

"When I wrote it, this part, I wondered."

"Go ahead. Read."

"Did you always know what you were going to feel when you wrote your books?" She was leaning back in the old overstuffed chair, slumped there now, out of the pool of yellow light in the gray afternoon.

"No, Wendy, I didn't."

She started now to read again, and he had to ask her to read louder. She sat up again into the light, holding the pages there, and she read the end of the story aloud.

Steve stands over Eve and bunches her jeans and underpants, stuffing them into the pickup bed with his left hand. When she says okay now, she adds, "But you'll have to hit me again, and then you can do what you want." Her head aches from the first time. He pretends not to hear, and she pushes him with her foot and tells him, "No. Steve, you have to hit me or give me my pants."

The last two sentences of Wendy's story were "Steve leaned in the open cab and placed his left hand heavy on her hipbone. His other hand was out of sight." Immediately upon saying these sentences, Wendy stood and put her papers away. "Thanks for listening," she said, already turned for the door.

"Wendy," Jimmy Brand said, "congratulations. Please sit. This story is solid and fine and finished, and now you get to do what real writers do."

"What is it?" she asked. "I'll do it."

"You get to write another and bring it next week. Or sooner. If you can. Wendy, I think you should make it sooner."

She was standing and looking at Jimmy Brand and said, "Thank you," and she went out and closed the door carefully behind her. And in the quiet now in his temporary quarters, Jimmy Brand felt lucky. I'm lucky to meet her this fall, he thought.

He heard voices outside, and then a moment later it was the next afternoon somehow, or much later the same day, and there literally was a drumroll, a snare, and the door opened again, full of his old friends talking and greeting him, Craig Ralston grabbing the milk crate at the door and Mason handing Jimmy a bright sheet of lyrics and stepping back so Larry could reach his guitar. Someone said, "Is Frank coming?" and then Frank said, "I've got forty minutes for my art," and then Mason saying or someone saying, "We should rename the band, to be honest, and call it the Half Hours, Three Days a Week." And someone said, "Forty minutes for my art."

Then the notes were firing from Larry picking at the Fender. Jimmy saw that the boy could link passages now, his fingers awkward half the time in the transitions. It was strange. The music halted and flowed. It sounded like it flowed. Jimmy had shown him how to work his left hand on the frets, using his thumb sometimes, and it had been unnatural at first, but now it worked.

Frank stood behind Larry with his bass. "You're hired," Frank said.

"Of course, the pay is abysmal."

"Abysmal, dismal, nadir, etc. Vocab deluxe."

Jimmy leaned back. He didn't dare close his eyes because the day would flee. They geared up and stumbled through a far-ranging version of "Johnny B. Goode." None of them could hear it, whether it was good or bad or even clear, but Frank's grin was magnified as the chords subsided. "This is such a crazy idea," he said. "Let's do one more."

And then the door shut and the light failed, and it was quiet even with small wind coming over the small shelter, and then another long quiet day and the air inside the garage a liquid blue, the quiet like a humming, and only the door turning white, the light of the world, and in the space a man saying something, "Are you all right out here?" Jimmy was floating; it was sweet not to hurt. He could see his father's face. "Are you all right out here?" He wanted to answer the question; his father was so close, the voice he hadn't heard in decades, and the humming silence filling up the room. His father was in the room a step and then back in the doorway. "Look at this." Then there was the patchy silence. "Craig did a good job," he said. Jimmy wanted to answer, but no air came in or out. He heard the door. The door was real.

When he heard his father's voice, inside his heart he felt as if something tore, a page of paper being torn, paper torn slowly, a page from a book, but the tear was so old. He had imagined talking to his father five thousand times or ten; it was all the same with him in his life. What he had done was out of a great empty helplessness and a hurt, the stab that was the start of the tear. There was that whole beautiful year with the band, the way the music had tightened everything in the world, and the pure ascending joy of learning the guitar, and every week hoping Matt would sail out of his drinking, fly out of it, step out, and it had all spun to a single moment at the reservoir when in the sun-struck afternoon Matt pushed Jimmy from the boat, cursing him with a phrase that burned Jimmy instantly and that instantly in deep reaction he forgot. When Jimmy swam ashore after his drunken brother pushed him from the motorboat, Mason helped him up, and Jimmy put his arms around his friend, but Jimmy knew like a brick in his throat that Matt was going to have an accident and that he was going to kill himself. Jimmy suspended his mind and played guitar with Mason in Frank's open jeep for those hours, sunburning his shoulders, in a way that would see them peel four days later when he was already on the bus and would earn him the scar with freckles which he still bore, but his head was blaring the whole time with a noise that came real in an hour in two friends running up the broad boat ramp, "It's Matt, Jimmy. It's Matt."

Then an hour of confusion, hell with kids, not one person standing still.

Frank Gunderson holding Jimmy back when they brought the body up in someone else's boat. And then the ambulance. And then the ambulance driving up the boat ramp slowly with none of its flashing lights, just a humble white station wagon, now turning for town without haste. Jimmy remembered Mason putting the guitars away in their cases, the lining of Mason's case was garish—whorehouse purple, they called it all that year. Jimmy heard the brass latches take. He was awake through the rest of the day, but he didn't remember how he got back to town, who drove, or what it was like standing in his kitchen, a goodbye torn from his mother—he had to go—and then two nights at the old motel with Mason, refuge, and then the bus away.

And now as a fact his father's hand on his shoulder, warm and heavy, and the real words, "Are you okay out here?" Sleep crushed him and his answer, but he had heard what he had heard.

NINE

Homecoming

Homecoming dance lit Oakpine for the two weeks beforehand with heady expectation, and it caught the whole town in its gears. The florist made his year with corsages and roses, and the two alteration shops watched the thirty dresses they'd been fussing and adjusting fly away on hangers in the yellow light of Saturday afternoon, and half the windows downtown were painted with colorful bulging letters in some version of Homecoming Sale Special, the bakery, the saddlery, and even the furniture and appliance outlet, as if the big home football game might be a first-rate reason to buy a new stove. This siege of preparation took an edge when the tailgaters began to arrive at the high school the morning of the game, eight hours ahead of time, setting up their households in the open air, all the furniture and the open fires for charcoal and the bratwurst to come, and then the smell of lighter fluid and burning charcoal and before noon the smell of cooking meat in the steaming crosshatched rising smoke.

Frank Gunderson had an outpost set up, chairs and folding tables under his canvas ANTLERS banner, and he and his barmen grilled hundreds of sausage sliders, heaped on platters for all of his patrons and their friends and their friends. Frank ran the grill for a while midday and then gave the spatula to Leander, his cook, and he washed his hands and stashed his apron and put on a beautiful gray Stetson with a small silver band and moved among the crowd like the mayor. There were a thousand plastic cups and samples of his new beer, one in the hand of the genuine mayor, who had graduated from Oakpine five years after Frank and his friends. "You know it's past noon when the mayor is younger than you are," Frank said, tapping the man's shoulder in lieu of shaking his full hands.

In the thin fall sunlight, the parking lot and three streets became a dense little village of their own, filling with tall characters in fresh cowboy hats who had been at the school going back through the decades and still owned this part of it; it never faded. Someone would start telling a story about a football play, a perfect slow-motion draw play or a wide-bellied double reverse, which had lasted twenty seconds twenty-two years ago in a game at homecoming, and before it was half told, there would be five tellers or six, with necessary flourishes including the names of the players and what they went on to do and where they now lived and how that place in its own way was inferior to Oakpine, and in some cases how they died, the kid who ran like a demon, low to the ground and fast, and could never be caught all that day so long ago, who later lost his life in the famous rail accident south of Gillette or all his toes on a late-winter elk hunt.

When the football game itself started, Oakpine was as deserted as a town in a movie about the end of the world, not a noise except for the train every two hours, and even the train sounded reluctant to move through, and the streets were empty north and south. Jackson Hole was being hosted *and toasted*, as the saying had it, and from the opening kickoff, in which Oakpine crushed the runback out at the six-yard line, Jackson Hole was in fact toasted and then just burned. The game was a deft display of Oakpine's speedy offense and their smashing defense, and the game was fully decided by halftime, but not a soul left the overcrowded little stadium. It was a rout, but a nasty one, thirty-nine to three, and when Jackson Hole saw their fate, they played every play to the death, with a grudge, piling on, hitting hard even when their strategy was soft.

Larry Ralston, breaking from the huddle for each play, scanned the arena, all these people, and he knew the names of two hundred or three, and beyond this shell, the tiers of the stadium, he could see the sun caught in yellow slashes on the rooftops of the little downtown and the hazy horizon smoking on the curved world's edge. He had a kind of vertigo, and even with seeing Stephanie Barnes waving and Wendy there beside her where the students stood behind the end zone, he felt removed, and he thought, I wonder if those girls know the guy they are waving to. Larry didn't know what to think about the minute he was in and he heard himself say, "High school," and he knew it to be just part of the craziness, the new craziness he realized was his life now.

Larry Ralston played weak side end, and early in the fourth quarter of the game he took a shot to the ribs, a knee after he had tackled the halfback, that had him wincing at the bottom of every breath, a pain and pleasure at once, which endured unto the final whistle, the three referees dancing out onto the field waving their arms making crazy shadows that ran twenty yards in squirming clusters: game over. Immediately the hometown crowd rushed the field, and the entire population of Oakpine was as densely packed as they ever became once a year, and a player or two appeared above the mob on shoulders as if pushed there perforce.

Larry Ralston never got his balance back after the game. There was the jamboree of bumping and twisting through the crowd, everyone batting his shoulders and tapping his helmet until it was pulled off his head and handed to him by Stephanie Barnes, who, jostled, kissed his sweaty neck, laughing, and then he went up the gym steps into the old locker room for the last time. He showered along with his exhilarated teammates, the room a riot, thirty-two animals scrubbing eye grease off their faces, spontaneous whooping and whistles and song, though the songs were hooted out and replaced by the names of these heroes called back and forth in the bright, tiled room. They threw their towels in the same game as always, trying to lodge them above in the hanging lights, so the room appeared to have exploded. Standing on his towel and buttoning his shirt, Larry put his fingers against his side and thought: *I broke a rib. Or two.* Then he said, "I broke a rib, but it does not matter."

He imagined the Jackson Hole team in their two buses, gray motor coaches crawling north in the cool fall twilight, wet hair, already past the loss, past football, scheming someplace to go tonight, that wonderful mix of hope and fatigue, sixty lives headed away. He knew that road as it rolled off the plains and into the first mountain junctions. Buses on a night, just any night, not homecoming, just a night.

Larry and all his mates had the homecoming dance, and soon the locker room was half empty and half again, and then just Larry and the center, Chuck Seebord, who had brought his suit to school and was lying in his dress shirt and his boxers on the wooden locker-room bench, his ankles crossed in gold-toed black socks. They had both played every down. Chuck pointed at Larry, and Larry nodded; it was the entire conversation. Larry loved the quiet room, the water still dripping in the showers and the hundred towels above and beneath. The air smelled like talcum powder and the mint of the trainer's balm. Larry sat down and pulled on his old school loafers. He was sharply sad for almost a minute, and he breathed until it lifted. He was smiling. For some reason he couldn't figure, Larry wanted to be the last one out of the room, but Chuck wasn't going to roll out for half an hour.

Outside in the twilight the cold air took his neck, and he drove home and showered again, running the hot hot water on his bruise, which was now a blue shadow. He watched his hands in the mirror button his shirt. With his hair combed back and his face rosy, he went down into the kitchen and did a turn for his mother and father, pointing out the dimple in his red silk tie.

"Here's a handsome young man," Marci said, kissing her son on the cheek, "who smells quite good."

"What happened to the life, Marci?" Craig Ralston said. "Play football all day and dance all night."

"My aging parents," Larry said. "The night of the prom their hearts were full of "—and he opened his hands to them—"something."

His father came up and put his hand inside Larry's jacket on his ribs, just a pressure. "Take a breath."

"I'm okay, Dad."

"Just one deep breath."

Larry inhaled and felt his father's fingers on his bones.

"It's just a bruise."

His father tapped the rib right where the fire was. "You still bend," Craig said. "That would be broken on most folks." He stood back and smiled. "More to the point, I happen to know Mr. Barnes and his curio store," Craig said.

"Antiques, Dad. And I know him too. I deliver bubble wrap there twice a month. You can get the full prom report from him later, as much as Stephanie will confess. For Pete's sake."

"She's a beauty," his mother said.

"She is," Larry said. "So many of these girls are."

"Is Wade drinking?" Craig said.

"He's driving."

"Is he drinking?

"Not with me in the car," Larry said. He pointed at his mother's merlot and the beer bottle on the table. "You two behave. I'll get the report on you." There was a honk, and Wade's headlights flared up the oak-lined drive.

"Romance awaits. Don't stay up. I'll see you later."

"Nice game, Larry," Craig said. "Have fun."

Larry went out again into the dark and thrilling cold and said to the shiny vehicle, all glass and billowing exhaust, "The next thing. Good luck to us all." He pulled the door open, and he said to Wendy and Wade, "Dear friends, classmates," which had Wendy laughing immediately. "I saw you both earlier today at Oakpine High."

"You are so full of shit," Wade said. "Get in."

"Despite that, I am glad to see you again." They drove to Stephanie Barnes's house, and they all went in and stood in the carpeted living room and listened to Mr. Barnes recap the game in a funny synopsis that featured each of Larry's plays and ended with his number: ". . . and the question was answered when number eighty-seven plucked the ball from the waiting arms of the receiver and went forty-five if not fifty yards with the interception." After every sentence Stephanie, in her strapless gown, said, "Dad, we were there, remember?"

"Yes, I remember, dear, but the excitement lingers. Or it should," he said. "Let's have something linger. I'm not going to be the one to say on whom youth is wasted."

"My parents have got the same thing, Mr. Barnes. You're not getting through to us. Not to worry. Nobody's getting through to us.

We're kids." Stephanie's mother lined the teenagers up every way she could and took a dozen flash photographs.

"Where are you going for dinner?" she asked.

"Probably the Tropical," Wade said. "It's a big night."

The homecoming dance was held in the Oakpine gymnasium, and the senior boosters, twenty juniors and seniors who wore their sweater vests every Thursday, had titled it Flames of Fall and colored leaves were the theme. In the eight thousand shadows of the two thousand leaves hung in the nylon netting over the room, Larry danced with Stephanie Barnes, stepping through the spotted pools of rolling lights, blue and green and red and yellow. They were fairly comfortable— that is, they moved without touching and mostly in time with the music—and they did not stick out from the crowd of dancing teenagers, all dressed up in the high middle of the evening. Immediately after they'd started dancing, Stephanie did a funny thing. She took his hand and pulled him out to the rear stairway and put her fingers on his cheek and made it clear he should kiss her, and he bent and they kissed. "I wanted that out of the way, Larry. Many thanks. I missed your mouth out there on the field. We've never kissed, have we?"

"Just this once," he said. "And now twice." He put his arms delicately around her bare shoulders and kissed her again. "It's surprising to be so good at it." She took his arm in both of hers, and they walked back into the dark dappled gym.

"Where'd you go?" Wade asked them.

"We had some housekeeping," Larry said, and they began again to dance. Couples and clusters of friends drifted by and put their hands on Larry's arm and shoulders and said things about the game and greeted Stephanie. She was number one in their class, having always been number one, and president of the Student Tutor Society. She was the only girl in AP physics and AP chemistry. Tonight she had her bright brown hair pinned back, and she wore a green satin dress. She smiled as she danced, catching Larry's eye from time to time, her old friend from every single grade in school. It was the night of the year when the boys at Oakpine High School saw more cleavage than any other night, and Stephanie Barnes, who'd had famous breasts since seventh grade, was a big part of that viewing.

Wendy and Wade danced nearby, Wendy in a conservative black dress with spaghetti straps but a high front. Wade danced as if he were hearing sudden noises from afar, but Wendy was the smoothest dancer in the room.

Stephanie's face was bright, and her look made him ask, "What is it, Miss Barnes?"

She put her mouth against his ear and said, "Perhaps you could help me with something else."

"Perhaps," he said. Larry's head was empty; he was thoughtless in the bottom of this speckled pool, his arm on Stephanie and then away and then her arms on him turning or meeting or touching as they danced. An hour into the affair, when the disk jockey changed tunes, Wade stepped across Larry and took Stephanie Barnes's hand for the next dance.

The charge had been up ever since Larry squeezed in the front seat of the double cab pickup with Wade and Wendy, but now Larry was in new territory. Something had been at him all day. He had never thought before about how people had different motives for things, different from his. He saw the way Wade treated Wendy now as different than he'd seen it before. He knew their public side, and the three of them did a lot of things together, like kids, but something in Larry now allowed him to see further, and this disturbed him in a way that

he'd been expecting. These new ideas made Larry feel slow and obvious, and now with his body buzzing after the game and his ribs glowing, and knowing how Stephanie felt in his arms, he held Wendy and
felt powerfully, oddly jealous. I'm too late to be having so many
thoughts for the first time. Was he like Wade and just waking to it? He
knew in the quiet center of his heart that he wanted Wendy too, and
now he was dancing with her. He'd known her for six years, and they
were easy together. The song was something half slow, and half of the
kids in the dark, gleaming gym elected to dance fast, but Larry took
Wendy in his arms, and with her right hand in his left, he stepped
with the spaced beat of the music.

"Name this tune," he said to her.

"No," she said.

His head was against the side of her head, and as he took in the big
wooden room, he knew he was different than he'd been even a week
ago. He knew he was different than he'd been an hour ago. He was a kid
who had always been on balance, and now he felt as if he were fighting
not to fall. There was a vague lump in his throat that had been there
since before the football game, that he had thought was excitement but
now felt like an urgent sadness; actually it felt like both. His whole
body glowed with bruises and this dim rushing joy. There was a clear
blue footprint along the bottom of his ribcage. He leaned back a few
inches to say something to Wendy, and she took the signal and leaned
back, and their faces in that proximity stunned him, and he only looked
at her for a startling second and pulled her close again. Closer, in fact,
than he'd intended. It was purposeful that he didn't kiss her.

"Larry?" she said.

It was all he needed, an opening. When he leaned back this time, it
was as if he were leaning out of an airplane with nothing beneath him,

and he knew he was going to say absolutely anything. What he said was her name, and he saw her face when she heard it, and now she put her head into his shoulder. But he was going on. "Do you think, at the advanced age of seventeen"—and he couldn't stop—"that love and sex are the same thing? Is one required before the other? Are they related at all?"

"Larry," she said.

"Do you know Wade talks about you?" They were still dancing somehow, but the room was subsumed in shadow and the music was far away, and from this place Larry went forward. "Do you know Wade said he bit you, your breast? Has he?" When Larry said the last, his voice broke, and the lump asserted itself as a clear anchor wanting him. Anybody who looks at me, he thought, will know what I am saying. Wendy was in his face now, her expression stern and ready, as if challenging him to say more. Now they had stopped dancing. "Don't let him," Larry whispered to her. Saying that winded him, left him nothing, and he was sure he was going to drop Wendy, who looked at him with horror and understanding. She shifted so she could put the flat of her hand on his chest, and he felt the lump, the pressure, double. Their eyes were welded.

"I'm sure he didn't say it that way," she said. Her face was hard. "And you're too late." And then as an awkward footnote, she again said his name, "Larry," as if calling roll, and she folded herself against him for the duration of the song. He could feel her four fingertips in the top of his shoulder. They couldn't speak again because the music stopped, and suddenly Wade and Stephanie were before them.

"This wild thing can dance!" Wade said. "She's a bona fide mover." There was a line of sweat along Wade's hairline, and Stephanie's face shone under the leafy canopy. Larry turned to Wendy one last time before claiming his own date, but he saw she was looking past him at

Stephanie, the significant tops of her breasts. "What say we depart these premises?" Wade said. "You guys ready to get some dinner?"

"In a minute," Larry told Wade. "One more dance with my date. May I call you my date?"

"I am your date," Stephanie said. "And you can call me that all night long."

Holding her now and moving away in the shadows calmed Larry. He liked the way she put the corner of her forehead against his cheek, and he held her floating as the music waved through the room. How many times had he danced? Not a dozen. It was a strange activity in which, listening to music and responding to your partner, you moved with no clear destination. He loved it. Larry knew immediately that he would not dance enough in his life.

"Did you go to the junior prom?" he asked Stephanie.

"No. Did you?"

"I didn't. What were we thinking of, missing that?"

"Let's go next year. We'd be alums—they'd give us a discount."

"Good plan. I'll meet you on the gym steps at seven o'clock."

He could feel her fingers climb his shoulder as she pulled herself closer to him. After a minute, he said, "Did Wade behave himself?"

"You know he didn't," she said. "I'm glad I'm your date." When the music stopped they stood in the loose embrace for a minute until he heard Wade call.

"That's fine, Miss Barnes," Larry said. "But please, watch out for me. I'm untamed actually. Efforts to tame me have failed—efforts by experts—and your efforts in that regard will fail."

"Excellent," she said.

At the door Red Harwood stopped Larry and Stephanie, as they walked by, and put both of his hands on Larry's shoulders, facing him.

"Ralston, whoa. Is Elvis leaving the building? You are the man." Red Harwood was the stalwart tackle on the football team, and he wasn't drunk yet, but he would be in half an hour. Now he took Stephanie's arm and started to say something but then stopped and threw a long glance over her breasts and down the front of her dress. "Stephanie," he said to her chest, a comic, "I need to have a word with you. I want you to be careful when you squeeze this man, because I know as a stone cold fact that he cracked a rib today under the foot of the barbarian nose guard from the republic of Jackson Hole." He looked up into her face. "I happened to be on the ground nearby, where I had been rudely thrust by that same giant, and I heard it snap." Red put his arm carefully around Larry and snuggled against him. Wade and Wendy stood arm in arm, closing this little circle. "So squeeze him like this." Young Harwood snuggled against Larry's neck. Larry looked at Wendy during this charade, and she looked back at him, their eyes a connection. "Not too hard, see? I missed that tackle today, I did. I missed it. I tried and I failed, and if in your postprom enthusiasm, you jump on him and break it further, well, it will still be all my fault."

"I'll be careful," Stephanie said. "Your wisdom is a great help, Red, as always."

"Cushion it all with some soft part of yourself, if possible," Red Harwood said, again checking her bosom and raising his eyebrows.

"Thanks, Red," Larry said, "We're headed out now. Be careful."

Red stood up straight and took Larry's hand and shook it. "I'm sorry you got hurt, man."

"Forget it. We beat them. It was a good game."

"A great game," Red added. "I'll see you all later."

In the parking lot of the old high school, Larry got Wendy's door and closed it after her, and then he helped Stephanie up into the backseat of Wade's dual cab truck, and when he stepped in beside her, she grinned and waiting a second before kissing him.

"I want it to just be a habit," she said against his face. "Tonight it can be our habit."

"You've got a smile," he told her.

The windows of the Tropical were steamed up and marbled with murky green light from the neon palm tree above the door; it looked as if the young people were going to enter an aquarium. The bells on the door rang in the little foyer, and behind the screen in the larger room Larry could see tables of kids from the prom sitting around in the little thatched huts, drinking sweet drinks out of ceramic skulls and playing around during the rainstorms. On the way to their table, thunder sounded in echoing layers. Stephanie laughed and took his arm tighter and said, "I love the rain."

"This goofy place," Wade said. "When was the last time you were in here?"

"The day we graduated from Overburden Junior."

It rained every twenty minutes in the Tropical, starting with distant thunder, the calls of birds, and then the first drops gave way to a regular downpour on each of the little cabanas. The rain dripped to one side into the series of connected pools, and a waterfall at one end of the two-tiered room hissed and splattered throughout the evening. Wade and Wendy and Larry and Stephanie sat near the wall mural opposite the fountain. The wall was painted as a Pacific seascape stretching to the golden blue horizon. When the rainstorms ended, the birds began again to chitter, now accompanied by a soft soundtrack of ukuleles. It was a fun place with the overwritten, oversize menus and the waitresses with their leis, but the whole evening Wendy cast sober looks at Larry while everyone else ate the pupu platter and the island teriyaki chicken. Wade poured his whiskey into his skull and offered around a pint of Jim Beam. "None for me," Larry said. "Not in the tropics. Remember that one guy."

Wendy laughed. "He went too far."

"That was the general opinion of Miss Argyle's class."

"Where are you going to college?" Stephanie asked Larry.

Wade said, "He's going down to Laramie with me—roommates. It is going to be a blast."

Larry felt the first part of his life end. It was a slow-motion moment. He'd never seen Wade in a tie before, and he didn't recognize him, and Wendy's face was shining. The word *blast* had made him angry; there was something stupid about it, and he felt stupid, and he knew whatever he said next would be crosswise. "We'll see," Larry said. "I've been such a good boy, as you can all attest, every day of my fucking life . . ."

"Larry," Wendy said.

"It's okay," Larry said. "I've been saving up. I've got a shitload of foul language to accompany the wild life ahead. I am going off the tracks big time. If you look for Larry in the good-boy line, you'll be disappointed." He leaned and poked the table softly with his finger. "Fucking disappointed."

Stephanie laughed and took his arm. "Good, you savage. You untamed savage." Her head collapsed against his shoulder, and she laughed and whispered, "Good-boy line."

"Oh, you're headed for prison all right, sunshine," Wendy said.

"Don't call me that unless you mean it."

Two waitresses appeared with four large and two small platters of kung pao chicken and kung pao beef and ham fried rice and kung pao shrimp and white rice and chicken curry and wontons and an orange bowl of sweet-and-sour chicken. Chopsticks were distributed, and the table was bumper to bumper as the young people filled their plates. The plates steamed in the rainy room, and they ate for a while.

Larry leaned and pointed at Wade. "A blast. I don't know. Wade's already got a scholarship at every two-year school in the state and a few in Idaho. He's got some choosing to do."

Stephanie leaned away from Larry, squinting. "You should be a teacher."

"Right," Wade said. "You could be Mr. Peck and give a ridiculous quiz every day." He held his ceramic skull in front of his mouth with both hands, sipping. "I think it's time to get out of school and into the real world."

"This is the real world, Wade," Larry said. "Look at the four of us. It could be thirty years from now."

"Wow," Stephanie said.

"No, it couldn't," Wade said. "High school is not the real world."

"This will be revealed to us," Wendy said.

Wade looked at her. He said, "Whatever. I'm going into business. You get the money, then you can do whatever else you want."

"What kind of business?" Stephanie said

"I don't know. What you got?" He laughed. "I think I'd like to buy some property. How hard could it be? You've seen some of the guys who run Oakpine?"

Larry felt Stephanie's leg shift against his leg, the warmth. "Are you going to study science?" Wendy asked Stephanie. "Is it medicine?"

"I think so. I'd like to do research."

Larry offered everyone the dish of hot mustard. "You were in Denver last summer at the hospital?" Larry said.

"Yeah." She turned to him now, closer, and put her arm along the back of his chair. "It was an internship, and I was in a lab where they were working on different kinds of diabetes. I liked it very much." She held on to Larry's forearm while they picked at the platters of sweet-and-sour chicken and wontons with chopsticks.

"Did you experiment on rats?"

"They have white mice in the lab, but I didn't work with them."

"You'd look good in a lab coat, doctor," Wade said. He downed his drink. He poured another lick into the cup and put his arm around Wendy's chair. "And we're going to be in business and then travel."

"I'll take some of that," Larry said.

"Good man," Wade said, handing him the bottle along the side of their crowded table. Larry took it and put it in his pocket. "Hey," Wade said.

"Where will you two travel?" Larry said, defending himself with his chopsticks.

"Give me the fucking bottle," Wade said to Larry.

"To the islands," Wendy said. She said it in such a way that Wade leaned back and looked at her. She pointed to one of the islands on the painted mural. "The one behind that one."

"What's its name?"

"I'm not going to tell you," Wendy said. "That's what happened to Pago Pago."

Stephanie laughed.

Wade said, "Hawaii'd be nice. They don't scrape ice off their windshields night and day all winter."

Larry felt his lungs fill with air, and he knew he was going to say something. "I have unlimited affection for the ice on my windshield, you halfback. I'm not going to have you saying anything about it. Do you even know what it is and where it comes from and what it means, you—"

"Islander," Stephanie said. She was grinning.

"Plus, they have ice in Hawaii and an ice festival." As Larry said this, he knew he was going to fight Wade; this whole year had been too much. Knowing he was going to fight made him terribly, urgently happy.

Wendy smiled and shook her head. "You guys." She lifted her eyes to Larry's. "Don't spoil Wade's dream."

"Are you drunk?" Wade said.

"Wade"—Larry lifted his hand open over the table to stop traffic—"what do you suppose Wendy is going to study in college, should she decide to go?"

"Anything she wants," Wade said. "Nursing, marketing . . ."

"Geology?"

"Wendy is going to be a writer," Stephanie said. "Where have you been?"

"Wendy?" Larry asked her.

"I want to be a writer."

"Seriously?" Wade said.

"Seriously," she said. "I want to write stories or for a paper, something."

"Don't you feel, though, that we're just kids?" Wade said.

"We are kids," Larry said. "This is the way kids talk. This is the way everybody in here is talking."

"Bullshit," Wade said.

"See," Larry said. He signaled the waitress and asked for takeaway boxes. "We're going to have some groceries."

"A writer," Stephanie said. "That's cool. You've always written well."

"It's just something I want to do," Wendy said. "I'm not very good, but it's what I want."

Wade said, "That's obvious."

"What?"

"You spend a lot of time on your homework or whatever."

"I see you almost every day," Wendy said.

Wade swirled his drink and drank it down. "Let's blow this place."

"Let the birds finish," Larry said.

Crossing the parking lot, Larry said to Wade, "I'll drive. Allow me."

"I don't think you'll be driving my truck, big boy. Gimme that bottle."

"Keys," Larry said.

"You're flipping out too," Wade said. He pushed past Larry and got into the driver's seat and started the truck. "You're fucking flipping out. What is it, time to flip out? Get in, everybody. Let's cruise." The three young people looked at Wade, who had closed his door and was setting his CD player for Byton Hartman, the country singer.

Larry assessed his friend, and it was fully decided in him. He felt it as a shock in his elbows: he didn't like Wade. He had his hand on the smooth glass bottle in his suit pocket, and he knew for the first time in his life that he didn't like someone, and he was sure it was a good decision. *Flipping out?* Now that phrase made him angry. He felt again at the top of a big wheel slowly turning. "How dumb can you be?" he said quietly to himself. "You dumb bunny." It was a phrase of his mother's.

"What?" Wade said. "What'd you say?

"I'm talking to myself, Wade. Again."

The girls' short rabbit fur coats bristled in the cold Wyoming breeze. A week ago it had been warm. "He's okay," Wendy said. "I've seen him drive worse than this. Let's just go." She went around and climbed into the cab of the truck. Larry looked at Stephanie, and she leaned against him and said, "It's okay, Larry. Come on." In the narrow backseat, she slid against him for warmth, pretending to chatter her teeth. "Turn on the heater," she said to Wade. "It's cold."

"I sort of thought it might be raining," Wendy said. She was sitting with Wade in the front seat. "It's been raining in there for two hours."

Wade wheeled them onto Main Street and said, "We can't go to Wendy's. Her mom waits up, and she'd get us all in a big game of Scrabble."

They passed Fendall's and the gaggle of shiny cars parked there. The big front windows were full of the A group having coffee and banana splits, the girls in primary colors going from table to table sampling the ice cream, their shoulders shining. Larry felt he was seeing some time capsule cartoon of a life he had known. He wondered how they could breathe in that bell jar. Wade then drove them down Main Street and through the gravel parking lot of the Dome, naming the cars there behind the old pool hall, a dozen friends inside in fancy clothes playing eight ball. You could drink there if you were careful. "Just drive," Wendy said. "We're not going in there tonight."

"There," Larry pointed. "Pull into the Trail's End." The old motel was dark as charcoal in the night. The windows of the office were broken out, and weeds grew along the walkway in front of all the rooms. "Should we get a room?" Larry said.

Wade was confused and did a U-turn to drive into the littered parking lot of the ruin.

"Yes. They told us to get a room, and we should get a room," Wendy said, laughing.

"I don't know how many people just told us to get a room," Stephanie said.

"Twenty. 'Get a room,' they said," Wendy added. "Twenty people. Trusted individuals."

"I get that," Larry said, "and it sounds like good advice. Who doesn't like a room? But what exactly do we do with a room? I've already got a room."

"Me too," Stephanie said.

"What is it?" Wade said.

"We're good," Larry said. "I just wanted my date to be able to say I took her to the Trail's End."

"Do you have a room?" Stephanie asked Wade.

"Let's can it, boys and girls," Wade said, and he floored it and spun his wheels onto the highway out of town. They felt the old prairie darkness swallow the car. He turned at the lane for the cemetery and eased, lights out, up the hill and around the fenced property. There were no other cars on the dark plateau. Usually on weekend nights in good weather there was a car or two parked off from each other above the speckled lights of town.

"I guess we're all alone," Wade said.

For Stephanie, Larry pointed out at the graveyard and whispered, "Except for." She was in his other arm, and he could feel her hand on his hot rib cage. There were a dozen antelope bedded down in the poplar grove behind the cemetery, and they were watchful but didn't get up. Byton Hartman was singing a song about his country and how much it meant to him, by god, and how it would always mean a lot to him. He had a voice so deep, it seemed to have been machined. Wade set the vehicle in park and left it running and pulled Wendy across to him. The cab was large but small, the rear seats close but separated by the high seatbacks, and the dark warm space smelled of the dry floral scent of the girls' perfume and the newness of the heater and soy sauce and ginger.

Larry saw Wendy slide to Wade, and then he turned to Stephanie, who had lifted her face up for the kiss. She had somehow gotten her hand inside his shirt, and he felt the impossibly smooth surface of her palm on his fevered ribs. For a while everything was shifting satin and breathing and the singing, a nonsense bass thumping, and the windows screened with condensation, and Larry let go a little and then a little more with Stephanie against him, sweet and more muscled than he'd imagined. He hadn't imagined anything really, and here now she arched up as if she had made a decision. She bumped his chin with her forehead in such a way that he knew to unzip the back of her dress a stroke. "Larry," she whispered into his mouth, "be careful of my dress," and she helped him slide his hand along the moist side of her breast; she gasped, or it seemed she did, and he stopped breathing to feel the weight of her, the contour and the wonderful warmth. Their kissing was seamless. He could hear the couple in the front seat, and he realized his ears were out for every noise from there, Wendy's breath and Wade's little directional "uh's" every once in a while.

The night wind on the old garage on Berry Street sucked and rattled the door like a visitor, and Jimmy woke with his lamp still on. He opened his eyes and heard the familiar rattling of the entry door with a clarity that surprised him. His head was clear. When he rolled his head, it didn't hurt or drift, and he sat up and saw that it was midnight exactly. He drew a breath and then another, and he felt as if he had slept all night. He hadn't felt this well for a year. He pulled his legs up and took his bare feet in both hands and stretched his neck down, and it didn't burn. "I don't know what this is," he said aloud. He put on his slippers and his robe and the jacket with a kind of pleasure, and he stood up, and his vision did not swim. The door still tapped, and he went to it and pushed a folded paper into the jamb, and it was silent. Then he opened the door and felt the fresh night in his face. He sat on the bed again and pulled the new walker over and tested it. There were wheels and a brake and a basket and a little padded seat that folded down. It was deluxe.

In New York he and Daniel would walk to the river sometimes instead of going straight home from the paper. Daniel would come to the office on West 22nd Street, and they'd strike west, kicking and talking about their days. Daniel had once done a piece for a slick travel magazine on the theme of island getaways, and he'd included a famous sketch of Manhattan, referring to the various possible beaches up and down the East and Harlem rivers and then the Hudson, making each shoreline something out of the guidebooks, cabañas and piña coladas optional. Jimmy would have already been to some off-off Broadway play and then come back to the office to write it up, and it was wonderful to be out in the late night, especially in winter, the streets theirs all the way to the water. Even after Daniel got sick, and he was sick a long time, they still went down to what they called the beaches when they could, arm in arm to the waterfront, the new docks on the old piers, and the luminous water and the serious smell of the Hudson, and the lights of New Jersey in electric palisades.

Jimmy directed the walker out to the driveway now in the windy midnight neighborhood. All Wyoming was night. The air quickened everything and Jimmy was thrilled to be out this way. There was no moon, and the wind kept finding the leaves in ranks and rolling them past him. "'Pestilence-stricken multitudes,'" Jimmy said, the old Shelley poem. It was cold, and at first it was pure tonic, and then it settled on his neck and his forehead and his hands. "Go on," he said. "I'm walking to the street. A person walks to the street. Just to the old street and back." Halfway he realized he should have worn gloves, and his hands cramped and opened and cramped. And then he felt a sickening pain rinse through his body, as if he'd spilled something on his shirt; he wasn't able to be able to be able. You're sick now, mister. It was a long way, he saw. He might have made a mistake.

At that hour Larry listened. He held Stephanie Barnes, but now sometimes her head was in his shoulder, and they sat close. In the front, he could hear Wendy and Wade whispering a little now and again, something like whispering. He kissed Stephanie, and she was smiling at him, and he was happy too, he supposed. He should be. He heard Wendy whisper, "Not here." Stephanie heard it too, and to cover, she kissed Larry and embraced him, shifting her weight then suddenly and sharply to her hand on his ribs. The white light went right to the tops of his eyelids, and he said a sharp "Oh!" and Wendy's face appeared over the seat.

"What?"

Wade pulled her sharply back, and she said, "Goddammit, Wade, no."

Wade said something that Larry couldn't hear, and Wendy's face was there again. "Are you all right?" she asked Larry.

He was breathing through his teeth, and Stephanie was apologizing, and then Wendy was jerked away, and she swore again, and then Wade said, "Okay," and then after a silence he said loudly, "Fuck this! Just fuck this!" It was loud, but Larry was not surprised. Wendy scrambled back to the passenger side, and he came across for her, and Larry said, "Wade. Hey, buddy."

Wade said to him, "Don't you talk."

Wendy said *no* again and *no* again, and Larry could hear them cuffing and pushing.

"Wade." Larry sat forward. "Wade, let's go back. Let's just go back." He saw Wade put his hand against Wendy's face and push her head back against the window. "Stop it, man."

"Don't you talk, you shit."

Larry slid to his door and jumped out of the truck, opening Wade's door and dragging him out onto the windy hillside. "Leave it," he said. "Cool down, and let's go home."

Wade hit Larry below the eye, following with his right hand to the ribs, and Larry went down, and Wade jumped on him, swinging down now and missing. Larry's chest was on fire, and he threw Wade off and tackled him, rolling in the dirt, beyond angry, way beyond like some old man looking at himself, and then standing and lifting his teammate by the arm and the collar and throwing him in a spin to the ground.

The girls had climbed from the truck. "Stop," Wendy said. The antelope had risen silently and leaped the cemetery fence and drifted through the tombstones, disappearing. "Stop."

Wade sat splayed on the ground and then got up. "Fuck you, Larry." Wade stood up, scooping up the little bottle of whiskey, and stepped into the driver's seat. He revved the engine and backed without closing the passenger door, rocking it closed when he wheeled out of the lonely place and down the hill toward Highway 31.

"Are you okay, Larry?" Stephanie asked. His eyes wouldn't quit watering from the pain, and he sipped shallow breaths as he brushed himself off.

"Yeah," he said. "We're good. I think I cracked a rib in that game today, but right now I can't feel a thing. I think, however, I might have torn these fine trousers."

Wendy had a hand over her face, her shoulders naked in the night wind. "I'm sorry. I'm sorry."

"Oh god, Wendy," Stephanie said, "it's not your fault." Wendy had left her purse and jacket in the vehicle, but Stephanie had hers. "I'll call my dad." Larry shrugged out of his suit jacket and put it on Wendy and pulled the collar up and buttoned the two buttons while she looked up at him, and then he tied the sleeves in a loose knot in front.

"And he'll be happy to come out in the night and find us up here at Memory," Larry said.

Stephanie smiled and fished her cell phone. "His daughter knows what she's doing," she said to Larry. Her face was bright and flushed in the dark. She turned so Larry could pull the back zipper up those five inches. "He'll be glad I got this far." She took his arm, and the three walked the perimeter fence with the wind at their backs.

"Those kids from Jackson Hole are just pulling into that town now, grabbing their gear, walking across to the doors of the gym."

"What?"

"Other people," Larry said. "Way out in the world." Then he added. "That was a short fight for such a long wait. Was it even a fight?"

The wind was pulsing through the cemetery shrubs, and when they came to the corner of the iron fence, Larry said, "This is where Jerry Wainwright is—this corner."

"He was a good kid," Wendy said. "He was in algebra two." Wendy moved alongside Larry, and he put his arm around her, and she pushed the side of her face into the hollow of his shoulder. Larry stopped again and looked over the fence at all the dark graves, and he pointed there. "I know what you're going to say," Wendy said.

Larry dropped his chin onto his chest in the gusting wind and said, "I think you do."

"It's from Miss Argyle's class last fall."

"It is," he said. "You must have been paying attention."

"I remember the story is all," she said.

The three young people stood close to each other in the dark place. "What story?" Stephanie said. "With Miss Argyle?"

"I don't remember the title. It's what the grandfather said in the story," Larry said. "He's old. He points at the graveyard and says, 'There's no sense lying there.'"

"Dylan Thomas wrote the story," Wendy said. "He wrote like an angel."

Stephanie was still warm from the car, and she stood with both arms around Larry and her face against his shoulder, but by the reference to the story she relinquished her claim and smiled at Wendy, who stood so close also against the boy.

"Look," Larry said to Wendy, "when you write this, give me a couple graceful moves, like I ducked the punch and caught him with a left jab. Just one. Maybe I said something clever. Oh god, make me clever. No coarse or shitty swearing, like 'fuck this' and 'fucking that.' My mother might read your story, and I'd get in trouble."

"You are simply full of it, Larry."

"I may write it up," Stephanie said. "This is my first prom, after all."

The night wind ran for a hundred miles and then met the town and tore into ragged gusts between the sleeping houses, shuffling and repacking the leaf banks along the hedges and withered flower beds, and Jimmy Brand sat burning on the walker at the edge of Berry Street. He'd made it to the street and was all out. He had closed the throat of his robe, but the wind bit his bare ankles, and he was waiting to pass out. There was no wind in his head, just the hot fog pressing his eyes, and he clenched for balance. The periphery of his vision was shredded and unclear, but he saw something more than the waves of leaves cracking by. A figure crossed between the houses. A figure in the backyards, loping, floating, a figure that became a man, all dark and out of focus, huge with a cape, and then gone. A figure stumbling silently to the old garage and wheeling its arms, a man throwing ashes, something—a lick of light against the structure. Jimmy drew a breath, and it wouldn't come. He opened his mouth, a child under the great bare trees, and it wouldn't work. When he opened his eyes again, he saw the flames, a yellow sheet flapping against the side of the little wooden building where he dwelt, fire, where he did dwell, fire, his dwelling. Fire. And then like an answer to his silent calls, the light in the kitchen came on, and he heard the back door and his name in his mother's voice.

TEN

The Dinner

Larry Ralston drove through the dark town. The big red SUV felt huge on the little streets now, a lumbering gargantuan machine from the future come to visit and terrify the past. He was going twenty and speaking to each of the houses, saying goodbye and goodbye, "and though you will see me around for a while, by next year you will look for me in vain for I will be away." The fingers of his left hand made guitar chords on the steering wheel, and he was singing the sentences. He pointed at a little wooden bungalow with pale pink siding and said, "Oh, I ate pudding in your tiny kitchen when I was seven or eight with Bruce McDougal, who was in Mrs. Dennis's class with me. Whoever heard of pudding for a birthday, not that it wasn't good. Goodbye!" He named the houses as he drove and kept talking to them. "We knew each other well, or fairly well, or not at all, I'm not sure, but I recognize you tonight and so: goodbye." He turned slowly onto Berry Street and stopped and then carefully backed his father's red Cherokee along the Brands' two-track driveway, a lane made for narrower vehicles. Now the ancient sycamores and poplars along Berry Street stood barren in the gloom. It was an early twilight, and the cold, ever-present wind had risen with the dark, sucking leaves along the ground. It was twenty-five degrees. As he stepped out of the vehicle, the back porch light came on, and Mrs. Brand came out that door in a sweater. Arms folded, she hurried to the garage and met Larry there. "It smells like snow," he said.

"We've had a gracious fall," she said, "but it is definitely over." They went into the warm little room where Jimmy Brand was sitting in the green easy chair in the lamplight. Beside him on the bed was his red Fender guitar. He leaned back watching the plastic ceiling as it billowed and then suddenly drew up against the rafters, the corrugated valleys looking like ribs. He wasn't dreaming, but it was easy to drift now, a short step from any light in the window to his rich compendium of memory. There'd been a lot of sweet quiet in his apartment with Daniel, their ritual reading with popcorn after ten o'clock at night. Popcorn. He smiled with his head against the chair, watching the clear plastic struggle against the staples. It made a muted flapping sound that was soothing and somehow domestic, and he thought: This would make anyone hallucinate. He breathed as the image drew air, and he was aware of his lungs in their workings.

"You'll need this," his mother said to him, holding open a brown car coat. It had faux wooden toggles for buttons. Still sitting, he leaned forward while she helped him into it. "Thank you, Mother," he said. Larry gave his arm, and Jimmy pulled himself up and straightened the coat. "Well," he said to Larry. "Standing up in real clothes. Who would have thought?"

"How do you feel, dear?" his mother asked.

He reached his hand and took hers. "I love you, Mother," he said. "Larry. Always, always, every chance you get, tell your mother you love her. It's always true, and it's the kind of fact that just improves everything, the room, the furniture, the task at hand."

"Yes, sir," Larry said. "I'll try it."

"And there ends the advice," Jimmy said. Outside, after they'd helped Jimmy into the big automobile, Mrs. Brand came around to Larry with a bag of vegetables and then another. "I know your mother doesn't have time for a garden now with her work at the museum. Your dad likes his squash."

"He does, Mrs. Brand. Thank you."

Jimmy Brand felt electric. The medicines Kathleen Gunderson had arranged for him were powerful; there was no way to take them and keep a balance. Some days he'd sleep for hours, a thin, almost waking sleep in which he could not move. Some days he'd speed, too wired to even write, and that's when the guitar was a blessing, and he'd pick it until his legs—under two pillows—could no longer stand the pain. He was giving Larry lessons. Now, he felt awake but off center. He was used to this feeling of being tilted, not quite sure he was standing straight and facing forward; and he was glad, as Larry drove them slowly in the large vehicle through the village and up Oakpine Mountain, past the strange yellow windows in the thick undergrowth, to be out in the night. To Jimmy, all the lights appeared to be sparkling ferries in the glowing harbor, ships coming, sailing for the sea.

There were four other cars in the Ralstons' big circular driveway, and when Larry Ralston helped him down from the car, they stood a moment, and Jimmy again pulled at the big coat to straighten it. The toggle buttons in his fingers sent him back forty years. "This is my father's dress coat," he told the young man. "If he knew I was wearing it, he'd burn it tomorrow." Seeing Larry's confusion at such a confession, he added, "Forget I said that. What I meant was, add your dad to the list—tell him you love him too, early and often. He's a big man and needs a double dose."

"That's going to come a little harder."

"Absolutely," Jimmy said. "But you're a strong guy and young—you can learn it."

Larry looked at Jimmy, and Jimmy added. "I know I can't walk, but I know who I'm talking to. We're friends now, like it or not, and you listen to me."

"You have my best interests in mind."

"You know I do."

They could now hear a thumping from the house that resolved itself into a muffled drumbeat, the slow rhythm of a song. " 'Help me, Rhonda,' " Jimmy Brand said. "He's got the drum kit out."

"Let's face it," Larry said, "my father is a drummer. He is drumming night and day. He hasn't drummed since I was a kid, and now this fall he shows his true colors. The hardware store has been some kind of twenty-year cover-up." He took Jimmy Brand's arm, but Jimmy stood and walked easily toward the house. "That is a great song," Jimmy said. "But as long as I've lived and as far as I've traveled, I've never met a woman named Rhonda."

"We've got one in my class," Larry said.

"Well, talk to her for me," Jimmy said. He was happy. "Look at me walk. This party has started."

The house was rich with the smell of a savory roast and the promised early turkey and something nutty and laden with butter; the air was loaded. Larry did have to help Jimmy up the stairs, and Jimmy measured each one. Halfway up, Jimmy could feel each step double and then double again. It was as if he were giving blood. At the top he stood in the bright kitchen, every counter full of dishes and carafes, and his eyes clouded in a way that made it seem simple just to fall back down. He was gone for a moment, unable to speak, the breath he needed badly only seeping in. Marci came suddenly to him as he started to fall, wiping her hands on her apron, but Larry caught him, and then with a sweeping lift he was in the overstuffed chair in the den, the fire in the grate another hallucination. He heard his name and felt Kathleen's hand on his forehead; he knew her hand. He knew to gather a big breath and hold it for three seconds. Then quietly, he came back.

"Hello," he said. "I wanted an entrance."

"And some ice water," Marci said, handing him a blue wineglass full of cold water. She kissed his cheek. "I'm so glad you could come up. Is this going to be too much?"

"No, not now. We're here. I can tell there's a turkey in the late stages of being roasted somewhere in this house, and your mushrooms sautéing in butter and garlic have revived me. And the music!" The drumming had continued, not always steadily, and now Jimmy could hear two men singing with it. From time to time a guitar rushed in, quit, rushed in.

"Craig!" Marci called. "Let it rest, dear. Jimmy's here."

"Send him in," Mason called. "We need that electric guitar." There was a flurry of drumming and a cymbal clash closer, and the two men, Craig and Mason, ambled in from the back, each with a drink, and greeted Jimmy, taking his hand. "Larry, my boy," Craig said, "there's a hole the size of your ten-year-old foot in my snare drum. What do you say to that?"

"That's no problem for duct tape," the young man said. He was spreading a cracker with cheese. "Plus: seven years ago? I think I'm innocent by now."

"You can get your innocence back?" Kathleen said to him.

"Oh yes, ma'am. I've read about it."

"Show me those books," she laughed. She had a glass of wine and settled onto the huge shaggy couch. The coffee table was the scarred walnut top of the stationmaster's desk from the old depot, and it was spread with glass dishes of olives and pickles and cheese on toothpicks and two open bottles of wine.

Mason sat down next to Kathleen. "What you've got with a drum set lying around the house is a classic case of the attractive nuisance. A ten-year-old is required to kick a hole in at least one of the drums. It's like gravity. It is unstoppable. I'm surprised he didn't jump in with both feet."

"Mason," Jimmy said, and reached to take Mason's hand.

"I think I did," Larry said. "Both feet."

"Don't you have someplace to be?" Craig asked his son.

"Ma said I could hang out."

"The football star doesn't have a girlfriend?" Mason asked him.

"Yes, he does," Jimmy Brand said over his glass. "But it's in the incipient stage."

"What?" Marci said. "Stephanie is really after you?"

"They're all after me, Mom."

"They should be. He rescues them two at a time."

Craig had passed a plate of cheese and smoked oysters and crackers, and Jimmy Brand was nibbling a wafer. He held it up. "Eating a cracker with you guys," he said.

They all heard a noise below in the entry, and then Frank Gunderson's voice called, "Larry, you got a hand?" Larry stood and went down. A moment later Frank stepped into the kitchen with a baking pan covered in foil: an antelope roast. After him came Sonny, tall and dark and twenty-nine, her long black hair in a single braid. She had two bottles of red wine in her right hand and a long loaf of French bread in the other. Behind her, Larry came in with a pony keg on his shoulder.

"Set that right here, and let's have the finest beer in Wyoming. Who's interested?"

Craig had gone into the kitchen and greeted them. Mason stayed on the couch, watching Kathleen as they heard the other woman arrive in the next room. He took her wrist and lifted her hand onto his knee and then took it away. They both looked at it, some joke in the air. "That's nice, Mr. Kirby, if it's an advance. But if you're being solicitous, keep your hands to yourself." She looked past him to Jimmy Brand. "We're fine here. This is a dinner party."

A round of beer was poured into little glass tasters, and the large coffee table filled with little dishes of horseradish and mustard and soy sauce and a platter of antelope strips. Introductions were made. It all stopped for a minute when Larry stood to shake Sonny's hand, and when it became clear who she was, he said, "Oh, sure. You're Sonny," and everyone heard it as *They've all talked about you*. Craig stood in the silence and made a little team project out of selecting the music, putting the Beach Boys CD on and then holding up another. "The greatest band with only one album," he said.

"The Zombies," Mason said. "Let's turn it way up a little later."

Jimmy held the little glass of beer up to the fire, turning it and sipping. "A couple pints of this, and I'd be back to fighting weight," he said. "Congratulations, Frank."

Everyone fell back into chairs, Larry giving his spot on the couch to the woman he'd embarrassed, and crackers were spread with Brie and chutney. Frank pulled up an ottoman and asked Kathleen how things were going at the clinic. "She has delivered unto me the Harley Davidson of walkers," Jimmy interrupted. "A sleek blue machine that I've already had to the street."

"In the middle of the night," Kathleen added, shaking her head.

"What was that fire?" Frank said.

"Some prank," Jimmy said. "Some kid found the lawn mower gas and went for a walk. We were lucky he didn't smash Ma's pumpkins and wax the windows."

"I'm not sure it's a prank," Mason said. "But it was stupid enough that it might as well have been."

"We'll repaint on the first clear weekend," Craig said. "It's not much, a lick of soot." He had a mouth full of cheese.

"Then I'll see you in May," Jimmy said. Everyone heard it, and in the bare silence Kathleen poured herself some wine and said to Frank, "We're fine at the clinic. Summer is injuries at home and work and up at the lake—this frost is as good as a vaccine." Mason could tell she'd gone into some kind of mode, because she could not look at Sonny, and she felt mechanical, forced. "We're still losing nurses," she went on. There was a steady turnover at the medical center because the women's husbands' jobs kept disappearing. "We're going to end up with a bumper crop of trainees and assistants."

"How's Mr. Brand here doing?" Frank asked her.

"He's been worse," Jimmy said. "This woman's an angel." He had spoken quietly, and the quiet now grew again.

"I've made an executive decision." Marci came in from the kitchen and leaned on the doorjamb "We are not going to sit in the dining room. We are going to eat right here. We'll make a little buffet table and be ready in a minute." Kathleen stood and sidestepped into the kitchen, and Sonny asked Marci if she could help with anything. Craig asked who needed any wine, and he put two more logs on the fire. Frank asked Larry if he'd tried the antelope. Mason looked across at Jimmy and said, "You here, or are you dreaming already?"

Jimmy's face broke, and he smiled. He was nodding faintly along with the song "In My Room." "This is too slow, what a gambit, and it requires a great vocal," he said.

"And a touch depressing," Frank said.

"Brian Wilson," Jimmy said. "He is a giant—the sad giant." Suddenly the room filled with the smell of steaming turkey, and the business of the dinner began. A hundred dishes from the depot desk were shipped into the kitchen, and forty others came the other way. Marci brought Jimmy his plate of turkey and mushroom dressing and five tender spears of asparagus under melting butter and flecked with pepper. As platters rattled and knives were dropped and wine poured, one by one the diners crept back into the den settling onto the corners of things. Larry came last with a drumstick as big as his fist, and when he sat on the floor, Jimmy tapped his glass and held it out to the room. "Friends," he said, "Thank you for moving this holiday up for me. Happy Thanksgiving. It is sweet for me to be here. Thank you, Marci." In the silence as the CDs changed, each person in the room leaned forward and touched his glass with theirs.

"Please eat," Marci said. "You'll be up here for real Thanksgiving too, big boy," she said to Jimmy, "unless you spill on the couch."

"This is so good, Mrs. Ralston," Sonny said. She sat beside Frank on the ottoman, her plate on her knees.

"It's Marci, please." Marci told her.

"I better make my announcement right now," Frank said, stabbing the air with his fork. Faces lifted in alarm, and the quiet was so strange that Frank said, "Hey. It's just this. Gentlemen, I am a liberty taker, and I have taken the liberty of entering us into the battle of the bands up at the world-famous Pronghorn Bar and Grill outside Gillette. I applied using twenty-five dollars of my own money, because the deadline was yesterday. I'm hoping you will all join me in thinking this a worthy, kick-ass venture that would be more than any of us has had lately, meaning the last thirty years, more or less."

"The what?" Craig said. His mouth was full of turkey. "What?"

"Let's just do it. Who's driving?" Jimmy said. "I'm in. Not that there's much of me."

"A battle of what bands?" Craig said.

"You play two songs." Frank said. "There's prizes."

"When is it?" Mason asked.

"In three weeks. The day after Thanksgiving. Friday."

"You want to?" Mason asked Craig.

"What the hell is it with this fall?" Craig said. He lifted and drained his wine. "I want to do everything."

"Suddenly all our practice assumes a focus," Jimmy said.

"Two songs," Craig said. "Hell, we knew six or seven in the glory days."

"Six," Mason said, "We knew all the words to nine, at least Jimmy did. And this would be one of them." Mason went to the CD player and adjusted the volume louder as the Zombies sang "Time of the Season."

"You know this?" Jimmy said to Larry.

He shook his head no. Mason and Frank were already singing along. Kathleen joined them. Craig mouthed the drumbeat, and Jimmy took the lead, his ghosted tenor blending with Kathleen's: " 'With pleasured hands . . . promised lands . . . It's the time of the season for loving!' " When Jimmy stopped, his heart was pounding in his arms, and he closed his eyes.

"We're in," Frank said. "Life on Earth is in. On the application I put that we'd had a professional career sometime ago, but we'd taken a little time off for personal reasons."

At this Jimmy Brand laughed out loud, the first time in a year at least, and it shocked him to laugh as if something had burst in his face, and he rode it out and along, his head against the back of the couch until he was coughing. "Oh god," he said settling down. "Oh god."

"Battle of the bands," Craig said again. "That is a road trip. Marci, you up for that?"

"We'll see. I may have to work."

"Let me see." Craig rose and stepped around the room pouring wine. "You can either road it with a dangerous rock 'n' roll band, hang out, tell people near and far that you're with the band, or you can go to work at a museum. A tough call for the modern woman. Kathleen, tell me what it is about the modern woman? What does the modern woman want?"

"The modern woman wants exactly what the modern man wants." Kathleen swirled the last of her wine in the bright stemmed glass. "She wants to put out the fire and rescue everybody, and then when it's safe, she wants to go back in and wait to be rescued. I know we're among friends, but it hurts to tell the truth."

"Is that it?" Craig said to Marci. "How do I arrange it?"

Marci turned quickly to Jimmy Brand, who had pushed his food around and eaten a bite of everything but not much more. "Jimmy?"

"I'm okay. It's a wonderful meal."

"Elizabeth, my wife, would have said a woman wants to have fungus-free toenails and the chance to dance once a season," Mason said.

"I've got that," Marci said, kicking her stockinged foot into the air. "It's like everything else. They say there's a cure, but there's no cure."

The basket of hot dinner rolls made a trip around the room hand to hand, and Craig brought in the gravy boat for a tour. "Take notes on this, Larry. It could save you some trouble."

"Could but won't," Frank said.

The coffee table was as laden with dishes as a table gets. If one more were pushed onto the surface, another would fall off the other side. They all looked at it as if it were some strange altar that had arisen for rites not fully explained. Mason crossed his legs and sank deeper into the couch, his wine in two hands on his lap. "I am well nourished," he said. Marci nodded at him, and he said, "What?"

"No 'what,' you innocent boy. You've had enough time to get your innocence back four times. What happened to you?"

"I played to win—that's what happened." Mason set his glass down carefully and looked up. "Everything I did. It was just me. When I got to Minnesota for school, I don't know whether it was because I was insecure or scared or arrogant, which I have certainly been since, but everything I did, I did to win." He looked around at his friends. "You know me. I studied people and I watched. I learned how to dress and I learned what to say, and as I met people, one by one, I won them. I made myself important to them in some way. The guys in the dorms, my professors, all my professors, the staff of the union building, the newspaper, the frat guys, and every single girl I ever met."

"You were an asshole?" Frank said. "I don't get it."

"Mostly," Mason said. "I got close to these people, mirrored something they needed. I was a good listener, and I was about half bright. They took it, as I did sometimes, as friendship. Something. The women took it as love. Don't mistake this. I didn't set out to hurt anybody. I was good to everyone. I had the three P's: I was prompt, polite, and I came with small but tasteful presents." Mason drank his wine. "So yeah, an asshole. You think I can get over it?"

"Prompt?" Frank said. "I didn't know that counted."

"Were you in love, ever?" Marci asked Mason. Everyone had sunk further into the couches. Jimmy Brand pulled his knees up with his hands and rearranged his legs.

"You okay, Jimmy?"

"Soaring," he said. "What's your answer?"

"The answer is I don't know," Mason said. "I should know in another month, living in my campsite on Berry Street. Here's the big news for me: I've never really been alone before. I see that somewhere in law school, first or second year, right in the thick of assembling my career, collecting options, tending them, keeping them open, I lost myself to what I thought I should be. I couldn't tell, even writing briefs, when I was acting. It all felt vaguely real. From time to time, I'd close an argument with the same notions, wording, and then I began to hear myself in restaurants saying the same thing to somebody, good things I mean, true for me, but nevertheless, the same. So I constructed a persona, and I think *he* was in love. He was certainly a fucking success. With Elizabeth, I kept hoping I could shove him aside, get close, get . . . what? Get in it, instead of next to it. I loved her as well as I could, which was probably as poorly as anything I've done."

Marci went to Mason's chair and put her hand on his shoulder.

"You're a little tough on yourself, Mason." Jimmy said. He was speaking quietly. "I think this is the astringent version you've given us." Marci now reached and turned down two of the lamps

"Thank you," Jimmy told her. "My eyes are something else." He turned to Mason. "You've done a lot of good."

"We're talking," Mason said. "I'm glad to be here."

Frank spoke. "I'm sorry you're sick, Jimmy."

"I feel good tonight, Frank," he answered, "But yeah, I'm sick."

Kathleen stood to take a dish into the kitchen, and Marci said, "Let's don't. Let's leave it and sit here with these people." She whispered, "The dishes will keep them here. It's been so long."

"The butter," Kathleen said.

"Let's leave the butter out too," Marci said.

"Remember that time you guys came to the hospital with the guitar?"

"I do," Jimmy said.

"What a year," Frank said. "It's hard to believe you're here." The silence that followed held them. Frank stood and drew a pint from the small keg on the counter. "Anybody else?" he said, getting no takers. "What is it, Jimmy? You know I just don't know. I can't see it from here. How did you know? Did it creep up on you, or did you always just know? Did you know in the day?"

"Jesus, Frank," Mason said.

"No," Jimmy said, "it's good. Frank said it: we're talking. Mason started it. What do you want to know, Frank?" Jimmy settled in and put his arm on the back of the deep couch.

"Wasn't Winger gay?" Mason said to Frank. "You knew him."

"Winger, Big Bob, who bartended for me for six or seven years, not to mention Duane Boorman, and Tim's brother. I've known plenty of gay guys, okay?" Frank said. "But I've never, ever talked to one about it. Have you?"

Mason looked at Frank. "This isn't truth or dare."

Everyone watched Frank push his beer onto the tabletop, shifting dishes two then three deep. When it balanced, he lifted his palms. "Let it go," Frank said. "I'm just not as evolved as you, Mason. You got out of town, had a big life. Jimmy, I'm so goddamned glad to see you again, no shit."

Jimmy pointed at Frank, his face a joyous smile. "When we showed you that guitar, you were scared of it." He nodded at Larry and continued. "We took him a bass guitar in the hospital, and he looked at it like it was a torture device."

"It was, for a while," Frank said.

"Only for our audiences," Craig said.

"A good bass player is key," Jimmy said, "and Frank was."

"Is," Sonny said, and everyone turned to her. "He still plays pickup with some of the bands."

"A ringer," Craig said. "Good deal."

"I knew in high school," Jimmy said. "I knew it, and I knew it wouldn't pass." He folded his hands in his lap and spoke again softly, just over the Zombies singing "Tell Her No." "You take it as a kind of unhappiness for a while. I've talked to a lot of people about this."

"You wrote about it," Mason said.

"You're a misfit, which is exactly what everyone is for a while. Everyone. Then you see your friends start to sort themselves out, get married, like that. I was alone for a long time. I knew what it was, and I was surprised when others started to see it in me. Pleased. I spent almost five years in St. Louis, working for the *Street Sheet*, learning to write, and I met some people at the paper who were great. It was incredibly sweet to belong."

"What were you doing?" Frank said. "You mean dating?"

"I saw a lot of people way before anybody got sick. Yeah, it's dating."

"When two gay guys go out to dinner, who pays?"

Marci laughed, and Mason rolled his eyes. "For god's sake."

"No, really," Frank went on. "Who pays?"

Jimmy was wide awake now, his fatigue burning in his knees and back; he could feel himself smiling. "The answer is the same for all of us, Frank. Whoever has come courting. That's universal etiquette. And etiquette is everything. Daniel, my partner, loved to quote the movie *Gigi*. 'Bad table manners, my dear Gigi, have broken up more households than infidelity.'" Jimmy regretted the joke immediately, but he was out of breath now.

The moment tipped on them all, but Craig Ralston righted it with "You mean if I knew which fork to use, I could have a girlfriend?"

"You can't have a girlfriend," Marci said, standing. "But you can help me with the pies."

In the kitchen she quickly set out platters of pie and topped some with ice cream as Craig held it all on a tray. With him standing before her like that, she pointed the ice cream scoop at his face. "You want a girlfriend?" It came out as she knew it might: serious, awkward. Not even a joke. What was she saying? But it felt good to say, scratching some spot within that she didn't even know was sore.

"Oh, yeah," Craig said. "Then I want to take her to a dinner party where you glare at me all night long. No thanks, one woman is plenty."

As he spoke, she looked into his face, knowing her secret was open to be read. She could not control her expression. It was a moment like she'd never had before; she could feel Stewart's hands. His face had been right there, his breath, and he had said, "Oh my, you are so fine." Her heart was beating. If she spoke again, one life would end, this life, and she wanted trouble like that—she wanted everything out and said.

"Marci," Craig said, indicating the tray and nodding at the corner piece of pie, "put another scoop on that one for me, will ya? You're hoarding the ice cream."

When she did that and he went back into the other room, Marci stood still until ice cream dripped from the scoop onto the hardwood floor.

In the den, pie ruled. Plates of it balanced on knees and in hands, floated over all the other dinner wreckage.

"This is Kathleen's pie," Frank said. "No question about that."

"Both are," Marci came in. "We'll have tea in a minute."

"Can I have some tea, Nurse Kathleen?"

"You're asking me after you chugged that beer? You can have some decaf."

"Yes, you can," Marci said. "How are you feeling?"

Jimmy was eating the moist pumpkin pie with a spoon. "I'll be no help with the dishes."

"That's what they use me for," Larry said.

"What did your partner do?" Frank asked Jimmy Brand.

"He ran a restaurant downtown, and he wrote freelance travel pieces," Jimmy said.

"An upscale place?" Frank said. "Nineteen-dollar martinis?"

"Sixteen," Jimmy Brand said. "Yeah, it was pricey. You needed reservations a week out."

"Just like the Antlers," Frank said. "How'd you meet him?"

"Jimmy met him at a big party at a famous playwright's apartment. They met in the kitchen." Mason said.

"Mason's done his homework," Jimmy said. He'd finished half his pie, and he handed the plate to Larry, who stacked it on one of the impossible dish mountains. "I met Daniel at an opening-night party many years ago." He smiled in the soft light. "It was as weird as anything I've known. I'd been in the city for a while, and it was strong stuff. For me. Anything you wanted—right there." Marci leaned over and set a cup and saucer in Jimmy's hand, and he sipped the tea. "And it wasn't weird to be gay. I mean, for the first time in a long time, I felt normal. Imagine. I loved it, but I didn't think I'd fall in love. There was a lot of hooking up, and I thought the random energy was enough.

"But Daniel changed it all. With the restaurant, he was the center of a lot of stuff, and this party was about him as impresario as much as anything. People wanted to be with Daniel, and who was I? Sometimes," he said to Larry, "it's like you never got out of high school. Anyway, at the party he told me to follow him into the kitchen, and I did. There was like a group headed that way, and after I got in the door . . ." Jimmy Brand paused and set his cup and saucer onto his leg with both hands. "He put his hand on the door and shut it, you know, with his hand straight out." Jimmy extended his arm. "He was strong, and he just held the door shut, and these people were bumping the door, like knocking. I could feel it, the door bumping against me. And he kissed me there. It was this kiss where he held the door shut and kissed me there. No big sexual kiss, just the finest kiss you get, a true kiss, the door absolutely thumping. When we stopped kissing, he looked at me and said, 'Do you understand?' And I saw his eyes, a look you don't forget, and I understood." Jimmy Brand said to Frank, "That's what we do. Sorry for the speech."

Kathleen moved onto the couch and put her arm around him.

"It's okay," he whispered, and tried some more tea. "We were to-gether for thirteen years. When he died, he weighed exactly one hun-dred pounds."

There was a heavy stillness as they all sat in their places. The fire broke and a log fell and the light redoubled against the curved edge of plates and glasses. Mason was deep in the couch beside Kathleen, and he found and lifted his wineglass half full. "Oh, a toast," he said, "to Daniel and to the writer Jimmy Brand."

"To Jimmy," Frank raised his glass of beer.

In the soft light the teacups and the goblets rose, and the members of the party drank. The room had settled on Jimmy like a shawl.

"You want me to take you home?" Mason asked Jimmy.

"Somebody's going to have to haul me," Jimmy said.

"You can stay up here," Larry said. "Camp in."

"Absolutely," Craig added. As he went to get up, he shifted the ot-toman, and his knee hit one of the tiered plates, sending a shiver through the fragile architecture of dirty dishes. They all watched it rattle, shift, and settle, spoons rolling in every cup.

"Larry," Jimmy said, "you and I are the lucky ones here. Because we're the only ones whose mothers still wait up." He handed his tea-cup to Kathleen. "I've got to go home."

Sonny had been sitting on the floor against Frank's knees. She climbed onto her knees and pointed at the clutter. "Shall we?"

Marci said, "Turn the music up, and let's clear the table."

In the immediate clatter, Mason turned to Jimmy and helped him up gradually. They held each other steady there, looking down on the jumbled coffee table, and then they just embraced, Mason's arms around his neck. For Jimmy Brand it was like being on stilts far above the forbidden city. Whenever he moved these days, his blood took a minute to catch up.

Mason took his friend at both elbows. "You up?"

"Up." Jimmy said. "Way up here."

ELEVEN

At the Pronghorn

It was a road trip, and that's what Craig called out when he finally shut the tailgate of his Cherokee. He was ready for the showdown, and there was a definite bounce in his step, had been all morning. "It is time for us to get out of town!" he called. He went over to Frank, who sat with Sonny in his idling Explorer and put his hand on his forehead by the driver-side window. "Do we know what we're doing, Sonny?" he said. "Shouldn't you have prevented this?" He didn't wait for an answer but held up both hands to show he was done and ready, and he said, "Follow us." His construction job with young Dr. Marchant had come through this week, and they had signed the contract. He was to build a large guesthouse, almost two thousand square feet, as well as remodel a kitchen and library in the main house. He'd even contracted the foundation work. It was top to bottom, and he was thrilled—the project he'd always wanted. At seven that morning Craig had ordered trusses and plywood and forty square Southwestern Rose tiles for the guesthouse roof. He was under way, and he'd periodically called out, "All right, Mama!" as they'd packed up. He came around the Cherokee as clouds pooled in charcoal banks over the gray town in the darkening afternoon. The forecast was snow, and the wind chittering through the bare scrub oak around the Ralstons' drive had the scent of ice in it. The SUV was running, the heater on, and everyone was aboard: Marci, Mason, Kathleen, and Larry.

"It takes a hardy man to be whistling about roofing all winter," Mason said when Craig climbed in into the driver's seat.

"Not all winter. Two weeks, and we won't have that privilege until spring. As you know, I'm looking for a nonunion crew. Do you lawyers have a union?"

"Fraternity," Mason said. "It's worse—it means we collude, party hearty, and cheat on the exams."

Craig wheeled the car around in the driveway and started down the mountain. Marci sat in the front seat. "The best thing you can do with a beautiful new house like this is leave it," Craig said. "It makes you a king."

"Who is talking like this?" Marci said.

Mason sat in back with Kathleen and Larry. Frank and Sonny, who had been waiting in his idling Explorer, followed. The guitars and gear were stowed along with everyone's bags and two coolers full of drinks and lunch and candy.

"You in, Larry? Dr. Marchant's guesthouse. I'm doubling what you make at the store."

"He's got school," Marci said. "He doesn't want to be on a roof in the snow."

"The great drama of American football is over, Mom. High school is closing down a chapter at a time. I'll have hours."

" 'Ralston and Son Construction. Guesthouses, add-ons, decks, garages. The best work in Wyoming.' "

Larry said, "What about 'Two Guys with Hammers'?"

"Or," Mason said, " 'Son and Ralston.' I've never seen that, some kid carrying his father. You guys could make it work." They wended through the frigid town to the highway and turned north past the hill and the cemetery and the ruined weed lots and wasteland and the turn-off of the reservoir, driving north under low clouds that all afternoon worked at a layer of pale yellow light between the dark sky and the dark earth, a car or two hurrying back toward Oakpine in the empty world.

"Seriously," Larry said to Mason. "You've just landed on this planet, and we've picked you up as you look confused standing beside the highway. Now, look at it, sir. Those lines are the railroad, the rest is about to be snowed on. We have snow here. We have winter here. If you can see a bush big enough to hide behind, you can imagine an antelope hiding behind it. We have antelope on this planet. I'd like your answer now: do you want to stay?"

Mason smiled. "It's a cold night coming on. But I'll need to know one thing: what's an antelope?"

Kathleen laughed, and Larry said, "See. You get out of town twenty minutes, and it's a planet with real short days and long wind. It's getting dark already."

"They'll have that big bar all warmed up," Mason said. "Ask me then."

Craig was slowly shaking his head.

"What?" Marci said.

"Oh my dear," he said. "Battle of the bands. What are we doing?"

"When was the last time anybody did one extra thing, something weird? Something not pragmatic?" The dash lights glowed, and the heater warmed the vehicle as it was swallowed by the closing weather and the heavy winter twilight.

"I went—" Craig started.

"Not a fishing trip," Kathleen said. "Something like this, a bona fide extra. Or are you planning on winning this thing and restarting your musical career?"

"Now she knows," Craig said. "Hardware was fun for a while, but get real. That trophy is going to look good in the front window of the store."

"I wish Jimmy could have come," Marci said. The car was quiet, and after half a minute Larry said, "I'm going to give him the report, which means you better all behave."

Jimmy's name had come over the car, and in the dark day they drove quietly through the plains. Larry had visited the little garage the day before and, with the Fender guitar, had shown Jimmy his four new chords, playing the muted strings in the gray light. Unplugged like that, it sounded like a ukulele. When he looked up, Jimmy was out, his neck arched back as if in pain. Larry checked his breathing and was relieved when Kathleen arrived. She checked Jimmy's vital signs while Larry watched. She adjusted Jimmy on the pillow and arranged the covers and left without speaking. Larry quickly followed her into the winter afternoon. "What?" he had said.

"Jimmy won't be going to Gillette tomorrow," she said. "He's too weak." They were standing on the Brands' old driveway, and Larry felt the news for what it was. You go along knowing, but when you do know, it still is a surprise.

Now, in the car with these people, Larry felt it again and felt it as a test. He was happy to have had this fall knowing his father in a new way, and he didn't plan on making a new friend and losing him. He listened to Mason talking to Marci about fund-raising and long-term issues at the museum—a donor strategy. And then Kathleen quizzed Mason about when he was returning to Denver. His only answer: "Whenever feels too soon." And then, unable to be glib about it, he added, "I don't know. The clock's off." Craig was silent, driving, laying out in his head his plan of attack on the construction job he had ahead. Larry wondered if these people would ever be together in this way again, five in a car in the snow late in the year on the old highway. Finally Larry said, "Jimmy taught me four new chords yesterday, and I gave my word to try them in public."

When they neared Gillette in the gloom, Craig drove right past the Pronghorn. "Dad," Larry said from the backseat, "that's it." Off to the left there had been a sixty or seventy cars parked in a jumble, the pink neon beer signs almost obscured.

"Really," Craig said. "All those cars? I thought it was a junkyard."

"No," Mason said from the backseat, where he sat with Larry and Kathleen. "That's it. He's got a crowd tonight." Everyone in the car was quiet, and he added, "When I was a kid, every time we drove by Mangum's junkyard west of town, my dad would say, "Oh boy, Agnes must have a roast on—they've got company."

Craig slowed and waited for Frank's black Explorer. As they pulled U-turns on the two-lane, Frank lowered his window and called out. "I thought the crowd scared you off. We're going to have an audience!"

As they approached the Pronghorn now, the huge sign lit up suddenly and began to flash, blue and white, the profile of an antelope, and as the two vehicles picked through the overfilled parking lot, snow began to fall, as a sudden graphic mist of a billion dots.

There were eleven bands. Three were from Gillette, three from greater Sheridan, two up from Laramie, one each from Casper and the hamlet of Sojourn, and Life on Earth in their reunion gig. The owner of the Pronghorn was Bobby Peralta, who had taken the place over from his dad. He wore a black satin shirt with silver button covers and a silver cow-skull bolo tie. They'd all met before. The Pronghorn was a place where you stopped on the way home from the antelope hunt, and all season you could see pickups parked there with game in the beds. Bobby had been in high school in Gillette and had actually heard the band the one time they'd played here thirty years before.

"This place used to be out of town," Craig said as he shook Bobby's hand.

"You can't get out of town in this sorry state," Bobby said. "It's all found out and built up. How you been?"

"Busy. Oakpine's exploded, and I supply the paint." He introduced everybody: Marci, Kathleen, Larry, Mason, Sonny, and Frank, whom Bobby knew because of his brewery.

"We're only playing," Frank told the man, "if you can guarantee that there're no talent scouts here. We're not interested in being plucked from obscurity."

"You're safe on that count. Here." Bobby gave them all string necklaces with yellow passes looped on each. "All your drinks are mine, including as much of Frank's new lager as you can drink. And I've got a table for you up front." He looked at his clipboard. "We'll start at seven and do four bands, break, four more, break and then finish with three. Craig, why don't you meet me on stage at about ten to, and we'll draw the order."

They'd been standing in the back hallway beside the kitchen and could hear the crowd in the main barroom. "I believe I'll use the house drum kit," Craig said. "No sense showing everybody what Larry did to my snare way back when."

"This is going to require a drink," Mason said. He looked at his watch. "Twenty minutes to live. This is going to require two."

As he stepped toward the barroom, Kathleen took his elbow. "I'll go with," she said.

"Hey, Kathleen," Frank said to his ex-wife.

"Hey, Frank. Sonny."

"Can you believe we're here, we're going to do this?"

"I have no trouble believing anything, Frank. My credibility has been tested."

"You sour bitch," Sonny said. It was crowded in the passageway, and everybody stood still.

Kathleen stopped and smiled. "I know," she said. "But I'm working on it, Sonny. It's not permanent." She touched the young woman's wrist. "Listen, I just said your name."

Craig and Marci were already at the bar when Mason and Kathleen came up. There was no place to sit or stand, but Marci had winnowed between two guys and got an elbow in and was talking to the bartender. The cowboy she'd leaned over looked to Craig and said, "She act this way at home?"

She turned to the man and rubbed his cheek with the back of her knuckles, smiling. "I'm only going to be a minute, darlin'." Craig liked this side of her, the cowgirl, although she'd hidden it for some time now. He hadn't heard her say darlin' for years. It had been too long since he'd done anything with Marci except go over the household accounts or call her parents. He was having fun—it was a road trip. This day was crazy, and then he was going to build a guesthouse in town.

Marci handed back beers to the men and lifted two white wines to her group, one for Kathleen.

The Pronghorn had been a little tavern three miles south of Gillette, a place the roughnecks could stop on the way back to town. Over the years it had grown, first with a room on one side for four pool tables and then a large quonset in the rear with a hardwood floor for dancing. This area was lined with tables behind a low wooden corral. There were neon beer signs everywhere, red and blue and green, so the general glow added to the odd effect of having three ceilings of different heights in the gerrymandered room. Tonight all the tables were full, two and three pitchers of beer on each, four, and the dance floor too was packed with a fluid, partisan crowd, groups of people churning forward, cheering their friends, under a glacial slip of cigarette smoke that drifted toward the high center.

Marci was lit, feeling her nerves ebb and flow as a physical thing. Ever since her long flirtation with Stewart, she'd been out of her life, beside it, and everything seemed simplified. She could easily shed one life and pick up another; there were times every day when it felt she already had. She could leave tomorrow. Craig was strong enough for any new thing, and she'd finished her work with Larry. He was a good kid and had been self-reliant for these last two years. There were times when she felt Craig would understand—she had to move on. And there were times some nights when she started awake in bed, seized by a terror that made her put her teeth into her lip. What was she doing?

Now, as they weaved though the tight throng toward their table, her face burned. She felt a charge she couldn't contain. This was better than being numb, she guessed, but god. She kept looking at Craig for a clue. If he gave her an opening, she'd tell him, but she was out of sync, and people knew it. On the way up she'd been silent in the car, afraid that if she spoke, her sentences would go right off the edge.

As they'd been packing the lunch, Kathleen had asked her what was the matter. Marci wanted to say that the matter was that she was in love. There were times, when she was alone in her car driving home from the museum, when she said that aloud, "I'm in love." It sounded good, and it felt good to say, but later she'd look at Craig when he came in or when they were watching television, and all the rush was gone. She wasn't in love; that was something from a cheap refrain. Stewart would have leaned her against his desk, closing his eyes as he did, and pulled at her needfully, whispering, "I want all of this. When can I have all of this?" They burrowed against each other. It thrilled her and repelled her and ultimately made her tentative, and she'd straighten until they both stood and adjusted their clothing. She felt brave and stupid. It was too late to be doing this; it was never too late. In the Pronghorn, she ducked under the rope where the bands had their tables and sat down with Larry. The others were just arriving too, and Craig was already on the stage. She looked at her son. "You're not drinking, are you?" she asked.

"Not really," he said. "Some pop. I'll be your designated son."

"Good." She put her empty wineglass on the table. "I am. Drinking. Where's that waitress?" The three guys in red T-shirts at the next table all turned and checked her out, her black satin western shirt. "Hello to you," one said.

"Where you guys from?" she asked them.

"Gillette." They were all about thirty, with short hair and sideburns. "We're the Coyotes, pretty lady, the band to root for if you want to know. You could even sit at our table. We encourage groupies." The speaker, a thin young guy with a goatee, waved a finger at the two full pitchers. "In fact, we look after our true fans without worrying about the expense. We are dedicated to them hoof, hide, and bone."

"Oh, shit," Marci flirted back. "And I'm already with a band, darn it."

"You won't be for long."

There was a drumroll, and Bobby Peralta came on the microphone: "Hey, everybody, welcome to the Pronghorn Bar and Grill, the only four-star establishment in Wyoming and North and South Dakota.

Tonight, as you all know, we are happy to host the Pronghorn Battle of the Bands!" There was a roar and clapping and ragged whistles until Bobby held up his hands. In one he had a pillowcase full of pool balls. "Ladies and gentlemen, we will now select the order for the Pronghorn Battle of the Bands!" Another upheaval, screaming and a howl or two, followed. Bobby then had a representative from each band reach into the bag and pull out a ball.

"What'd he get?" Frank said. "Is it solid or stripe?"

Craig, like everyone else on the stage, was holding his choice high over his head in two fingers. The noise was impenetrable.

"Is it the eight ball? Tell me it's the goddamned eight ball."

"It's the nine," Mason leaned forward and said loudly. "We're late in the lineup."

"We should have got you shirts that matched," Marci said to Frank.

"What?"

"We should have got you shirts that matched!" she yelled. One of the red shirts at the next table stood and bent to Marci. "What'd you draw?"

"Nine," she said.

"It's not too late to drop out," he toasted them with his glass of beer.

"You're drunk," she told him.

"It's the only way. We're the Coyotes, and we will not perform unless inebriated."

"Good luck," Mason told the man.

"Well, yeah," the guy said thoughtfully. "But we're still going to kick your ass and take this girl here as a trophy. Please excuse my frankness."

Bobby Peralta named the bands, each to an explosion, sometimes a small explosion, from some quarter of the jammed barroom. Then he introduced the judges: a deejay from Jackson Hole, the owner of a record store in Laramie, and his own wife, Mrs. Annette Peralta, a happy blond woman in a full turquoise body suit. He tried to say something about the categories they'd be judging on, but no one could hear, and then he showed the three trophies, which brought a roar, general yelling, and applause. The dance floor was cleared or almost cleared, and for a few minutes there was relative quiet in the Pronghorn, as snow settled on the arched tar roof and waitresses with trays of drinks worked the room.

Frank leaned over to Larry and said, "Are we ready for this?"

Larry nodded. "Not really. But it's two songs. We're tight. Jimmy said to let it rip. I have a feeling this is our last gig forevermore. Whether we know what we're doing or not, let it rip."

Frank scanned the cordoned tables of bands. A couple groups had cowboy hats, and one band wore sharkskin suits. Sonny had topped everyone's beer, and Frank said, "Thank you, dear, but you're not working tonight. I'll pour."

"It's fine," Sonny said. "It's not a problem." She slid into the chair at the end of the table and touched Kathleen's arm. "I'm sorry for that remark earlier," Sonny said. "I didn't mean it. I'm so fucking touchy. I don't want to fight with you or your friends." Kathleen didn't move, so Sonny slid closer so no one else could hear her. "Every week I've been in town, every week for two years, somebody in the bar will start it. You've got more friends than anybody I've ever known, that's for sure. You're an angel, I guess, and they do not like me, even though they don't know me. They have said things near me and to me, and I haven't said anything back. But Kathleen, I just want to say one thing to you. I didn't do anything to you. I know it must be hard to see me with

Frank, but I didn't wreck your marriage, did I? Everybody says that, but we got together November two years ago, I swear. Not a day earlier. No joke. He told me that he'd been out of the house all summer. Is that wrong?" She had whispered all this urgently, and as she stopped speaking and lifted her chin, tears glossed her eyes.

Kathleen looked past Sonny for a minute: Larry, Mason, Marci, Frank. Larry had unfolded the playlist: six songs they knew. They all had a finger on the sheet as if it were a map. They had to choose two. Kathleen smiled weakly at the younger woman and then stood up and pulled her. "Let's get a drink," she said, and the two of them disappeared into the smoky room.

Craig came back to the table and plunked the nine ball into the ashtray. "We're hitting clean up," he said. "We'll know what we're up against." He sat down and squeezed Marci's shoulders. "We're going to need some support from our fans." He looked her over. "My, but you look fine," he said. "Am I right, Mason?"

"You both look good. Marci here," Mason said, toasting her with his glass of beer, "was class . . ."

"Historian," she filled in.

"I've seen the yearbook," Larry said. "What did you record?"

Marci gave him a look as the first band, a group called Mountain Standard, rattled into John Denver's "Rocky Mountain High." It took them a full minute to put it all to the beat, but they did and finished the song going away. After the whooping and applause faded, Craig said, "If that's what we're up against, we're taking a trophy home for Jimmy. These guys are soft." As if on his cue, the band now tried "Take It Easy," making it sound as if they were reading the lyrics for the first time, and making the whole a vague exercise. At the end Mountain Standard bowed and bowed until there was no one clapping. They were still waving at their friends when the second band, Wind Chill Factor, six guys in black T-shirts, walked onto the stage.

Wind Chill Factor was all bass, heavy bass, so much so their songs were unidentifiable, a beat and a thrum that simply shook the room, every table and every glass. Larry felt it in his cracked rib and listened through the gridlock vibration and thought he heard "Layla," but it would have had to be at double time. The six band members stood like mourners at the noisiest funeral of all time, feet planted, raking their instruments, the drum player hunched mostly out of sight. When their second song came in for a landing, the air was immediately filled with white static. Everyone's ears were ringing. A moment later the applause came as a kind of relief, and it was touched up with laughter. As the artists in Wind Chill Factor filed off the stage, nodding their heads in recognition of their significant contribution to the world of rock 'n' roll, Mason told his table, "Count your fillings."

Larry was writing the name of each band on a card in his shirt pocket so he could give the report to Jimmy Brand, as promised. He also had told Wendy he'd give her the news.

The third band was four guys who looked like brothers; they all had identical razored goatees. They could sing. They started a reasonable, if slow version of "Blue Eyes Crying in the Rain," and when the three lead men met at the mike for the chorus, people listened. They got it all and changed the mood in the room for those minutes. Then they made the strategic error of singing a folksy ballad full of strange religious references. "God did a lot of stuff in that song," Craig told the table when the goatees were through.

Then it was a two-man band—the Experts, they called themselves—and they tried to cover "Sweet Home Alabama," which was a curious choice because they lacked the punch for it, and the guitar player was rusty and behind the lyric, and it emerged as a kind of tender credo, a dirge, which wasn't unpleasant. After their second song, Bobby Peralta came up and announced a twenty-minute beer break, and the intermission was louder than the bands, and the room stood up and was at the bar four deep. The sound system filled with Johnny Cash singing "I Walk the Line," the only one of his songs that would be heard all day. Frank came back from the men's and said, "Armando Jensen is here. Somewhere."

"Goddamned pennies in the urinal," Sonny said.

"He does that?" Marci said.

"Everywhere," Sonny said. "Some men won't piss without marking the spot."

"I can't afford it," Craig smiled. They were all speaking loudly, the room a roar.

Frank laughed. "He calls it his tithe."

"Jimmy should write about this place. There's some characters."

"He did," Mason said. "And you're looking at them." He lifted his coffee cup. They all touched every glass. Mason showed the group his hands, which were trembling, and said, "Look. This is very fine. I'm nervous."

"It has been a long time," Frank said, "but nobody's paying attention, so we'll be all right."

Shirley Stiver appeared through the mob, dragging a younger man by the hand. She was done up proper in a golden western dress with tiny beaded fringe along the scalloped pockets. Her partner was all denim, the new shirt stiff, and he shook everyone's hand.

"Your honor," Frank said, "out among the people." He said to Mason, "Tom's the mayor."

"I'm undercover," the man said.

"And out of town," Frank added. "Good to see you."

"When do you guys play?" Shirley asked Mason, tousling his hair.

"Too soon," he said. "You're going to want to get a drink, more than one."

"Break a leg, Oakpine. We're working the room."

"Everybody's working this room," Mason said.

"And Shirley," Frank called to her, as the couple moved back into the crowd, "I already broke my leg. We're just going to make some noise and stay out of the weather."

The milling around didn't really stop after the break, as the room had filled even more now. All the latecomers out of the dark shook off snow in the entryway and called out to their friends. The next band was called the Cutbank Cowboys, and they had some difficulties, stopping their first number right in the middle so somebody could hand the bass guitarist a glass of whiskey. They tried to start over, and there was hooting, and Bobby Peralta came up and said, "Just go to your next song." The drinking musician looked at Bobby and took the microphone and drank and said, "I'd rather have this glass of jack than the goddamned trophy, Mr. Peralta." He was drunk and got a huge cheer by his remarks, so he added, "Besides, we are filing a protest. Are there any lawyers in the house?" This got a huge cheer as well. He drank again and dropped the empty glass and said, "Goddamned lawyers!" This raised the roof, and Mason called out, "Amen!" The Cutbank Cowboys finished with "Tie a Yellow Ribbon," and the dance floor was shoulder to shoulder.

The next band took a while to set up as they changed the drum kit to their own, with their name enameled on the facing, the Moonlight Gamblers. "Hey, we've got troubles," Frank said. "I've seen these guys down in Laramie. They're for real."

"I thought this was amateurs," Craig said.

"No, it's all comers."

The room filled with the sinister prelude to "Hotel California," and it got as quiet as it had been for an hour. It was clear these guys were good, and while the dance floor overflowed again, a group of three dozen adoring fans stood in front of the stage. Mason rolled his eyes at Frank. "Fate is speaking." The song closed, and the ovation rocked with whistles and calls for two minutes.

A woman came up to the varnished wooden lounge corral. She had on a tricolor cowboy shirt and snug white levi's. She folded her arms, waiting for Larry, who was bent making notes on the jam-packed table. "Can I help you?" Marci asked her.

"Not really, ma'am. Unless you want to dance. I'm waiting on this gentleman." Larry looked up. "Yeah, you. Let's just dance, if you will?

"You go, boy," Frank said. "We've got two bands to go."

Larry colored slightly and shrugged and lifted himself over the rail and said, "Okay then."

Marci watched the couple melt into the clog of dancers, as the lead singer of the Moonlight Gamblers lifted his hand for silence, which he received, and then sang the word, "Maybe," as the soulful beginning of Willie Nelson's song "You Were Always on My Mind." Marci's face bore a version of astonishment. "He's underage," she said.

"This is Gillette," Frank said. "No such thing."

"We're dancing," Marci told Craig, and she stood up.

Craig smiled. "I think we're on surveillance," he told the table as he led his wife around to the floor. "But hell, I'll hold you close, and you can spy all night."

Frank stood and took Sonny's hand. "We'll spy on them."

Kathleen and Mason were alone at the table, which was a landslide of glasses and bottles. "You know Shirley Stiver then," Kathleen said.

"She's my realtor, but I'm letting her go."

"Why's that."

"I'm keeping the house."

"What for?"

"I need a place to take you to dinner."

"I'm not ready for dinner, Mason." She put her hand on his elbow.

"I know, Kathleen. But every day has a dinner, and there'll come a day."

"You're so sure?"

"No, I am not. But I know what is good for me, and I'm going to stay up in Oakpine and work at it."

"Good luck," she said, leaning to him to kiss his cheek. "Good luck to you."

Now a young woman in a blue cloth coat came up behind them, unbuttoning it. "Hello," she said. "Have you played yet?" It was Wendy Ingram.

"Wendy," Kathleen said. "You've got snow in your hair."

The girl stepped back and brushed herself off. "It's snowing. Some-body's in the ditch a mile out. There was a backup."

"No, we're up in a band or two," Mason said. "Sit down."

"Is Larry here?"

"He's out there somewhere." Mason pointed at the mob. "But he'll return."

"Jimmy gave me this note," the girl said, and handed the folded paper to Mason.

The Moonlight Gamblers were perfect with the song, and the sixty couples on the dance floor moved imperceptibly in a fluid shuffle to the extended apology. Craig held Marci close. Everyone was being held close. She craned her neck for a while and then gave it up, her son out there somewhere with a woman. Her face was on Craig's shoulder. "We haven't danced in ten years," he said. "Twenty."

"It's like a joke," she said, holding him. Her mind was afloat, and it was a pleasure and a pain. It was as if she could feel the snow falling all over Wyoming and on into South Dakota, where they had gone once on a trip when Larry was a baby, taking a picture of him with the four stone presidents. This snow would be covering them now and on the ground until May, June in the hills, and she felt it falling, keeping them all in this strange room. She was weary of walking the tightrope, and she could feel it in her arms and chest, the wasted energy.

"You're a good dancer, Craig," she said.

"Are you going to be okay?" he said.

The question went through her as if someone had opened a door on the storm, and she put her teeth in her lip to stop the tears. What she did then was drop his hand and put her arms up around his neck while they made little steps and the singer sang and her eyes were closed.

Again, the Moonlight Gamblers got a long and steady applause and calls for an encore, and Wendy stood and waited at the edge of the dance floor and found Larry as he escorted his partner back to her table. The young woman had a good hold of his arm.

"Hey," she said.

"Hey," he smiled, and turned to her. "You came. I'll be right back."

She watched him walk the young woman to her table and wrestle her chair free so she could sit with her friends.

When he came to her, she said, "Your ribs must be healed."

"I'm good," he said. "Where's Wade?"

"Get real," she said happily. "He's not interested in music."

"I should get real," he said. "But how does one do that? How far from here is it? Is grinning part of it? I'm glad to see you." He wanted to grab her up and twirl her around, and he shook his head and held the grin.

"What is it?" she said.

"Nothing," he said. "Let's get you a coke." He led her to the bank of folks waiting at the bar, and they were squeezed together for a moment, pushed, and they were laughing, and finally she said, "Let's just go back and find your folks. I'm good. You can owe me a coke."

By the time they rejoined the others and found an extra chair, the next band was set. The lights went down and came up on four women in white shirts with string ties, one with long brown hair and a fiddle, and after the calling from the audience had subsided, the lead singer, her dark hair parted right down the middle, opened "Desperado," with a pure note that held the room still, and it remained still. "Whoa," said Larry, and Wendy pulled his arm to her and whispered in his ear: "Hey, let her sing. You're with someone."

"What?" he said loudly. "What did you say?" The table looked at him, interrupting the song. He stood and pulled Wendy with him to the side of the room under three mounted antelope heads. "I'm serious," he said in her ear. "What did you say?"

"It's true," she said, her face victorious. It was like using walkie-talkies; she speaking in his ear, he in hers.

"Say it," he said.

"You're with someone," she said, and smiled ridiculously.

He looked into her eyes.

She tapped his chest. "I put you in a story."

He looked around at the people near them by the wall, every face in the room focused on the amazing singer in her stunning white shirt. The room was shoulder to shoulder, knee to knee, packed.

"Is that a good idea?"

She nodded—it was easier than yelling.

"Want to hear something?" he said. It was intoxicating for him, because whatever he was going to say, he wanted to hear it too.

"I can hear everything," she said.

"I want to kiss you," he said. "I'm trying to get real."

"Here I am."

He pulled her past a group stamping their boots in the side doorway and out the tracked entryway into the sudden silence of the cascading snow. It was so quiet it hurt, and even in the new dark the world glowed as an underwater scene. Every three seconds the entire snowfield flashed blue and then white in the pulsing neon profile of the huge pronghorn antelope that was the bar's sign. The dark sky was layers of fat flakes now floating in unending echelons, tons as ounces, an ocean of it all, and they were snowy in a minute. "Have you felt like this before?" he asked her.

"You haven't and I haven't."

"You haven't and I haven't," he said. His ears were ringing. He put his hand on her elbow and leaned and watched her face in the snowfall. "Snowy people," he said, and they were both briefly dizzy as if the planet had shifted or become some other cold place rich with falling snow. "Stand still," he said. "Watch me closely. Study my resolve." Then he said, "Resolve," again and put a finger up between them as if it were the key to the lesson. "Watch me not kiss you." And then his lesson disappeared as she grinned and pushed his finger aside, and their faces fused, and they kissed standing in that parking lot until they were capped with snow.

"I watched you," she said."I studied your resolve."

"Good, because I forgot. But come on, who am I in the story? I hope I'm a detective. Shy but brilliant, right?"

"You're the young man who dances with the girl and scolds her all the while."

"What does she do?"

"He's a character who runs everywhere, and he's a scolder. But she can't hear him because her ability to hear has been canceled out by his hand on her back. She can feel his hand on her back, right where it's supposed to be from dancing class. She can only feel his hand." She reached and brushed the snow off his hair. "I love the snow," she said.

"It's snowing," he said. "But the snow has nothing whatsoever to do with what just happened."

In Oakpine it was snowing hard. There was a thing with Jimmy's eyes now every time he woke up, and it was that the light hurt them in a way that he almost felt as pleasure. He could feel the muscles in his eyelids working, and then the patterns struck his eye like a cold wind, burning in a blurred focus for a few seconds into the resolution of the room. The shimmering plastic that formed the ceiling and covered the large door was always moving like water, and Jimmy turned his head when he was lying down so he could see the hard outline of the chair or the table or the sill of the pretty little window. He was amused by the illusive beauty his eyes brought, and he was patient with their weariness.

Now he heard a sound, a human sound, and he opened his old eyes again. There was always a little vertigo, and he turned to anchor himself. There was someone in the chair, a shadow, only gray, unmoving. Jimmy Brand could hear a hissing now, a friction he realized was his own blood working everywhere he touched the sheets. The shadow in the chair did not move, but Jimmy knew it was no hallucination. It was a person made of charcoal sitting still, both feet on the floor, square and sound as Lincoln's statue in his temple. Jimmy's eyes ached against the light, the air, and he squinted them down as if to focus, trying to focus, but they would not be hurried. He tried to swallow and could not, and then he tried to breathe, and he could. With special energy, he lifted his hand from under the covers and brought it to his face, where two fingers rubbed his eyes. He could feel his sharp cheekbone. When he dragged his hand away, the lights were sharper, and now the man in the chair was three shades of gray, four, five, and now some blue.

"What line of work were you in?" The voice was deep and soft.

"I was a writer," Jimmy whispered. "I worked every day at a newspaper for years, eighteen years." He cleared his throat. His hand appeared again and lifted toward the little bed stand and his cup of water. The water was sharply cold, and he registered it and thought: Good, I still can tell cold. Now he was fully awake, and he looked across the room at his father.

"How does that go? Did you write the news? Did you have an office?"

"Dad?" Jimmy Brand said.

"Yeah," his father said. "I just come out for a minute. You okay?"

Jimmy shouldered his pillow so he could sit up slightly. His eyes were settling, but there was still a terrific ripping blur at the peripheries. "Is it snowing?" The window shimmered and flared with fabulous light, lifting the room.

"Yeah, it started when your buddies left. It should go all night now."

"Snow."

"Yeah, a real storm."

Jimmy looked at his father, sitting in his overalls like always and always. Now his big hands were in his lap like a boy's, and his face was still and serious and new with an expression Jimmy knew there were no words for, and his father started to speak and Jimmy also knew what he would say, and he said it quietly, "I just come out for a minute."

"I'm glad you did. How do you like my room?"

"Old Craig done a good job, I'd say."

"Do you want to hear about my job?"

"Was it good work?" his father asked.

"It was a good job," Jimmy said. "I loved to write, but it wasn't exactly news. I covered events like the museum shows and art galleries. One time I covered the Metropolitan Car Show, early on, about 1984, all the new cars and actors and a big show. You'd have gotten a kick out of that. Women in costumes opening the car doors. It was deluxe."

"Were you working days?"

Jimmy smiled. His father hadn't moved. "It was a day shift for a long time," he answered, "but then I started reviewing plays. It was good work, Dad. That was more of a swing shift. The plays were at eight, and then I'd go back to the office or home and write up the review. Sometimes I had the whole next day, but I like writing for a midnight deadline. I got pretty good at it."

"Mom said you won some awards."

"I did. Four awards. You get a glass statue and a little raise."

"A raise," his father nodded. "That never hurts."

Jimmy was trying to keep track of the conversation and he felt it slipping. He'd had a custom all his life of slowing down at moments he wanted to capture, stepping aside and identifying them, so he wouldn't miss anything, so he could know what it meant, and now he wanted this, his father talking to him, but it was slipping away like smoke. He was tired, and his heart, he could hear it trying to pound him softly into the bed. He closed his eyes, and they burned for a moment.

"You tired?" his father said.

"I'm fine," Jimmy said, his eyes still shut.

"I just come out for a minute," his father said again. "Your mother said you might like to go up to Gillette for the band, for the show up there."

"What?" Jimmy said.

"If you wanted to go up and see the band, I could drive you up. Mom has made a kit, some sandwiches and that. If you want to, I could drive you up. The weather's not great, but I could drive you up."

Jimmy's eyes were open now, and he tried to draw a deeper breath. The air came in strings, and his legs were faintly trembling. He pushed himself in three motions up so he sat facing his father. "Dad," he said, "you know I'm sorry about coming back out here and making problems for you. If I'd had anything else or another way . . ." Now Jimmy's voice skipped out on him, and he waited. Something new was burning in his spine, and the pain was like static. "That's all. I'm sorry."

His father was a stationary silhouette. "If you'd like to go up there, I could drive you. I'd like to drive you. Shit, I've driven to Gillette when they wouldn't take the mail. The day you were born I was out in Stayner with a freight train stopped by the blizzard, and your mother called from Holy Cross downtown."

"They'd stopped the train," Jimmy said. He hadn't heard this story for forty years.

"That was a snow that stopped every damn thing." His father's voice was like a hand on his arm. "But your mother had walked seven blocks to Hildy's house."

"Aunt Hildy," Jimmy said, remembering the woman now dead twenty years.

"There was a woman could manage," Edgar said. "She called me up there and said they were going over to Holy Cross to pick up a baby."

Jimmy struggled on an elbow to sit up. His eyes were fine now, and he focused on his father as he told his story.

"I told the foreman. It was Sid Jakowski, remember?"

"I remember Sid," Jimmy said. "I knew his daughters in school." Something was happening to Jimmy's face; he could feel it. Strange, he knew at last, I'm smiling. But his back and his chest were knotted in a cramp. His father sat before him, an old man. My father is an old man, and I am an old man. "They were tough girls, Polly and Lucinda."

"He was a tough guy. Scared-of-nothing Jakowski. But not in that storm. We had the one company International, and he wouldn't drive me down. I argued with the man. We were in the switching shack by the roundhouse, and he wouldn't budge. He wouldn't lend me the damn truck."

"So you took it."

"I took the truck. He knew I was going to and just gave me the keys."

"Didn't he say—"

"He said, 'Don't take the truck,' and he gave me the keys. I was having a baby. You were on the way, Jimmy."

The garage ceiling made a quiet chuffing as the plastic filled and emptied.

Jimmy's face felt strange again, and he heard himself speak. "We could go up there. It's only a little snow."

"Sure we could." Mr. Brand stood up. "I'll warm up the car."

He exited the little room, and Jimmy leaned back against the head-board. He felt the electricity in his arms and legs, but he could not move. Finally, by counting down from five, he slid one leg to the edge of the bed and over. The floor was ridiculous, so far down there.

It was a minute later that Mr. Brand came back into the garage, saying, "I like a good storm—it'll keep the traffic down." Then he closed the door and he knelt on the floor where his son lay. "Jimmy," he whispered. He felt for a pulse and then stood up. He didn't know what to do with his arms, and he folded them. Then he knelt again and lifted his son into an embrace, and he sat on the floor that way against the bed.

Inside the Pronghorn, there was news. Bobby Peralta was at their table with a bulletin. "Craig, you guys are up next." He stood with his hands on the back of Kathleen's chair.

"No we're not, Bob. We're after the break." Craig tapped the nine ball in the ashtray and lifted his glass. "We need these good people drunk."

"The gang from Sheridan put their car into the fence a mile down the road, and they're here but shaken up. Somebody's sprained his wrist, and we've got a bruise on the drummer's forehead you won't even want to see, and so what about you guys stepping up?"

"Are they okay?" Kathleen said, looking up at Bobby.

Seeing her, he said, "Can you come see? They're in the kitchen, and the drummer's got this head."

"We are good to go," Frank said. He stood up. "Gentlemen?"

"Jimmy made a request," Mason said. "Let's go play."

They took a minute setting up, plugging in, and Craig adjusted the drums and ran a few rounds. When Larry took the Fender out, a few guys stood and came up to the stage to see the classic, and Mason wired up and went to each of his friends and said, "Plenty loud now. I cannot sing."

Bobby Peralta made the announcement, thanking this band from

Oakpine, Life on Earth, and there was some applause and a call or two. "A garage band," he added. Larry stood behind Mason on the right, and he could see Wendy at the front of the stage, but it was hard to see back very far under the stage lights, which was just fine with all the men. The drums and the bass rocked into "Help Me, Rhonda," and in a minute it sounded just like a song, and they forgot themselves and pounded it out without reservation. Larry thought he could see people dancing, and when they stuck the ending, there was a wild clapping and periodic ya-hoos, which sounded strange and distant, and Mason walked to Frank and said, "Was that for us?"

From his place in the drums, Craig said into his mike, "Our second song is dedicated to the other member of our band, Jimmy Brand, Oakpine High School class of 1970." Again there was noise, some calling, and the band exchanged glances, and Larry thought, *This is just unreal. How long have we been up here in this light?* His father started the snare, and Frank nodded to the beat and then gave them aloud the one, two, three. The first word of the song "Let Him Run Wild," was "When . . ." and Larry heard it and knew he had stepped forward and was singing with Frank. It was way too slow and quiet for this big room, but they didn't care about that now. It was a song they knew, but when they'd practiced it, they'd all sung together, no one leading, and now they bogged down almost immediately waiting for each other. It was like they were just talking, talking in slow motion. It was very quiet in the room and impossible to tell if it was just falling flat.

Then Larry saw Wendy's face and knew it was falling flat. They stalled, and Frank cranked his hand, and the tempo ascended, but the singing was still slow and threatening to fail in each line. Then it did fail, or seemed like it failed: the end of the first verse, which was the part of the song Larry loved, should have had a snap, and it was dry as toast. Larry made a face at Wendy, motioned to her, and hauled her up with a hand onto the stage, and when Frank gave her the microphone, the song went crystal all the way to the back wall, and everybody heard the girl's voice take an edge and then sing the old warning about what the boy would do to other girls, and the guitars focused at once, explosive and precise, and her voice rang. Larry loved the final verse, the wicked rhyme of "need him" and "freedom," and they all crushed it together and threw themselves into the chorus urgently one more time. Frank steered them around to do the last verse again, and she followed perfectly. Craig brought it all in for a landing with the drums and in the flaring silence was able to say, "Thank you," and was going to say it again when the crowd sound came again, the clapping, whistles, and cries in a sharp crescendo.

Then they were off the stage, Larry carrying his guitar with Wendy down the far side, and Frank and Mason off the back. Craig went to the bar but got pushed by the crowd into the kitchen hallway. Someone grabbed him from the back, Marci, her face laughing, and she hugged him, focused, and kissed him. "Let's get a beer," he said. He was sweating. "My god. Did we do that?"

"You were great, honey." The hallway was booked solid, and Craig backed against the ladies' room door off balance, and the two of them were pushed into the room, but before the next woman could follow them, Craig reached past her and put his hand on the door holding it, and pulled her up with an arm, and kissed her against it as they felt the bumping traffic. "Yes," she said, "I love you." She felt the words in her elbows, her neck, and she took a deep breath.

He examined her face. "That's good news for this drummer." They kissed again, and a woman tapped him on the shoulder waiting to exit.

"Whenever you two are through," she said.

"We're just starting," he said to her, "but let's all get out of here."

Back at the table it was strange: they were quiet. People came by and said things about the way they played, but they all looked at each other knowing something had happened that they didn't need to talk about. Two of the red-shirted Coyotes from the next table raised their glasses, and one of them called, "Okay, okay, keep the lady. We knew she was pretty. We didn't know she was smart."

"How do you feel?" Marci asked her son.

"I see now why anybody has a band," Larry said. "I get it. It's like anything that scares you so much, you want a little more. Let me tell you, for old guys you did very well. I have it in the report." They ordered another round, and then a Pronghorn special Round the World pizza, but before it came, Larry and Wendy stood up. "We're going to drive back, go tell Jimmy how it went."

"It isn't over yet," Frank said.

"That'll make it a better story," Larry said.

"You be careful," Craig said to his son.

"It's four-wheel, Mr. Ralston," Wendy said. "And the plows have been through by now."

"Tell him about the girl who saved the day," Mason said. "Tell him we sang his song."

Memory

The afternoon winter wind was slow and ponderous and unrelenting and ultimately called fierce, though it was nothing except the icy air moving along the frozen plates of the world, and the snow had crusted and blown into waves against the fences along Berry Street in Oakpine, Wyoming. The day was closed. It was five days since the battle of the bands, and it had snowed every day since. Mason Kirby stood in his kitchen listening to the arctic air work his old house with the ghostly sounds of joists first nailed together during the Great War, short cries and groans he remembered from his boyhood. He turned from his reflection in the glass of his perfect kitchen window, and he pulled slowly the cork from a bottle of red wine in the warm room, and poured a glass, which he handed to Kathleen.

"You've done a nice job on this place," she told him. "I like these counters."

"I could never design a room," he said. "It is a published fact, but this will be my place." He pointed to the large framed photograph of Mickey Mantle over the stove. The ballplayer was in full swing, his forearms bulging in the black and white print.

"It should be."

He touched her glass, and they tasted the wine. "Oakpine," he said. Outside the kitchen windows, which were cornered with snow, they could see two dozen cars parked crazily along the drifts in the gloomy twilight on Berry Street, as if part of some sudden winter disaster.

"And I might get a dog. This is a good street for one. And a dog improves this weather."

"You had one."

"I did. Old Buddy. I knew him from a pup."

"He was some kind of black Lab, right?"

"He was, and a good dog. He certainly knew where the school was at three in the afternoon." He stood facing the window. "I need more of that in my life. Shall we walk down?" he said.

Kathleen lifted her scarf and coat from the chair. When she was wrapped up, she grabbed the shopping bag from the chair.

"What'd you bring?" he asked.

"Cholesterol. Sausage and scalloped potatoes."

"Perfect for the season."

"In thirty years of bringing this dish to parties in this town, I've never had to take any home." Kathleen opened her hands to the pretty kitchen. "You wanted to show me that you're staying."

He put his suit-coat collar up and tied a black scarf around it. "I just wanted you to see my home. I'm fishing for design tips. I need to get some rugs for that dog to lie on."

It was a pleasure to fight the old front door in the wind and to bump out into the uncompromising night. The wind was frigid and cut at their noses as soon as they stepped out onto the porch. Kathleen took his arm and put her head against his shoulder as they marched through the stiff sheets of snow three houses toward the Brands.

"Oh wind," Mason said.

"Right," Kathleen said. "Welcome home."

"This is the little walk that counts," Mason said. "Hold on to me."

"I will, but they all count." She spoke in phrases as the wind cut through. "If a person was raised here, he knows the way the light falls in this town on any given week, even you who have been absent for years. That isn't true for any other place for you. Knowing that, you can choose, wind or no wind, and let's just say: there'll be wind. This is a big week, Mason, with the trip and Jimmy gone, and now as always the big weather."

He stopped walking to turn in front of her to block the snow for shelter. There was the shadow of a kiss in his posture, but she nudged him out of it. "Let's walk and talk. Mason, I'm glad you're here, and I'd like to meet that dog." She held his arm tight, and they kicked through the drifts. "This is a good little walk that we won't ruin in any way."

"Good enough," he said. "You're right about the daylight. And the wind."

The Brands' house was full of noise, all their friends and Jimmy's friends, and the aromas of dozens of covered dishes. There was just room to take off their coats a shoulder at a time in the tiny entry and turn to give them to Sonny. The two women looked at each other and embraced. "Hello, hello. Good luck finding these things later—they'll be on the bed with a thousand others."

Kathleen threaded through the close room to the kitchen with her casserole. Mr. Brand, in his Sunday suit and tie, came up and shook Mason's hand. "You've got some people in here," Mason said to the older man.

"It was a good service."

"It was," Mason said. "He was a good man."

The remark caused Edgar Brand to put his hand on Mason's

shoulder, and Mason recognized the touch, that approval, from days lost to memory. "He was a good man," Mr. Brand said now. "He made many things." He was searching Mason's face for information.

"What they will say about Jimmy," Mason said to the old man, now seeing that the red and blue tie was an old union tie, AFL-CIO, a tie from 1953 or 54, when foremen wore ties to work on Mondays, "was that he had leverage. And his work will last. He was clear and fair as a reviewer of all of the arts, and his own writing will last."

"I know it," Mr. Brand said. He said the three words, and Mason saw the older man's eyes flush with tears. Now Mason put his hand on Edgar Brand's upper arm. After a moment Edgar said, "I'm good, Mason. Thank you for your remarks."

The old world phrase made Mason smile.

"I'm glad you're here, back in town. Now, get some food."

"I'll find it, I'm sure."

The sofa and every chair in the living room were full of an older generation, friends of the Brands, and a face or two was familiar to Mason. Craig and Marci were in the kitchen doorway talking to Mrs. Brand, the story of the snowy day at the bar in Gillette coming out in episodes. "We got rushed, a little because one band drove off the road."

"Before that," Marci said, "the girls' band knocked everybody flat. They were heartbreakers."

"Women?" Mrs. Brand said. "The whole band?"

"Exactly," Craig said. "They were good. They'd probably studied music in school."

"It doesn't seem fair, does it, dear?" Marci said to her husband.

"Then we played, two complete songs, and we didn't stop, and we didn't fall down, and I was feeling pretty good about that. I mean it," Craig said. "Jimmy would have been proud."

Mrs. Brand's face was rosy in the warm room, braced and smiling. She reached for her husband's sleeve and pulled him over.

"So then," Craig went on, "some characters from Lander . . ."

"Wearing red suspenders and yellow shirts . . ." Mason added.

"About half the bands had costumes." Frank had come up. "Mrs. Brand, I'm already into the zucchini brownies, and they are prizewinners." He held up his last bite and then spoke, chewing. "What we should have done is got some sequined outfits, something. We looked too normal."

"That's stretching it," Mason told him.

The group shifted as neighbors and friends slipped into the kitchen, where Mrs. Brand's table brimmed with steaming dishes and two sliced hams.

"Get a plate, Mason," Mrs. Brand told him. Kathleen was back and hugged Mrs. Brand. "This place smells wonderful," she told her.

"But suspenders were just the start." Craig handed Marci his glass and held his hands before him, as if to level the conversation to new seriousness. "They set up and strummed a little intro, like bing, a bing-bing, and then, are you ready for this?"

"Finish the story, big boy," Marci nudged him.

"Mrs. Brand, and this is the truth before these witnesses: two kids bounce onto the stage . . ."

"Suspenders, shirts . . ." Frank added.

"Little kids, like ten years old," Craig said.

"They were seven, tops," Frank said. "Here." He handed Mason a bottle of his new lager.

"One of these kids runs around and climbs into the big drum kit, and you couldn't even see him, just the sticks waving up there."

"They were really cute," Marci told Mrs. Brand.

"He could drum, and his sister could sing," Mason said. "They tore through that train song."

"They did. They were good."

"But kids," Craig said. "That's the sympathy vote."

"We were lucky to get third place," Mason said.

"This year," Frank said. "Where's that trophy?"

"Larry's got it," Marci said. "They're still up at the cemetery."

"That'll be windy enough."

"Not for those two," Marci said. "They're on a mission."

"I wish I was up there with them putting that trophy on Jimmy's grave." His phrase stopped the conversation. Jimmy was dead. Mason held up his bottle. "To Jimmy Brand, our friend." One by one each of the glasses touched every glass. Marci said his name, Jimmy, and she heard it whispered throughout the room. It was quiet in the little house; they could only hear the muffled hauling of the storm. Marci saw Mr. Brand's face and put her arms around the older man.

He took the embrace and patted her back and whispered to her, "I'm good."

Frank said, "You want to get that boat back in the garage, Mr. Brand?"

"Snow won't hurt that boat," Edgar Brand said. "I wonder, Frank, if you could just haul it away?"

"Done," Frank said. "This week. I'll see to it, snow or no. It is not a problem." He shook Mr. Brand's hand.

"Jimmy Brand," Mason said again quietly, an echo. Kathleen took his arm. "He taught me the guitar, made me want to learn it that year."

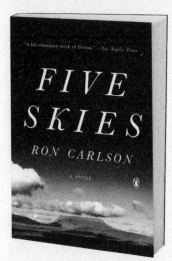

Five Skies

It is summer in the Rocky Mountains. The giant, silent Arthur Key flees from a spectacular betrayal and lands in Idaho where he will work on an ambitious construction project, alongside shiftless and charming Ronnie Panelli and the rage-filled Darwin Gallegos. During the course of their time together, one man will triumph over his dark nature; another will fall beneath the weight of his own.

"Bluntly beautiful . . . like one of those heartbreaking Raymond Carver stories."
—The New York Times

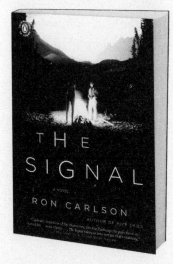

The Signal

The Signal follows Mack and Vonnie, a married couple who, after ten years together, are taking their last hike in the mountains of Wyoming to say good-bye. As the troubled elements of their past gradually come to light during their journey, Mack keeps a secret: he is tracking a signal, sent via a beacon, that will lead them both into a wood far darker than they have ever imagined.

"Has a lingering elegance and power."
—Los Angeles Times

**PENGUIN
BOOKS**